The yellowbacks... classics of popular fiction

The yellowjackets or yellowbacks were a great series of bestselling adventure and crime thrillers that had its origins in the mid to late 19th century following on from the 'penny dreadfuls'. They virtually began the mass market revolution of the early 20th century with a clear standard format and imprint/series livery (what would today be called branding). Hodder & Stoughton published the yellowjackets in two main series with series run dates of: 1923-1939 and later 1949-1957.

As the tagline ('where thrillers really began') on the back cover implies, the imprint and series focused on thrillers that were the bestsellers of their time. This current reissue or retro revival if you will, brings back many of these masterpieces, now classics in their own way and extends it further by including key titles from that period that were either great crime or thriller or even general commercial fiction (including sub-genres of noir, horror, gothic, romance, westerns, etc.) influences of their time. There are some perennial favourites and many rarities either lost or not easily available being revived in the current series. Writers and characters ranged from adventure heroes like Bulldog Drummond, Allan Quatermain, Richard Hannay or the Saint through thriller grandmasters Edgar Wallace and E. Phillips Oppenheim, crime and mystery maestros like Patricia Wentworth, G.K. Chesterton, Agatha Christie and the Detection club, to western and swashbucklers like Zane Grey, Max Brand, Captain Blood and even romance or general fiction classics like Hermina Black, Denise Robins, Marie Corelli or Stella Morton. These were books that had storytelling at their heart and always entertained.

The yellowbacks had both hardback (with varying design elements) and paperback (which built the series look) versions with the latter still carrying the imprint 'yellowjacket'. The current reissues pay tribute to both and use an amalgam of elements from both editions while retaining the complete yellow (or 'mustard-plaster') livery with the author's name in blue beveled type with a 'simulated emboss' effect and a white outer 'outline', and the book title in black. These reissues retain the distinctive size of the original mass market paperback and follow the three main category variations—the thrillers (crime, westerns, mystery, adventure) had blue lettering for the author's name, while Romance and softer general fiction had red; and other categories like humour had green.

For more details and a full list of titles visit https://www.hachetteindia.com/home/yellowbacks

ARSÈNE LUPIN
THE COUNTESS OF CAGLIOSTRO
(aka Memoirs of Arsène Lupin)

ARSÈNE LUPIN, THE COUNTESS OF CAGLIOSTRO
(aka Memoirs of Arsène Lupin)

Maurice Marie Émile Leblanc was a French novelist and writer of short stories, known primarily as the creator of the gentleman burglar, adventurer and detective Arsène Lupin, often described as a French counterpart to Arthur Conan Doyle's Sherlock Holmes and E.W. Hornung's Raffles.

Refusing the career that his father had set up for him at a card factory, Leblanc instead went to Paris in 1888, to pursue writing as a journalist. But he soon turned novelist and storyteller. His first novel, *Une femme (A Woman)*, published in 1893 was a success and was followed by other works, such as *Des couples (The Couples)*, *Voici des ailes (Here are Wings)* and a play *La pitié,* released in 1902, which was a flop. In 1905, Pierre Lafitte, the director of the monthly *Je sais tout,* commissioned a short story from Leblanc, with the brief that he was to combine the appeal of A.J Raffles by Ernest William Hornung and Sherlock Holmes. The result was 'L'Arrestation d'Arsène Lupin' ('The Arrest of Arsène Lupin') which was a huge success. Two years later, *Arsène Lupin, Gentleman Burglar* was released, and the rest was history – with one of the most successful series being born.

ARSÈNE LUPIN
THE COUNTESS OF CAGLIOSTRO
(aka Memoirs of Arsène Lupin)

Maurice Leblanc

translated by
ALEXANDER TEIXEIRA DE MATTOS

Arsène Lupin, The Countess of Cagliostro (aka Memoirs of Arsène Lupin)
First published as *La Comtesse de Cagliostro* in French in 1924 and translated from French in 1925 by Alexander Teixeira De Mattos in English as *The Countess of Cagliostro* (aka Memoirs of Arsène Lupin). Published in English in 1925.

This Hodder Yellowback edition © Hachette India 2023
(Registered Name: Hachette Book Publishing India Pvt. Ltd.)
An Hachette UK Company www.hachetteindia.com

1

All rights reserved. No part of the publication may be reproduced, stored in a retrieval system (including but not limited to computers, disks, external drives, electronic or digital devices, e-readers, websites), or transmitted in any form or by any means (including but not limited to cyclostyling, photocopying, docutech or other reprographic reproductions, mechanical, recording, electronic, digital versions) without the prior written permission of the publisher, nor be otherwise circulated in any form of binding or cover other than that in which it is published and without a similar condition being imposed on the subsequent purchaser.

The texts in these editions in most cases have been reprinted as is, with minimal editorial changes and by and large no bowdlerizing for political correctness; though in some editions, a few words and phrases considered archaic, or those considered offensive now, along with archaic punctuation may have been modified in places to make the text more accessible to today's readers. The narratives, language, beliefs, social mores and/or cultural depictions, in these volumes are a reflection of their times and must be viewed as such. They may also contain certain cultural, racial and gender prejudices and stereotypes that may be outdated or clearly wrong then and wrong today; but their removal would be tantamount to claiming these prejudices never existed. The Publisher does not endorse or support those depictions or stereotypes; and these books have been made available for a discerning audience that will read it for entertainment value and a chronicle/record of popular fiction of past times.

Cover design by Priya Singh adapted from the original classic yellowjacket by Hodder & Stoughton.

Cover illustration by Ishan Trivedi.

Series note: Some of the books in the series (unless otherwise credited) may have cover or inside illustrations from the original yellowbacks or early editions, and while full restoration has been attempted, some images may be grainy or faded due to the condition of the original material. The end notes or bonus material or blurb details may have been sourced from the public domain or free use publications such as Wikipedia and attribution is hereby made also allowing similar free use reproduction from here. Sources requiring further specific attribution may write in and further detailing and/or corrections shall be made in subsequent printings/editions.

Reprint specifications may be subject to change including but not limited to finishes, paper, colour sections.

ISBN: 978-93-5731-213-4

Hachette Book Publishing India Pvt. Ltd.
4th & 5th Floors, Corporate Centre,
Plot No. 94, Sector 44, Gurugram - 122 003, India

Typeset in Electra LT STD 10/12.5 pt by Manipal Technologies Limited, Manipal

Printed and bound in India by Manipal Technologies Limited, Manipal

PREFACE

This is the story of the first adventure of Arsène Lupin, and undoubtedly it would have been published before the stories of the others if he had not so often and so resolutely opposed it.

"No," he would say, "there are one or two little matters yet to be settled between the Countess of Cagliostro and me. We must wait."

The waiting lasted longer than he foresaw. More than a quarter of a century passed before the final settlement; and only today am I permitted to relate the frightful duel of love and hate which brought a boy of twenty to grips with Cagliostro's daughter.

ARSÈNE LUPIN
THE COUNTESS OF CAGLIOSTRO
(AKA MEMOIRS OF ARSÈNE LUPIN)

CONTENTS

I.	Arsène Lupin at Twenty	1
II.	Josephine Balsamo Born in 1788	18
III.	A Tribunal of the Inquisition	33
IV.	The Sinking Boat	51
V.	One of the Seven Branches	67
VI.	Detectives and Policemen	82
VII.	The Delights of Capua	100
VIII.	Two Wills	118
IX.	The Tarpeian Rock	138
X.	The Mutilated Hand	158
XI.	The Old Lighthouse	176
XII.	Madness and Genius	194
XIII.	The Strongbox of the Monks	220
XIV.	The Infernal Creature	240
Epilogue		266
Endnotes		270

I

ARSÈNE LUPIN AT TWENTY

Ralph d'Andresy extinguished the lamp, and thrust his bicycle behind a bank. At that moment the clock of Benouville struck three.

In the deep shadow of the night he followed the lane which led to the estate of La Haie d'Etigues and so came to the wall which ran round it. He waited a little—the sound of horses pawing the ground, of wheels which rang on the pavement of the courtyard, the sound of harness bells. Then the two leaves of the big door were thrown open and a carriage passed out. It passed so quickly that Ralph barely caught the sound of men's voices and perceived the barrel of gun before the vehicle reached the highroad and took the way to Etretat.

"Come," said he. "Shooting gulls is an attractive sport and the rock where they shoot them is a long way off. At last I'm going to know the meaning of this improvised shooting-party and of all these odd comings and goings."

He took his way along the boundary wall to the left, turned a corner and then another, and stopped forty yards along the wall. In his hand he held two keys. The first of them opened a small, low door. He went through it up a staircase hollowed out of the wall, half fallen to ruin, which, running along its left wing, had formed one of the old defences of the château. The second key opened for him a secret door in the first floor of the château itself.

He lit a small bull's-eye lantern and without taking any special precautions, since he knew that the staff of servants lived in the other wing and that Clarice d'Etigues, the only daughter of the Baron, had her rooms on the second floor, went down a passage which brought him to a large study. In that very room some weeks previously he had asked the Baron for his daughter's hand in marriage. His proposal had been received with an explosion of indignant anger of which he retained a most disagreeable recollection.

A mirror showed him the pale face of a young man, even paler than usual. However, inured to emotion, he remained master of himself and coolly addressed himself to his task.

He was not long about it. In the course of his interview with the Baron he had observed that that gentleman now and then cast a glance at a large mahogany roll-top desk of which the top had not been drawn down. Ralph knew all the places in which it is possible to put a secret drawer and all the mechanical devices that work such secret drawers. In a very short time he discovered in a cranny of the desk a tiny drawer which held a letter written on very thin paper and rolled up into the shape of a cigarette. No signature. No address.

He studied this letter, which at first appeared to him too commonplace for anyone to have taken so much trouble to hide it, and after working on it with the most minute care, giving the most earnest consideration to certain words which seemed significant and ignoring certain phrases evidently intended to fill the gaps between them, he was able to disentangle the following:

I found at Rouen traces of our enemy and I have had published in the local newspapers a story that a peasant in the vicinity of Etretat has dug up in his field an old copper candlestick with seven branches. At once she telegraphed to the livery stable at

Etretat to send, at three o'clock in the afternoon on the twelfth, a brougham to meet her at Fécamp station.

On the morning of that day I will see that the livery stable receives another telegram, countermanding this order. Therefore it will be your brougham that she will find at Fécamp station and which will bring her to us, under a sufficient escort, at the very moment at which we are holding our meeting. We shall be able to constitute ourselves a tribunal and pronounce upon her a relentless sentence.

In those days in which the greatness of the end justified the means, the punishment would have been immediate. Dead men tell no tales. Choose what end you please; but remember the conclusions to which we came during our last interview and bear in mind that the success of our enterprises and our very existence itself depends on this infernal creature.

Be prudent. Arrange a shooting-party to divert suspicion. I will arrive by way of le Hâvre at four o'clock exactly, with two of our friends. Do not destroy this letter. You will give it back to me.

"An excess of precaution is a mistake," thought Ralph. "If the Baron's correspondent had not been so distrustful, the Baron would have burnt this letter and I should not have known about this scheme of abduction, this scheme of an illegal tribunal and even, heaven help us! this scheme of assassination... Hang it! My future father-in-law, devout Catholic though he may be, seems to me to be entangled in combinations that are not Catholic at all... Will he go as far as murder?... All this is devilishly serious and may very well give me a hold on him."

He rubbed his hands. The business gave him considerable satisfaction and excited in him no great astonishment, since for several days he had been noticing some queer facts. He resolved then to return to his inn and sleep there and then to come back in good time to learn what the Baron and his guests were plotting and who this "infernal creature" was whom they desired to suppress.

He rerolled the letter, cigarette-wise, carefully, and put it back in the drawer, but, instead of departing, he sat down in front of a small round table on which there was a photograph of Clarice, and drawing it directly in front of him contemplated it with a profound tenderness. Clarice d'Etigues, very little younger than he was himself... eighteen. Voluptuous lips... eyes full of dreams... a clear-skinned, pink, and delicate fair face, crowned by a mass of fair hair such as the hair of those little girls who run about the roads in the neighborhood of Caux... and such a sweet expression and such charm!

Ralph's eyes grew fonder and fonder as he gazed. Thus, naturally, the desire came to him to be with the object of his adoration. Why not? Clarice was alone in her isolated suite of rooms above him. Twice already, making use of the keys which she had entrusted to him, he had made his way to them in the afternoon. What was there to hinder him now? No sound they would make could reach the servants. The Baron would not return till the afternoon. Why go away? Compromise her? Why should he compromise her? No one could possibly know that he had been with her.

Besides, it was such a delightful night. The moon, nearly at the full, was shining with all its brightness. On such a night, under an even brighter moon and clearer sky, Romeo had made love to Juliet. He went quickly, but quietly, up the stairs.

Before the closed door of her boudoir he hesitated. Suppose someone should learn that he had been with her? No one could. He knocked with a rather uncertain hand. He waited. He knocked again louder and again waited. There was a sound in the room. The door opened, revealing Clarice, candle in hand, dressed in a lace peignoir, her charming face enframed in the silken mass of fair hair loosely held together by a ribbon.

"Ralph?" she murmured softly. "It seemed impossible. But I knew it was you. But—you oughtn't to have come."

"I couldn't keep away. I wanted so to be with you. It's quite safe. No one saw me come. No one can know I'm here," he said in pleasing accents.

She smiled at him adorably and stepped back. He entered and shut the door and turned the key. He took the candle from her, blew it out, and set it on the table. Then, gently, he put his arms around her, drew her to him, and kissed her eyes and her lips with long, lingering kisses.

Then he drew her to a couch in front of the long, low window, and they sank down on to it, his arm round her waist, and her arm round his neck; and in the intervals between their languorous, passionate kisses, they gazed down on the plain and across the sea bathed in the silver radiance of the queen of the night.

They sat, murmuring to one another the lovely thoughts which their nearness in the night evoked in their ardent souls, thrilling and intoxicated, till the moonlight faded in the golden dawn and the sun rose over the seat.

They had loved one another for three months—since the day of their meeting in the south, where Clarice was spending some time at the home of a schoolgirl friend. Forthwith they felt themselves united by a bond, which was for him the most delightful thing in the world, for her the symbol of slavery which she cherished more and more fondly. From the beginning he appeared to her to be an extraordinarily elusive creature, mysterious, one whom she would never understand. He grieved her by occasional moods of flippancy, of malicious irony, of deep gloom. But in spite of that, what a fascination he had! What a gaiety! What bursts of enthusiasm and youthful exaltation!

All his faults assumed the appearance of qualities in excess; and his vices had the air of virtues ignorant of themselves and about to expand.

After her return to Normandy she was surprised one morning to perceive the slender figure of the young man, perched on a wall in front of her windows. He had chosen an inn a few kilometers away, and from there, almost every day, he came on his bicycle to find her in the neighborhood of La Haie d'Etigues.

A motherless girl, Clarice was not fortunate in her father, a hard man, gloomy in character, a fanatic in religion, inordinately proud of his title, greedy of gain to the point that the farmers who rented his land looked upon him as an enemy.

When Ralph, who had not even been introduced to him, had the audacity to ask his daughter's hand in marriage, the Baron fell into such a fury with this beardless suitor, without a career and without relations, that he would have horsewhipped him if the young man had not quietly held him with something of the gaze of a tamer of wild beasts.

It was in consequence of this interview and to efface the memory of it from Ralph's spirit that Clarice had entrusted to him the two keys which gave him secret access to her suite.

Later in the morning, pretending that she was not feeling well, she had her midday déjeuner brought up to her boudoir while Ralph hid himself in a room at the end of the corridor. After the meal they returned to the couch in front of the window and renewed the transports of the magical night.

A fresh breeze, rising from the sea and blowing across the high ground, caressed their faces. In front of them, beyond the great park enclosed by the wall, and among the plains all golden with the blossom of the colza, a depression allowed them to see, on the right, the white line of the high cliffs as far as Fécamp, on the left Etretat Bay, Aval Harbor, and the point of the enormous Needle.

A cloud fell on Clarice's spirit. The tears welled up into her eyes.

He said to her gently:

"Don't be sad, my dearest darling. Life is so sweet at our age; and it will be sweeter still for us when we shall have swept away all the obstacles. Don't be sad."

She dried her tears and, gazing at him, tried to smile. He was slender as was she, but broad-shouldered, of a build at once elegant and solid. His face, full of character, displayed a mischievous mouth and eyes shining with gaiety. Wearing knickerbockers and an open jacket over a white woollen sweater, he had an air of incredible suppleness.

"Ralph," she said in a tone of distress, "at this very moment even while you are looking at me, you are not thinking about me! You are not thinking about me any longer, even though you are with me. It hardly seems possible! What are you thinking about, darling?"

He laughed gently and said:

"About your father."

"About my father?"

"Yes: about the Baron d'Etigues and his guests. How on earth can men of their age waste their time killing off poor innocent birds on a rock?"

"It's their amusement."

"Are you sure of that? For my part I'm rather puzzled about the matter. In fact, if we were not in the year of grace 1892 I should be inclined to think rather... You're not going to feel hurt?"

"Go on, dear."

"Well, they have the air of playing at conspirators! Yes; it really is so... the Marquis de Rolleville, Matthew de la Vaupaliere, Count Oscar de Bennetot, Rufus d'Estiers, etc., all these noble lords of the Caux country are up to their necks in a conspiracy!"

She looked at him with incredulous eyes.

"You're talking nonsense, darling," she murmured.

"But you listen so prettily," he replied, assured of her complete ignorance of the plot. "You have such a delightful way of waiting for me to tell you serious things."

"Things about love, darling."

He drew her to him almost roughly.

"The whole of my life is nothing but love for you, darling. If I have other cares, other ambitions, they are to win you outright. Suppose that your father, this conspiracy discovered, is arrested and condemned to death and all at once I save him. After that how would he be able to refuse me his daughter's hand?"

"He will give way someday or other, darling."

"Never! I have no money... no means of support."

"You have your name: Ralph d'Andresy."

"Not even that."

"What do you mean?"

"D'Andresy was my mother's name, which she took again when she became a widow, and at the bidding of her family whom her marriage had outraged."

"Why?" said Clarice somewhat dumbfounded by these unexpected revelations.

"Why? Because my father was only an outsider... as poor as Job... a simple professor... and a professor of what? Of gymnastics, fencing, and boxing!"

"Then what is your name?"

"An uncommonly vulgar one."

"What is it?"

"Arsène Lupin."

"Arsène Lupin?"

"Yes; it's hardly a brilliant name, is it? And the best thing to do was to change it, don't you think?"

Clarice appeared overwhelmed. It made no difference what his name was—to her. But in the eyes of the Baron the particle "de" was the very first qualification of a son-in-law.

She murmured however:

"You ought not to have disowned your father. There's nothing to be ashamed of in being a professor."

"Nothing to be ashamed of at all," said he, laughing cheerfully, but with a rather hard laugh which hurt Clarice. "And I can assure you that I've benefited to the greatest possible extent by the lessons in boxing and gymnastics which he gave me when I was still at the bottle. But it may be that my mother had other reasons for denying the noble fellow. But that is nobody's business."

He hugged her with a sudden violence and then began to dance and pirouette. Then coming back to her:

"But smile, little girl—laugh!" he exclaimed. "All this is really very funny. So laugh. Arsène Lupin or Ralph d'Andresy, what on earth does it matter? The main thing is to succeed. And I shall succeed. About that there is no doubt. Every fortuneteller I have ever come across has predicted a great future and universal renown for me. Ralph d'Andresy will be a general, or a minister, or an ambassador... Always supposing that he does not remain Arsène Lupin. It is an affair settled before the throne of Destiny, agreed on, signed by both parties. I am quite ready. Muscles of steel and a number one brain! Come, would you like me to walk on my hands, or carry you about at arms' length? Or would you prefer that I took your watch without your perceiving it, or shall I recite by heart Homer in Greek and Milton in English? Heavens, how sweet life is! Ralph d'Andresy... Arsène Lupin. The statue with two faces! Which of them will be illumined by glory, the sun of those who really live?"

He stopped short. His lightness seemed all at once to chafe him. Silent, he looked round the quiet little room, the security of which he was troubling, as he had troubled the young girl's pure and peaceful heart; and with one of those unexpected changes which were the charm of his disposition, he knelt down before Clarice and said to her gravely:

"Forgive me. I did wrong to come here... But it is not my fault. It is so difficult for me to keep my balance... Good and evil, they attract me in turn. You must help me, Clarice, to choose my path, and you must forgive me if I miss my way."

She took his head between her hands and in passionate accents cried:

"I have nothing to forgive you, darling. I'm happy. You will cause me bitter suffering—I'm sure of it—and I accept beforehand and joyfully all those sorrows you will bring upon me. Here, take my photo, and act in such a way that you never need to blush when you look at it. For my part, I shall always be just what I am today—your sweetheart and your wife. I love you, Ralph."

She kissed him on the brow. But even now he was again laughing; and as he rose to his feet, he said:

"You have armed your knight, lady. Behold me henceforth invincible and ready to confound my enemies. Appear, men of Navarre!... I enter the lists!"

Ralph's plan—let us drop the name of Arsène Lupin since at that moment, ignorant of his destiny, he himself held it in some contempt—Ralph's plan was very simple. In the park, on the left of the château, and resting against the boundary wall, of which it formerly formed one of the bastions, there was a truncated tower, very low, roofed over, and almost hidden by waves of ivy. Now he had no doubt that the meeting fixed for four o'clock would take place in the great chamber inside it, where the Baron interviewed his tenants. And Ralph had also observed that an opening, an old window or air-hole, looked over the country.

The ascent to it was easy for a young man of his agility. Leaving the château and creeping along under the ivy, he raised himself, thanks to the huge roots, to the opening in the thick wall. He found it deep enough to allow him to stretch himself at full length in it. So placed, nearly twenty feet from the ground, his head hidden by the leaves, he could not be seen, and he could see the whole of the chamber. It was furnished with a score of chairs, a table, and in the middle of it was set a great bench from some church.

Forty minutes later the Baron entered with his friends. Ralph had foreseen exactly what would happen.

The Baron Godfrey d'Etigues enjoyed the muscular development of a strong man of the music-halls. His face was brick-red and the lower part of it was covered with a red beard. His eyes shone with a strongly vital intelligence. He was accompanied by his cousin, whom Ralph knew by sight, Oscar de Bennetot, who had the same air of the Normandy squire, but was of a commoner and duller type. Both of them appeared to be in a state of considerable excitement.

The Baron walked up and down restlessly and ran over the arrangements: "La Vaupaliere, Rolleville and d'Auppegard are on their way to join us. At four o'clock Beaumagnan will arrive with the Prince of Arcola and de Brie, by way of the park of which I have left the big gate open... And then... then she will arrive... if by good luck she falls into the trap."

"That's doubtful," murmured Bennetot.

"Why? She has ordered a brougham; the brougham will be there and she will get into it. D'Ormont, who is driving it, drives her here. At the edge of the four crossroads Rufus d'Estiers jumps on to the step, opens the door, and overpowers the lady. The two of them truss her up. This is bound to happen."

They came right under Ralph's hiding-place; so that he caught Bennetot's murmur:

"And then?"

"Then I explain the situation to our friends, the part that this woman is playing," growled the Baron.

"And you imagine that you will be able to get them to agree to condemn her?"

"It doesn't matter whether they agree or whether they don't; the result will be the same. Beaumagnan demands it. How can we refuse?" said the Baron.

"That man will be the ruin of us," affirmed Bennetot.

The Baron d'Etigues shrugged his shoulders and protested:

"We need a man like him, to struggle against a woman like her. Is everything ready?"

"Yes. The two boats are on the beach at the bottom of the priests' staircase. The smaller is scuttled and will sink ten minutes after it is set afloat."

"You have put a stone in it?" asked the Baron.

"Yes, a good-sized boulder with a hole in it, through which you can run the rope."

They were silent, casting uneasy glances at the door of the chamber.

Not one of the words they had spoken had escaped the keen ears of Ralph d'Andresy and not one of them had failed to put a keener edge on his already keen curiosity.

"Hang it all! I wouldn't give up this box on the first tier for an Empire," he murmured. "What hot stuff they are! They talk about murdering as other people talk about putting on a clean collar."

Above all Godfrey d'Etigues astonished him. How could the gentle Clarice be the daughter of this gloomy soul? What end was he trying to compass? What were the dark motives on which he was acting? Hate, greed, the lust for revenge, the instinct of cruelty? He brought to one's mind an executioner of bygone days ready to set about some sinister task. His brick-red face and red beard seemed to be lit up by internal flames.

Then three other guests arrived together. Ralph knew them as frequent visitors at La Haie d'Etigues. They sat down with their backs to the two windows which lighted the chamber as if they desired their faces to be blurred in the shadow.

On the very stroke of four two newcomers entered. One, a man of considerable age and of a soldierly stiffness, tightly buttoned up in a frock coat and wearing on his chin the little beard which in the days of Napoleon III was called an imperial, stopped short on the threshold. Everyone rose and stepped forward to greet the other. Ralph did not doubt for a moment that he was the author of the unsigned letter, the man for whom they were waiting, whom the Baron had called Beaumagnan. Although he was the only one of them to have no title, nor even the "de" before his name, they welcomed him as one welcomes a leader, with a respect which his air domination and his imperious eyes seemed naturally to exact. His face was clean-shaven; his cheeks were hollow; there was in the glances of his fine black eyes a quality of passion. In his manner and in his dress there was something severe, even ascetic; he had the air of a dignitary of the Church.

He begged them to sit down, apologized for having been unable to bring his friend the Count de Brie, beckoned his companion forward and introduced him:

"The Prince of Arcola... I believe you know that the Prince of Arcola is one of us, but, as luck would have it, was unable to be present at our meetings and that his activities were exercised at a distance and with the happiest results. Today his evidence is necessary to us, since twice already, in eighteen-seventy, he met the infernal creature who threatens us."

Ralph was conscious of a slight disappointment; working it out, the "infernal creature" must be more than fifty years of age, since her meetings with the Prince of Arcola had taken place two and twenty years before.

Thereupon the Prince sat down beside Oscar de Bennetot; and Beaumagnan drew Godfrey d'Etigues aside. The Baron handed him an envelope, containing doubtless the compromising letter. Then they held in low voices a discussion of a certain liveliness, which Beaumagnan cut short with a gesture of virile command.

"There is no doing anything with the gentlemen," said Ralph to himself. "The verdict is fixed. Dead men tell no tales. The drowning will take place, for it seems quite clear that that is the solution on which he is resolved."

Beaumagnan sat down behind the other conspirators. But before sitting down he said in cold and measured tones:

"You know, my friends, to what a degree this hour is serious for us. All of us, in complete agreement and of one mind about the magnificent end which we wish to accomplish, have undertaken a common task of immense importance. It appears to us, and rightly, that the interests of our country, those of our party, and those of our religion—I do not separate the one from the others—are linked with the success of our schemes. Now these schemes have for some time been brought up short by the audacious and implacable hostility of a woman, who, being in possession of certain evidence, has set herself to discover the secret which we are on the very point of discovering. If she discovers it before we do, it means that all our efforts have been wasted, utterly. Her or us: there is no room for the two. Let us pray earnestly that the struggle in which we are engaged may be decided in our favor!"

He sat down, and resting his two arms on the back of a chair, bent his tall figure as if he wished to remain unseen.

Some minutes passed.

The silence of these men met together for reasons which should have excited them to lively converse, was absolute, so keenly was the attention of all fixed on the distant noises which came from the surrounding country. The capture of this woman obsessed their minds. They were in a hurry to hold and to see their adversary.

The Baron d'Etigues raised his hand. They began to catch the dull rhythm of a horse's hoofs.

"It is my brougham," he said.

Yes: but was their enemy inside it?

The Baron rose and went to the door. As usual the Park was empty, since the servants' work kept them busy in the courtyard in front of the château.

The sound of hoofs grew louder. The carriage left the high road and came along the lane. Then it suddenly appeared between the two pillars of the entrance to the Park. The driver waved a reassuring hand; and the Baron exclaimed:

"Victory! They've got her!"

The brougham stopped at the door. D'Ormont, who was driving it, jumped smartly down. Rufus d'Estiers stepped out of it. With the help of the Baron they drew from the interior a woman whose wrists and ankles were bound. A gauze scarf covered her face. They carried her to the church bench which stood in the middle of the chamber.

"Not the least difficulty," said d'Ormont in a tone of triumph. "She came straight out of the train and stepped into the brougham. At the crossroads we tied her up before she had time to let out more than two squeals."

"Remove that scarf," said the Baron; and as D'Ormont stooped to do so, he added: "After all, we may as well restore her freedom of movement. We have her safe."

He himself untied the cords.

D'Ormont raised the veil and uncovered her face.

There came a cry of amazement from the spectators; and Ralph, up in his observation post, from which he had a view of the prisoner in full daylight, was hard put to it not to betray his presence by a similar exclamation, when there was revealed a young woman in all the splendor of her youth and beauty.

Then a voice rose above the murmurs of astonishment. The Prince of Arcola stepped forward, and his starting eyes glaring in a twitching face, stammered:

"It's she!... It is she... I recognize her... But what a frightful thing it is!"

"What is it?" snapped the Baron. "What's frightful? Explain!"

And the Prince of Arcola uttered these incredible words:

"She is no older than she was two and twenty years ago!"

The woman was sitting, and sitting quite upright, her clenched fists resting on her knees. Her hat must have fallen off in the course of the attack on her, and her hair, half-undone, fell behind her in a thick mass, partly held up by a gold comb, while two rolls with tawny gleams in them were drawn back evenly above her brow, and were waved a little above her temples.

Her face was of a wonderful beauty, its lines of an astonishing purity; and it was animated by an expression which, even in her impassibility, even in her fear, appeared to be a smile. With her rather delicate chin, rather high cheek bones, deep-set eyes, and heavy eyelids, she recalled those women of Leonardo da Vinci, or rather of Bernardino Luini, all the charm of whom is in a smile you do not actually see, but which you divine, which at once moves and disquiets you.

She was simply dressed: a dust cloak which she let fall, a gray woollen dress which, fitting tightly, gave the lovely curves of her figure their full value.

"Well!" said Ralph, who could not take his eyes off her, softly to himself. "She appears quite inoffensive, this magnificent and infernal creature! And they're nine or ten to one against her!"

She scrutinized with keen eyes the group of men round her, d'Etigues and his friends, and strove to see clearly those others in the shadow. Then she said:

"What is it you want? I do not recognize any of you. What have you brought me here for?"

"You're our enemy," declared Godfrey d'Etigues.

She shook her head gently.

"Your enemy? There must be some mistake. Are you quite sure that you're not making a mistake? I am Madame Pellegrini."

"You're not Madame Pellegrini."

"But I assure you..."

"You're not!" the Baron exclaimed in a loud voice.

Then he added—and the words were little less disconcerting than those uttered a little while before by the Prince of Arcola:

"Pellegrini was one of the aliases adopted in the eighteenth century by the man whose daughter you pretend to be."

She did not answer for a few seconds, seeming to be taken aback by the absurdity of the statement. Then she said tartly:

"Then what is my name—according to you?"

"Josephine Balsamo, Countess of Cagliostro."

II

JOSEPHINE BALSAMO BORN IN 1788

Cagliostro! The astonishing man who puzzled all Europe and so thoroughly upset the Court of France in the reign of Louis XVI! The Queen's necklace... Cardinal de Rohan... Marie Antoinette... some of the most obscure episodes in history!

A strange man, and enigmatic, dowered with a veritable genius for intrigue. A man who exercised a genuine power of domination. A man on whom full light has not yet been thrown. Impostor? Who knows? Have we the right to deny that certain beings of more delicate sensibilities than ourselves can peer into the world of the living and the dead in a fashion which is forbidden to us? Is one to treat as charlatan or fool the man in whose mind rise the memories of past existences, who, recalling what he has seen, reaps the harvest of acquisitions in the past, of lost secrets, and forgotten knowledge, and exploits a power which we call supernatural, but which is merely putting into action, hesitating perhaps and stumbling action, forces of which we are, it may be, on the point of becoming masters?

If Ralph d'Andresy, from the bottom of his post of observation, remained sceptical, if he laughed in his heart, not perhaps without certain reservations, at the fashion in which events were shaping themselves, it seemed that those taking part in them were accepting on the instant and without question, as realities beyond all discussing, the most extravagant assertions.

Had they then proofs and an understanding of this matter peculiar to themselves? Had they found in her who, according to them, laid claim to be the daughter of Cagliostro, gifts of clairvoyance and divination which, in days gone by, the world attributed to that celebrated worker of wonders, and by reason of them treated him as magician and sorcerer?

Godfrey d'Etigues, who was the only one of them standing, bent towards the young woman and said:

"Your name really is Cagliostro, isn't it?"

She pondered. One would have said that, taking thought how best to defend herself, she was seeking the best counterstroke; that she wished, before definitely plunging into the struggle, to know what weapons the enemy had at his command. Then she answered quietly:

"Nothing compels me to give you an answer, since you have no right whatever to question me. However, why should I deny that on my birth certificate is the name Josephine Pellegrini and that it is my whim to call myself Josephine Balsamo, Countess of Cagliostro? The two names Cagliostro and Pellegrini complete the personality of Joseph Balsamo, a personality in which I have always taken the greatest interest."

"Then it follows that, contrary to certain declarations you used to make, you are not his direct descendant. Is that what you wish to imply?" said the Baron.

She shrugged her shoulders and said nothing. Was it prudence? Was it disdain? Or was it a protest against such an absurdity?

"I do not care to consider this silence either an avowal or a denial," said Godfrey d'Etigues, turning towards his friends. "What this woman says is of no importance; and it is a waste of time to refute her statements. We're here to make our decisions, most important decisions, in a matter which we all know in its entirety, but of which certain details are unknown to the majority of us. It is then necessary to run over the main facts. They are set forth as shortly as possible in the memorandum which I am going to read to you, and to which I beg you to give your most earnest attention."

And he read quietly a document which—at least Ralph had no doubt about—it must have been drawn up by Beaumagnan. It ran:

At the beginning of March, 1870, that is to say, four months before the outbreak of the Franco-Prussian war, among the crowd of strangers who, as was usual every spring, descended on Paris, none excited greater interest than the Countess Cagliostro. Beautiful, charming, lavish of her money, generally alone, but sometimes accompanied by a young man, whom she introduced to people as her brother, everywhere she went, in every house into which she was welcomed, she was the object of the most lively curiosity.

First of all her mere name excited people's interest, then the truly impressive fashion in which she emphasized her relationship to the famous Cagliostro by her mysterious bearing, by certain miraculous cures she effected, and by the answers she gave to those who consulted her concerning their past or their future. The novel of Alexander Dumas had made Joseph Balsamo, that is to say the Count of Cagliostro, the fashion. Employing the same methods, even more boldly, she boasted that she was Cagliostro's daughter, declared that she knew the secret of eternal youth, and with a smile spoke of this and that meeting, of this and that event which had befallen her in the days of Napoleon I.

Such was her prestige that she forced open for herself the doors of the Tuileries and appeared at the Court of Napoleon III. People even talked of private séances at which the Empress Eugenie gathered round the beautiful Countess her most faithful intimates. A secret number of that satirical journal, the

Charivari, which was instantly suppressed, tells the story of one of the séances in which an occasional collaborator took part. I quote this passage from it:

'She is truly a wonderful woman, with something of *La Joconde* about her. Her expression changes very little but it is very difficult to describe. It is quite as caressing and ingenuous as perverse and cruel. There is a wealth of experience in her gaze and a bitterness in her unchanging smile—such a wealth of experience, indeed, that one is willing to allow her the eighty years she allots to herself. Now and again she draws from her pocket a small golden mirror, lets fall on it two drops from a tiny flask, dries it, and look at herself in it. And once more she is Youth in its most adorable perfection.'

When we questioned her about it, she replied:

"This mirror belonged to Cagliostro. For those who look at themselves in it with assured confidence, time stands still. Look: the date is engraved on the back, 1783, and it is followed by four lines which are the list of the four great enigmas. These enigmas which he had set himself the task of solving, he had from the lips of Queen Marie Antoinette herself; and he was wont to say, so at least they told me, that the man who found the key to them would be a King of Kings."[1]

"May one hear them?" somebody asked.

"Why not? To know them is not to solve them; and Cagliostro himself hadn't the time to do so. I can only give you their titles. They are:

"*In Robore Fortuna*.

"The Flagstone of the Bohemian Kings.

"The Fortunes of the Kings of France.

"The Candlestick with Seven Branches."

Afterwards she talked to all of us in turn; and to each she made astonishing revelations.

But that was only the prelude; and the Empress, though she refused to put the most trivial question about matters which concerned her personally, asked her to throw some light on the future.

"Would your Majesty be so good as to breathe lightly on this," said the Countess, holding out the mirror.

And forthwith, after examining the mist that the Queen's breath had spread over its surface she murmured:

"I see many excellent things... In the summer great war... Victory... The return of the troops under the Arc de Triomphe... They are cheering the Emperor... The Prince Imperial..."

Godfrey d'Etigues folded the paper and went on:

"Such is the document which has been communicated to us. It is a disconcerting document since it was published several weeks before the war it foretold. What was this woman? Who was this adventuress whose dangerous predictions, acting on the somewhat feeble mind of our unfortunate sovereign, played their part in bringing about the catastrophe of 1870? Someone—you will find it in the same number of the *Charivari*, said to her one day:

"'Granted that you are the daughter of Cagliostro, who was your mother?'

"'For my mother,' she replied, 'you must look high among the contemporaries of Cagliostro... higher still... Yes: that's right... Josephine de Beauharnais, the future wife of Bonaparte, Empress that was to be.'

"The police of Napoleon III could not remain inactive. At the end of June they sent in a report the facts of which were established after a difficult inquiry by one of their best agents. I'll read it. It runs:

'The Signorina's Italian passport, while making reservations about the date of her birth, describes her as Josephine Pellegrini-Balsamo, Countess of Cagliostro, born at Palermo on the 29th of July, 1788. Having gone to Palermo, I succeeded in discovering the old registers of the Parish of Mortarana; and in one of them, under the date of the 29th of July, 1788, I found the entry of the birth of Josephine Balsamo, daughter of Joseph Balsamo and Josephine de la P., subject of the King of France.

Was it Josephine Tascher de la Pagerie, the maiden name of the young wife who was separated from the Vicomte de Beauharnais, and of the future wife of General Bonaparte? I made investigations from this point of view. They required considerable patience; but at the end of them I learnt from the manuscript letters of a Lieutenant *de la prévôté*, of Paris, that in 1788 they had been on the point of arresting the Count of Cagliostro, who, though he had been expelled from France after the affair of the Queen's Necklace, was living in a little house at Fontainebleau under the name of Pellegrini; and at that house he was visited everyday by a tall and slender lady. Now Josephine de Beauharnais was at this time living at Fontainebleau. She was tall and slender. On the eve of the day fixed for his arrest Cagliostro disappeared. His departure was the very next day followed by the departure of Josephine de Beauharnais.[2] A month later the child was born at Palermo.

These coincidences cannot fail to be impressive. But how much greater is the weight of them, when one considers them in the light of these two additional facts—ten years later the Empress Josephine brought to La Malmaison a young girl whom she declared to be her god daughter. This child won the heart of the Emperor to such a degree that he took the greatest pleasure in playing with her. What was her name? Josephine, or rather Josine. Secondly, on the fall of the Empire, the Czar Alexander II received this Josine at his Court. What title does she take? That of the Countess de Cagliostro.'"

The Baron d'Etigues laid great stress on these last words. They had listened to him with the deepest attention. Ralph, taken aback by this incredible story, tried to catch a shade of emotion or of some feeling on the face of the Countess. But she remained impassive, her beautiful eyes always faintly smiling.

The Baron continued: "This report and probably the dangerous influence which the Countess was beginning to acquire at the Tuileries, were to cut short her brilliant career. A decree for her expulsion was signed and for the expulsion of her brother. Her brother went away to Germany, she to Italy. One morning she arrived at Modena, whither she had been conducted by a young officer. He bowed, saluted her, and left her. This officer was the Prince of Arcola. He it was who was able to procure these two documents, the suppressed number of the *Charivari* and the secret report, the original of which is actually in his possession, with the official seals and signatures. Lastly it is he who a little while ago assured you of the indubitable identity of the woman he left that morning at Modena with the woman he sees here today."

The Prince of Arcola rose and said gravely:

"I am no believer in miracles; nevertheless what I say is the affirmation of a miracle. But the truth compels me to declare on my honor as a soldier that this is the woman whom I saluted and left at the railway station at Modena two and twenty years ago."

"Whom you saluted and left without anything in the nature of a polite farewell?" said Josephine Balsamo. She had turned towards the Prince and asked the question in a tone of mocking irony.

"What do you mean?"

"I mean that a young French officer is too courteous to take his leave of a pretty woman with just a formal salute."

"Which implies?"

"Which implies that you must have uttered some words."

"Perhaps. I no longer remember," said the Prince of Arcola with a touch of embarrassment.

"You bent down towards the exile, Monsieur. You kissed her hand rather longer than was necessary; and you said to her: 'I hope, Madam, that the hours I have had the pleasure of passing near you will not be without a tomorrow. For my part, I can never forget them.' And you repeated, emphasizing by your accent your gallant meaning: 'You understand, Madam? Never.'"

The Prince of Arcola appeared to be a man of admirable manners. However, at this exact revival of a moment that had passed a quarter of a century earlier, he was so upset that he muttered:

"Well, I'll be damned!"

But, recovering himself on the instant, he took the offensive, and in a bitter voice he said: "Madam, I have forgotten. If the memory of that meeting was pleasant, the memory of the second occasion on which I saw you has blotted it out."

"And this second occasion, Monsieur?"

"It was at the beginning of the following year, at Versailles, whither I accompanied the French plenipotentiaries entrusted with the task of negotiating the peace of the defeat. I saw you in a café, sitting at a table, drinking and laughing with some German officers, one of whom was an officer of Bismarck's staff. That day I understood the part you played at the Tuileries and on whose errand you came."

All these revelations of the vicissitudes of a life which seemed fabulous, were set forth in less than ten minutes. There was no structure of reasoning. No attempt, either logical or rhetorical, to impose this in credible thesis on those who were listening. Nothing but the facts, nothing but the bare proofs, violent, driven home like the blows of a fist, and all the more terrifying that they evoked against a quite young woman memories some of which went back more than a century!

Ralph d'Andresy was almost amazed. The scene appeared to him to savor of romance, or rather to be long to some fantastic and gloomy melodrama. These conspirators, who accepted these fables as if they had been indisputable facts, seemed to him the creatures of a dream. Truly he was quite alive to the poorness of the intelligence of these country bumpkins, relics of an epoch that had passed away. But all the same how on earth could they bring themselves to ignore the very data of the problem presented by the age they attributed to this woman? However credulous they might be, had they not eyes to see?

Again the attitude of the Countess to them appeared even more strange. Why this silence which, when all was said and done, was an acceptance of their theory, practically, at times, a confession? Was she refusing to demolish a legend of eternal youth which was pleasing to her and helpful to the execution of her plans? Or was it that, ignorant of the terrible danger hanging over her head, she looked upon all this theatrical display as merely a practical joke?

"Such is this woman's past," continued the Baron d'Etigues solemnly. "I shall not dwell on the intermediate episodes which link that past with today. Always keeping behind the scenes, Josephine Balsamo, the Countess of Cagliostro, played a part in the tragicomedy of Boulangism, in the sordid drama of Panama. One finds her hand in every event which is disastrous to our country. But in these matters we have only indications of the secret part she played. We have no direct proof. Let us leave them and come to this actual epoch. One word before we do so, however. Have you no observations to make about any of these matters, Madam?"

"Yes," she said.

"Let us have them."

"Well," said the young woman, with the same note of mocking irony in her delightful voice, "I should like to know, since I appear to be on my trial and you to have formed yourselves into a really medieval tribunal—of the German brand, of course—whether you attach any real importance to the charges you have heaped up against me. If you do you may as well condemn me to be burnt alive on the spot, as a witch, a spy, and a renegade—all crimes which the Inquisition never pardoned."

"No," replied Godfrey d'Etigues. "I have only narrated these different adventures of yours in order to paint, in a few strokes, as vivid a picture of you as possible."

"You think you have painted as vivid a picture of me as possible?"

"Yes; from the point of view that concerns us."

"You are certainly easily satisfied," she said in a faintly contemptuous tone. "And what are the links you think you see between these different adventures?"

"I see three kinds of links," said the Baron with some heat. "First there is the evidence of all the people who have recognized you, thanks to whom we can go back, step by step, to the end of the eighteenth century. Next your own avowal of your claims."

"What avowal?"

"You have repeated to the Prince of Arcola the very terms of a conversation which took place between the two of you in the station at Modena."

"So I did!" she said. "And then?"

"And then I have here three portraits, all three of which are portraits of you. Are they not?"

She looked at them and said: "Yes. They are portraits of me."

"Well," said Godfrey d'Etigues in a tone of triumph, "the first is a miniature, painted at Moscow in 1816, of Josine, Countess of Cagliostro. The second is this photograph taken in the year 1870. This is the last, taken recently in Paris. The miniature has your signature on the back, after the words presenting it to Prince Serge Dolgorouki; the two photographs have your signature across the face. All the three signatures are letter for letter the same with the same flourish."

"What does that prove?" she asked in the same mocking, ironical accents.

"That proves that the same woman retains in 1892 her face of 1816 and of 1870."

"Then to the stake with her!" she cried and laughed a silvery, rippling laugh.

"Do not laugh, Madam. You know that between you and us a laugh is an abominable blasphemy!" cried the Baron sternly.

She struck the arm of the bench with an impatient hand.

"Look here, Monsieur: we've had enough of this nonsense!" she exclaimed, frowning at the Baron. "What is it exactly that you have against me? What am I here for?"

"You're here, Madam, to pay the penalty of the crimes you have committed."

"What crimes?"

"My friends and I were twelve, twelve men who were seeking the same end. Now we are only nine. The three others are dead. You murdered them!"

A shadow, perhaps—at least Ralph d'Andresy thought that he saw one—veiled for a moment, like a cloud, the smile of the Giaconda. Then on the instant her beautiful face resumed its usual expression as if nothing could ruffle its serenity, not even this frightful accusation launched at her with so violent a virulence. You might very well have said that the ordinary feelings of humanity were unknown to her, or that at any rate they did not betray themselves by those symptoms of indignation, revolt, and horror with which all human beings are overwhelmed. What an anomaly she was! Guilty or not, any other woman would have risen in revolt. She said never a word. It might have been cynicism; it might have been innocence. There was no saying.

The friends of the Baron remained motionless, their brows knitted, their faces stern. Behind those who hid him almost entirely from the eyes of Josephine Balsamo, Ralph perceived

Beaumagnan. His arms still resting on the back of the chair in front of him, he kept his face buried in his hands. But his eyes, gleaming between his parted fingers, never left the face of his enemy.

In a complete silence Godfrey d'Etigues proceeded to develop his indictment, or rather his three terrible indictments. He did so coldly, without raising his voice. It was as if a clerk were reading an indictment in which he had no personal interest.

"Eighteen months ago," he began, "Denis Saint-Hébert, the youngest of us, was out shooting on his estate in the neighborhood of Le Havre. At the end of the afternoon, he left his bailiff and his keeper and went off, with his gun over his shoulder, to look at the sunset over the sea, from the top of the cliff. He did not turn up that night. Next day they found his body among the rocks uncovered by the ebbing tide.

"Suicide? Denis Saint-Hébert was rich, in the best of health, and of a happy disposition. Why should he have killed himself? A crime. No one dreamt of such a thing. An accident, then.

"In the following June we were again plunged into mourning under analogous conditions. George d'Isneauval, while shooting gulls in the early morning, slipped on the seaweed in such a disastrous fashion that he struck his head against a rock and fractured his skull. Some hours later two fishermen found him. He was dead. He left a widow and two little children.

"Again an accident, I suppose. Yes: an accident for his widow, his children and his family. But for us? Was it possible that Chance should for the second time have attacked the little group we had formed? Twelve friends form a league to discover a great secret, to attain an end of considerable importance. Two of them are struck down. Are we not compelled to presume the existence of a criminal conspiracy which, in attacking them, at the same time attacks their enterprise?

"It was the Prince of Arcola who opened our eyes and set us on the right path. He knew that we were not the only persons to know of the existence of this great secret. He knew that, in the course of a séance in the suite of rooms of the Empress Eugenie at the Tuileries, someone had revived the list of the four enigmas handed down to his descendants by Cagliostro, and that one of them was called by the very name of the enigma in which we are interested—the enigma of the Candlestick with Seven Branches. Must we not therefore seek among those to whom the legend could have been handed down?

"Thanks to the excellent means of investigation which we had at our disposal, our inquiry bore fruit in barely a fortnight. In a private hotel in a quiet street in Paris was living a lady of the name of Pellegrini. Apparently she was leading an almost secluded life and often disappeared for months at a time. Of uncommon beauty, her behavior was discreetness itself. Indeed it appeared to be her main effort not to attract attention. Under the name of the Countess of Cagliostro she frequented certain circles which busied themselves with magic, the occult, and the black mass.

"We managed to get a photograph of her—this one. We sent it to the Prince of Arcola, who was traveling in Spain. He was amazed to recognize the woman he had formerly known.

"We made inquiries about her movements. On the day of Saint-Hébert's death, in the neighborhood of Le Havre, she was staying at Le Havre. She was staying at Dieppe when George d'Isneauval met his death at the foot of the Dieppe cliffs!

"I questioned the dead men's families. The widow of George d'Isneauval confided to me that her husband, towards the end of his life, had had an affair with a woman who caused him, according to her, an infinite amount of suffering. In the other quarter a written confession of Saint-Hébert, and up to then kept secret by his mother, informed us that he had been so foolish as to jot down our twelve names and some facts about the Candlestick with the Seven Branches on one of the leaves of his pocketbook and that pocketbook had been stolen from him by a woman.

"After that everything was clear. Mistress of a part of our secrets, and desirous of knowing more, the woman who had been loved by Saint-Hébert had thrown herself across the path of George d'Isneauval and been loved by him. Then, having wormed their secrets out of them, in her fear of their denouncing her to their friends, she murdered them. That woman is here before us."

Godfrey d'Etigues paused again. The silence once more became oppressive, so heavy that the judges seemed to be paralyzed in that burdensome atmosphere so loaded with anguish. Only the Countess of Cagliostro maintained her air of aloofness, as if no single word had concerned her.

Always stretched at full length in his post of observation, Ralph admired the young woman's delightful and voluptuous beauty; at the same time he could not help feeling some distress at perceiving such a mass of evidence being piled up against her. The indictment gripped her tighter and tighter. From every quarter facts thronged to the assault; and Ralph suspected that she was threatened by a yet more direct attack.

"Am I to tell you about the third crime?" said the Baron.

She replied in weary accents:

"If you like. Everything you have been saying is quite unintelligible. You have been talking about people whose very names I never heard before. So a crime more or less—"

"You didn't know Saint-Hébert and George d'Isneauval?"

She shrugged her shoulders and did not answer.

Godfrey d'Etigues bent closer to her and in a lower voice he said:

"And Beaumagnan?"

She raised limpid eyes to his face:

"Beaumagnan?"

"Yes—the third of our friends you murdered. And only a little while ago... A few weeks... He died poisoned... You did not know him?"

III

A TRIBUNAL OF THE INQUISITION

What was the meaning of this accusation? Ralph looked at Beaumagnan. He had risen, without raising himself to his full height, and sheltering himself behind his friends drew nearer and nearer to Josephine Balsamo. With her eyes fixed intently on the Baron, she paid no attention to him.

Then Ralph understood why Beaumagnan had hidden himself and the formidable trap they were laying for the young woman. If she had really tried to poison Beaumagnan, if she really believed him dead, with what a fear she would be stricken when he stepped forward in person to face her, living, ready to accuse her! If, on the other hand, she remained untroubled and Beaumagnan appeared to her as great a stranger as the others, what a proof of her innocence!

Ralph found himself extraordinarily anxious. Indeed so keenly did he desire her to succeed in foiling the plotters that he tried to find some method of conveying a warning to her.

But the Baron d'Etigues did not loose his prey; and he continued with scarcely a pause: "Then you don't remember this crime either, do you?"

For the first time displaying a touch of impatience, she frowned at him; but she said nothing.

"Perhaps you never even knew Beaumagnan?" said the Baron, bending towards her like an examining magistrate watching for a clumsy sentence. "Come, speak up! You never knew him?"

She did not speak up; she did not speak at all. The effect of his obstinate insistence must have been to awaken her distrust, for a shadow of anxiety dimmed her smile. Like a hunted beast, she scented an ambush; and her eyes searched the shadows.

She studied Godfrey d'Etigues, then turned towards de la Vaulpalier and de Bennetot, then to the other side where Beaumagnan was standing. On the instant there was a gesture of dismay, the start of one who sees a phantom; and her eyes closed. She stretched out her hands to thrust away the terrible vision which menaced her and they heard her mutter:

"Beaumagnan! Beaumagnan!"

Was it the avowal? Was she going to weaken and confess her crime? Beaumagnan waited. With all the force of his being, so to speak, visible, with clenched fists, with the veins on his forehead swollen, with his stern face convulsed by a superhuman effort of will, he demanded that access of feebleness in which all resistance crumbles.

For a moment he thought he was succeeding. The young woman was weakening; she was yielding to her tamer. A cruel joy illuminated his face. A vain hope! Recovering from her faintness, she drew herself slowly upright. Every second restored to her a little of her serenity and little by little freed her smile; and she said with a reasonableness which appeared the very expression of the obvious truth:

"You did give me a fright, Beaumagnan! I read in the newspapers the news of your death. Why did your friends try to trick me?"

Ralph realized at once that everything that had passed up to that moment was of no importance. Now the two real adversaries found themselves face to face. Short as it must be, given the weapons of Beaumagnan and the isolation of the young woman, the real struggle was only just beginning. And this was not the cunning and sustained attack of the Baron d'Etigues. But the wild onslaught of an enemy exasperated by rage and hate.

"A lie! A lie!" he cried. "Everything in you is a lie. You are hypocrisy, vileness, treason, vice! Everything sordid and repulsive in the world is masked by your smile. Ah! That smile! What an abominable mask! One longs to tear it from you with red-hot pincers. Your smile is death! It is the everlasting damnation of the man who lets himself be charmed by it... Heavens! What a wretch this woman is."

The impression that Ralph had had from the beginning of being a spectator in a scene from the Inquisition, grew infinitely stronger in face of the fury of this man who hurled his anathema with all the violence of a monk of the Middle Ages. His voice trembled with indignation. His gestures were a threat, as if he were going to strangle the impious creature whose divine smile brought madness on her victim and doomed him to the fires of Hell.

"Calm yourself, Beaumagnan," she said with an excess of gentleness that infuriated him more than if she had hurled an insult at him.

Nevertheless he struggled to restrain himself and to control the words which surged up in him. But they rushed from his mouth, storming, headlong, or muttered so faintly that his friends, whom he now addressed, had sometimes great difficulty in understanding the strange confession he was making, beating himself on the breast exactly like the penitents of the days of yore making public confession of their sins.

"It was I, I, who deliberately entered the arena after the death of d'Isneauval. Yes: I was sure that this sorceress was still raging on our trail... That I should be stronger than the others. Safer against temptation... And I was right! You know I was right!...

You all knew my intention at that time. Already dedicated to the service of the Church, I was desirous of assuming the robe of a priest. I was, then, secure from the evil, protected by formal undertakings and even more by the intense ardor of my faith. In that temper I betook myself to one of the Spiritist meetings at which I knew I should find her.

"She was there; and there was no need for the friend who had brought me, to point her out to me; and I confess that, on the very threshold of my enterprise, an obscure apprehension made me hesitate. I watched her. She spoke to few of the people present and wore an air of reserve, content seemingly to listen, smoking cigarettes.

"In accordance with my instructions my friend went and sat down beside her and entered into conversation with the persons among whom she was sitting. Then from a distance he called me by my name; and I saw from her troubled look, without any possibility of being mistaken, that she knew that name. She had read it in the pocketbook stolen from Denis Saint-Hébert. Beaumagnan was one of the twelve associates... One of the ten survivors. And this woman who appeared to live in a kind of dream, suddenly awoke. A little while after she spoke to me. For two hours she displayed all the charm of her spirit, she used every weapon that beauty gives a woman, and in the end induced me to promise that I would go to see her the next day.

"At that instant, at the very second at which I left her, that night, at the door of her house, I ought to have fled to the end of the world. It was already too late. There was no longer in me either courage, or will, or foresight, nothing but the insane desire to see her again. It is true that I disguised this desire in fine phrases: I was accomplishing a duty... It was necessary to know the enemy's game, to bring home her crimes to her and punish her for them, and so forth... Mere pretexts! In reality at the first assault I had fallen a victim to her fascination; at the

A TRIBUNAL OF THE INQUISITION

first assault I was convinced of her innocence. A smile such as that was clear evidence of a soul of crystal purity.

"Neither the sacred memory of Saint-Hébert, nor that of my poor d'Isneauval cleared my vision. I would not see. I lived for some months in obscurity, tasting the most infamous joys, without even a blush at being an object of reproach and scandal, at renouncing my vows and denying my faith.

"Inconceivable sins in a man like me, I swear it, friends. Nevertheless I committed another which perhaps surpasses them all. I was a traitor to our cause. I broke that vow of silence which we took when we formed our union for that common end. This woman knows as much of the great secret as we know ourselves."

At these words a murmur of indignation ran round the room. Beaumagnan bent his head.

Now Ralph understood better the drama which was unfolding before him; and the characters who were playing their parts in it assumed their right proportion. Country squires, rustics, bumpkins? Yes—without a doubt. But Beaumagnan was there—Beaumagnan who inspired them with his own spirit and filled them with his exaltation. In the middle of these vulgar lives and these absurd figures he stood forth the prophet and the seer. He had forced on them as a duty some conspirator's task to which he had devoted himself body and soul, as in the old days one devoted oneself to God, and left one's castle to go on a crusade.

Mystic passions of this kind transform those in whom they burn into heroes or executioners. In Beaumagnan there was a veritable inquisitor. In the fifteenth century he would have persecuted and mangled to tear from the impious the confession of faith.

He had the instinct of domination and the bearing of a man for whom no obstacle exists. Did a woman rise between him and his end? Let her die. If he loved this woman, a public confession absolved him. And those who listened to him succumbed to the ascendancy of this hard master all the more easily because his hardness appeared to be directed quite as much against himself.

Humiliated by the confession of his fall, he was no longer angry; and he continued in a dull voice:

"Why did I fail? I do not know. A man like me ought not to fail. I have not even the excuse of being able to say that she questioned me. She did not. She often talked about the four enigmas mentioned by Cagliostro; and one day almost without knowing what I was doing, I spoke the irreparable words... like a wretched weakling... just to make myself agreeable... just to seem important to her eyes... that her smile might grow more tender. I said to myself: 'She shall be our ally... She shall help us with her counsel, with her clearsightedness, refined and heightened by years of practice of divination. I was mad. The intoxication of sin had set my reason tottering.

"The awakening was terrible. About three weeks ago I had to go to Spain on a mission. I said goodbye to her in the morning. In the afternoon, towards three o'clock, having an appointment in the center of Paris I left the set of rooms in which I was living in the Luxembourg. Then it chanced that, having forgotten to give some orders to my man, I returned to my rooms through the courtyard and up the servants' staircase. My man had gone out and left the kitchen door open. As I came through it, I heard a noise. I went forward quietly. There was someone in my bedroom. It was this woman. I had a good view of her in the looking glass. What was she doing, bending over my trunk? I watched. She opened a small cardboard box which contained the cachets which I take when I'm traveling, to cure my insomnia. She took out one of these cachets and in its place she put another, a cachet which she took from her purse.

"My emotion was so great that I never even dreamt of seizing her. When I grew composed enough to enter the room, she had gone. I could not overtake her.

"I hurried to a chemist and had the cachets analyzed. One of them contained poison enough to destroy me.

"So I had the irrefutable proof. Having been so imprudent as to tell her everything I knew about the secret, I had been condemned. It was just as well, was it not, to clear out of her path a useless witness and an associate who might one day or other take his share of the spoils, or, it might be, reveal the truth, attack the enemy, and vanquish her. Death then. Death—as for Denis Saint-Hébert and George d'Isneauval. A stupid murder for no sufficient reason.

"I wrote from Spain to one of my friends. Some days afterwards certain newspapers announced the death of a Frenchman named Beaumagnan at Madrid.

"From that time I lived in the shadow and followed her step by step. She betook herself first to Rouen, then to Le Havre, then to Dieppe, that is to say to the very places which bound the scene of our researches. From what I had told her she knew that we were on the point of ransacking an ancient Priory in the neighborhood of Dieppe. She spent the whole of a day there, and profiting by the fact that the building had been abandoned, searched it. Then I lost sight of her. I found her at Rouen. You have heard what followed, from d'Etigues. How the trap was laid and how she fell into it, attracted by the bait of this Candlestick with Seven Branches, which, as she believed, a peasant had unearthed.

"Such is the character of this woman. You realize the reasons which prevent us from handing her over to the law. The scandal of the proceedings would reflect on us, and throwing the full light of day on to our enterprises, would render them impossible. Our duty, however dreadful it may appear, is to judge her ourselves, without hatred, but with all the severity that she deserves."

Beaumagnan was silent. He had ended his indictment with a seriousness more dangerous to the accused than his anger. She appeared undoubtedly guilty, almost a monster in this series of useless murders. For his part, Ralph d'Andresy no longer knew what to think; but he cursed in his heart this man who had loved the young woman and who had just recalled, trembling with emotion, that sacrilegious love.

The Countess of Cagliostro rose and looked her adversary full in the face, always with a faintly mocking air.

"I was quite right," she said. "It is the stake?"

"That will be according as we decide," he said. "Nothing at any rate can prevent the execution of our just sentence."

"A sentence? By what right?" said she. "There are judges for that. You are not judges. You talk about the fear of scandal. What does it matter to me that you need darkness and silence for your schemes? Set me free."

"Free? Free to continue your work of death? You are in our power. You will suffer our sentence," he said sternly.

"Your sentence for what? If there were a single judge among you, a single man who had any sense of reason and probability, he would laugh at your stupid charges and your unconnected proofs."

"Words! Phrases!" he cried. "What we want are proofs to the contrary... Something to disprove the evidence that my eyes gave me."

"What use would it be to defend myself? You have made up your minds."

"We have made them up because you are guilty."

"Guilty of pursuing the same end as you; yes, that I admit. And that is the reason why you committed that shameful action of coming to spy upon me and play that comedy of love. If you were caught by your own snare, all the worse for you. If you have revealed to me facts about the enigma, of which I already knew the existence from the document of Cagliostro, all the worse for you! Now it is an obsession with me; and I have sworn to attain that end, whatever happens, in spite of you. That and that only is my crime—in your eyes."

"Your crime is murder," asserted Beaumagnan, who was again losing his temper.

"I have not murdered anyone," she said firmly.

"You pushed Saint-Hébert over the cliff; you fractured d'Isneauval's skull."

"Saint-Hébert? D'Isneauval? I never knew them. I hear their names for the first time today," she protested.

"And me! And me!" he exclaimed violently. "Didn't you know me? Didn't you try to poison me?"

"No."

He lost his temper utterly and in an access of fury he roared: "But I saw you, Josephine Balsamo! I saw you as clearly as I see you now! While you were putting that poison in the box, I saw your smile grow ferocious and the corners of your lips rise in the grin of the damned!"

She shook her head and said firmly:

"It was not I."

He appeared to choke. How dared she say such a thing?

But quite coolly she laid her hand on his shoulder and said quietly:

"Hate is making you lose your wits, Beaumagnan. Your fanatical soul is in a wild revolt against the sin of love. However, in spite of that, I suppose you'll allow me to defend myself?"

"It is your right, but be quick about it," he said less loudly, but coldly.

"It won't take long. Ask your friends for the miniature, painted in 1816, of the Countess of Cagliostro."

Beaumagnan obeyed and took the miniature from the hands of the Baron.

"Good. Look at it carefully," she went on. "It is my portrait, isn't it?"

"What are you driving at?" he said.

"Answer. Is it my portrait?" she said impatiently.

"Yes," he said with decision.

"Then if that is my portrait it means that I was alive at that time? It is eighty years ago; and from that portrait I was then twenty-five or thirty? Consider carefully before answering. What! In the face of such a miracle you hesitate, do you? You dare not assert that it is a fact; now, dare you?"

She paused, gazing at him with compelling eyes; then she continued:

"But there is more to come. Open the frame of this miniature, the back of it, and you will find on the other side of the porcelain, another portrait. The portrait of a smiling woman, wearing a veil, an almost invisible veil, which descends as far as her eyebrows, and through which you can see her hair parted into two waving rolls. It is me again, isn't it?"

While Beaumagnan carried out her instructions she had put on a light veil of tulle, the bottom of which touched the line of her eyebrows; and she lowered her eyes with an expression of charming reserve.

Beaumagnan compared her face with the portrait and stammered: "B-B-B-But it is you! It is!"

"Is there any doubt about it?"

"Not the slightest. It is you," he declared.

"Well, read the date on the right side of it."

Beaumagnan read out: "Painted at Milan in the year 1498."

She repeated: "In 1498—that's four hundred years ago?"

She laughed outright, a clear, ringing laugh.

"Don't look so astonished," she said. "I have known of the existence of this double portrait for a long time, and I have been hunting for it. But you may take it from me that there is no miracle about it. I am not going to try to persuade you that I was that painter's model and that I am four hundred years old. No: that is merely the face of the Virgin Mary; and it is a copy of a fragment of the Holy Family of Bernadino Luini, a Milanese painter and a pupil of Leonardo da Vinci."

Then, with a sudden gravity, and without giving her adversary time to breathe, she said to him: "You understand now what I am driving at, don't you, Beaumagnan? Between the Virgin of Luini, the young girl of Moscow and myself, there is that elusive, marvellous, and yet undeniable bond, a likeness—an absolute likeness... Three faces in one. Three faces which are not those of three different women, but which are the face of the same woman. Then why do you refuse to admit that the same phenomenon, after all a perfectly natural phenomenon, should not reproduce itself in other circumstances, and that the woman whom you saw in your bedroom was not me, but another woman who resembles me so closely as to deceive you. Another woman who knew and murdered your friends Saint-Hébert and d'Isneauval?"

"I saw... I saw!" protested Beaumagnan, who had come so close to her that he almost touched her, and he drew himself up, pale as death and quivering with indignation. "I saw! I saw with my eyes!"

"Your eyes also see the portrait of twenty-five years ago and the miniature of eighty years ago, and the picture of four hundred years ago. Is that me too?"

She presented to Beaumagnan's gaze her young face in all its fresh beauty, that perfect row of white teeth, her delicately tinted, rounded cheeks, her clear and limpid child's eyes.

Weakening, he stammered: "T-T-There are moments, sorceress, when I b-b-believe in this absurdity. With you one never knows! Look: the woman of the miniature has, low down on her bare shoulders, on the white skin of her bosom, a black mark. That mark, it is there, low down on your shoulder... I have seen it there... Come... Show it to the others and let them see it too and be edified!"

He was livid and the sweat was trickling down his forehead. He stretched out his hand towards her high necked bodice. But she thrust it back, and speaking with considerable dignity, she said:

"That's enough, Beaumagnan. You don't know what you're doing and you haven't known for months. Listening to you just now I was simply amazed, for you spoke of me as having been your mistress, and I haven't been your mistress at all. It's all very fine to beat your bosom in public, but it is also necessary that the confession should be the truth. You hadn't the courage to tell the truth. The demon of pride forbade you to admit the humiliating check you received; and like a coward, you have let them believe in a thing that never happened. During the months you were crawling at my feet you entreated and threatened without your lips having ever once brushed my hand. That's the secret of your behavior and your hate.

"Failing to move me, you tried to destroy me and for your friends you painted a frightful picture of me as criminal, spy, and sorceress. Yes, as sorceress! A man like you, to use your own words, could not fail; and if you did fail, it could have been brought about by the action of diabolical witchcraft. No, Beaumagnan: you no longer know what you are doing, or what you are saying. You saw me in your bedroom substituting the cachet which was to poison you, did you? Come now, by what right do you invoke the testimony of your eyes? Your eyes? But they were obsessed by my image; and that other woman showed you a face which was not her own, but mine, and you could not help seeing it. Yes, Beaumagnan: I repeat it, the other woman... There is another woman on the path we are all of us following... There's another woman who has inherited certain documents from Cagliostro and who also uses the names that he assumed. Marquise de Belmonte, Countess de F... look for her, Beaumagnan. For she it was whom you saw; and it is really upon the stupidest hallucination of a deranged brain that you have reared this structure of so many lying accusations against me. In fact all this business is merely a childish farce; and I was quite right to remain unmoved in the midst of you all, as an innocent woman in the first place, and in the second place as a woman who was in no danger. In spite of your airs of judges and torturers and in spite of the enormous personal interest each of you has in success of your common enterprise, you are at bottom honorable men who would never dare to murder me. You would perhaps, Beaumagnan; because you're a fanatic who lives in terror of me. But you would have to find here executioners capable of obeying you. And there are none here. Then what are you going to do? Imprison me? Shut me up in some out-of-the-way corner. If that amuses you, do so. But you may make up your minds that there is no cell from which I cannot escape as easily as you can leave the room. So go now: judge me and sentence me. For my part, I am not going to say another word."

She sat down, pushed up her veil, and setting her elbow on the arm of the bench, rested her face on her hand. She had played her part. She had spoken without any vehemence but with a profound conviction, and in a few sentences, of a really irrefutable logic, she had connected the accusation brought against her with this inexplicable legend of longevity which was the keynote of the affair.

In effect she had said: "It all holds together; and you yourselves have been obliged to base your indictment on the story of my adventures in the past. You had to start it with the narration of events which go back a hundred years, to come to the criminal actions of today. If I am mixed up in the latter it is because I was the heroine of the former. If I am the woman you saw, I am also the woman that my different portraits show you."

What were they to answer?

Beaumagnan was silent. The duel was ending in his defeat; and he did not try to disguise it. Besides his friends no longer had the implacable and harassed faces of men who find themselves forced to the terrible decision of death. Doubt was stirring in them; Ralph d'Andresy was distinctly conscious of it and he would have derived some hope from it, if the memory of the preparations which Godfrey d'Etigues and de Bennetot had made, had not lessened his satisfaction. Beaumagnan and the Baron conversed in low voices for a few moments; then Beaumagnan made his answer in the manner of a man for whom the discussion was closed.

"You have before you, my friends, all the facts of the case," he began. "The prosecution and the defense have said their last word. You have seen with what genuine conviction Godfrey d'Etigues and myself brought these charges against this woman and with what subtlety she defended herself, entrenching herself behind an inadmissible resemblance and so giving a striking example of her resourcefulness and her infernal cunning. The situation then is quite simple: an opponent of this strength of will and intelligence and disposing of such resources, will never let us rest. Our task is compromised. One after the other she will destroy us. Her existence implies inevitably our ruin and destruction.

"Does that mean that there is no other solution but death and that the punishment she deserves is the only one that we can consider? It does not. Let her disappear, let her be unable to make any fresh attempt. We have no right to demand more; and if our consciences revolt against such an indulgent solution, nevertheless we ought to be content with it because, when all is said and done, we are not here to punish, but to defend ourselves. These then are the arrangements we have made, subject to your approval. Tonight an English ship will be cruising off the coast. A boat will be lowered from it, and we shall row out to it and meet it at ten o'clock at the foot of the Needle of Belval. We shall hand over this woman; she will be taken to London, set ashore during the night, and shut up in a madhouse until our task is accomplished. I do not think that any of you will oppose this arrangement, which is not only generous and humane but also makes our task safe and ourselves secure against perils we should never escape."

Ralph perceived at once Beaumagnan's game and he thought to himself: "That means death. There is no English ship. There are two boats, of which one with a hole in its bottom will be towed out to sea and sink. The Countess of Cagliostro will disappear without anyone ever knowing what has become of her."

The duplicity of the scheme and the deceitful fashion in which it had been set forth frightened him. Why should not the friends of Beaumagnan agree to it when they were not even asked to answer in the affirmative? Their silence sufficed. Let none of them make any objection to it and Beaumagnan was free to act through his intermediary, Godfrey d'Etigues. None of them did raise any objection. Without knowing it they had pronounced sentence of death.

They all rose to go, manifestly delighted to have got out of the business so cheaply. No one made any comment. They had the air of leaving a gathering of friends at which they had discussed matters of no moment. Some of them moreover had to catch a train at the neighboring station. At the end of a couple of minutes they had all of them gone except Beaumagnan and the two cousins. So it came about in a fashion which Ralph found disconcerting that this dramatic meeting in which a woman's life had been dealt with in such an arbitrary manner and her death sentence obtained by so odious a subterfuge, came to a sudden end, like a play the dénouement of which is brought about before the logical moment, like a trial in which sentence is pronounced in the middle of the evidence.

This disingenuous juggling revealed to Ralph d'Andresy the subtle and crafty nature of Beaumagnan with entire clearness. Inexorable and a fanatic, ravaged by love and pride, the man had decided on death. But there were in him scruples, cowardly hypocrisies, confused fears, which obliged him, so to speak, to hide himself from his own conscience and perhaps also from the eyes of justice. Hence this dark solution of the difficulty, this free hand obtained by this abominable trick. Now, standing on the threshold, he was gazing at the woman who was about to die. Livid and scowling, the muscles of his jaw twitching nervously, his arms crossed, he had as usual the rather theatrical air of a romantic personage. His brain must be teeming with tumultuous thoughts. Was he hesitating at the last moment?

In any case his reflections did not last long. He gripped Godfrey d'Etigues by the shoulder and drew him over the threshold, flinging this order over his shoulder to de Bennetot as he went out: "Guard her! And no nonsense! Understand? If there is—"

During the departure of the conspirators and then of their leaders the Countess of Cagliostro did not stir; and her face preserved that thoughtful and serene expression which was so little in keeping with the situation.

"Assuredly she has no suspicion of the danger that threatens her," Ralph said to himself. "All that she is looking forward to is confinement in a madhouse, and she is not worrying at all about the prospect of that."

An hour passed; the shades of evening began to darken the chamber. Twice the young woman looked at her watch. Then she tried to enter into conversation with de Bennetot, and of a sudden her face assumed an expression of incredible fascination and her voice inflections that moved one like a caress.

De Bennetot grunted boorishly and did not answer.

Another half-hour passed; she looked round and then gazed at the open door. It was quite clear that she had made up her mind that flight was possible, that she was drawing herself together to spring for the door. For his part, Ralph was trying to find some method of helping her in the effort. If he had had a revolver he would have made no bones about dropping de Bennetot. He thought for a moment of jumping down into the chamber; but the opening of his post of observation was too narrow. Besides some instinct seemed to awake de Bennetot to the danger and he pulled out his revolver, growling:

"A movement, a single movement, and I shoot. By God, I will!"

He was a man to keep that oath. She did not stir.

Ralph, in a growing, torturing anxiety for her, gazed at her untiringly.

Towards seven o'clock Godfrey d'Etigues returned, carrying a traveling rug over his arm.

He lit a lamp and said to Oscar de Bennetot: "Get everything ready. Go and fetch the stretcher. It's in the coach-house. Then you can go and get some dinner."

When he was alone with the young woman the Baron appeared to hesitate. Ralph saw that his face was haggard, his eyes wild, and that he was on the point of speech or action. But the words or the acts must have been of a kind from which one shrinks, for he was for sometime restless and fidgeting. Then his opening was brutal.

"Pray to God, Madam," he said suddenly.

She replied in a puzzled tone: "Pray to God? Why are you telling me to do that?"

Then he said in a very low voice: "Do as you like... Only I must warn you—"

"Warn me of what?" she asked gazing at him in a sudden anxiety.

"There are moments," he murmured, "when one ought to pray to God as if one was about to die that very night."

She was stricken with a sudden panic. The facts of the situation suddenly flashed on her. Her arms seemed to stiffen and she clasped her hands in a kind of feverish convulsion.

"Die?... Die?... But there is no question of that, is there?... Beaumagnan never spoke of death... He spoke of a madhouse."

He did not answer.

The unfortunate woman murmured:

"Heavens! He has deceived me. The madhouse was a lie... It's something else... You're going to throw me into the sea. At night... It's horrible! But it isn't possible... Me die—me?... Help!... Help!"

Godfrey d'Etigues caught up the traveling rug and with a furious brutality he covered the young woman's head with it and pressed his hand over her mouth to smother her cries. As he was doing so, de Bennetot returned carrying the stretcher on his shoulder. The two of them stretched her out on it and tied her down securely and in such a way, that through an opening between the slats, there hung down the iron ring to which a heavy boulder was to be fastened.

IV

THE SINKING BOAT

The darkness was thickening. Godfrey d'Etigues lit a lamp. Oscar de Bennetot went to the château to get some dinner. He must have made a hasty meal, for he was back in about a quarter of an hour. The two cousins settled down to the death vigil. Even in that dim light Ralph could see that their faces were sinister. He could see the nervous twitchings which the thought of the crime so near at hand provoked.

"You ought to have brought a bottle of rum," growled Oscar de Bennetot. "There are occasions on which one had better not perceive too clearly what one is doing."

"This is not one of them," said the Baron coldly. "On the contrary, we shall need to have all our wits about us."

"It's a nice business," growled de Bennetot.

"Then you ought to have argued it out with Beaumagnan and refused him your help," said the Baron impatiently.

"It was impossible," murmured de Bennetot.

"Then obey," said the Baron sternly.

The time passed slowly. No sound came from the château or from the sleeping countryside.

Once de Bennetot rose, went to their prisoner, and bending down, listened. Then he turned to the Baron and said:

"She is not even groaning. She certainly is a woman of character."

He went back to his chair and added in a low voice in which there was a note of fear: "Do you believe all these things they say about her?"

"What things?"

"About her age?... And all those stories of bygone days?"

"They're rubbish!" said the Baron scornfully. "Beaumagnan believes in them at any rate."

"Who knows what Beaumagnan believes, or what he doesn't?" said the Baron impatiently.

"Nevertheless you must admit, Godfrey, that it's an infernally odd business... and that everything goes to show that she was not born yesterday."

"Yes: that is so," murmured Godfrey d'Etigues.

"For my part, when I read that paper Beaumagnan drew up, I spoke to her as if she really had been living all those years ago."

"Then you do believe it?"

"More or less. But stop talking about it. I've already had a good deal more than I bargained for in getting mixed up in this affair. If I had only known what it meant before I started on it, I swear to you—" he raised his voice—"I would have refused to have anything to do with it, and made no bones about it. Only—"

He broke off short. The subject was in the highest degree distasteful to him and he did not wish to say a word more about this infinitely painful business.

But de Bennetot went on: "Yes, and I swear to you that for two pins I'd clear out now; and all the more, look you, because I've a notion that Beaumagnan has us all nicely hooked. As I told you before he knows a lot more about the business than we do; and we're just puppets in his hands. One day or other, when he no longer has any need of us, he'll bid us a fond farewell and we shall see that he has worked the whole business for his own advantage. I'd bet on it. However—"

Godfrey put his finger to his lip and murmured: "Be quiet. She can hear you."

"What does that matter?" said de Bennetot. "In a little while she'll—"

The words died away on his lips; and they seemed no longer to dare to break the silence. Every quarter of an hour the clock of the village church chimed. Ralph fancied he could see their lips move as they counted the strokes, gazing fearfully at one another without saying anything.

But when that clock struck ten, Godfrey d'Etigues banged his fist down on the table with a violence that made the lamp jingle.

"Hell take it! It's time we started."

"What a disgusting job it is!" growled de Bennetot. "Are we going by ourselves?"

"The others want to come with us. But I shall send them back from the top of the cliff, since they believe in that English ship," said the Baron.

"I should much prefer that we went in a body," said de Bennetot.

"Oh, be quiet! My instructions are that only you and I are to handle the matter. The others might get talking; and that would be a pretty kettle of fish. Hullo! Here they are!"

The others turned out to be the three who had not taken the train, that is to say d'Ormont, Rufus d'Estiers, and Rolleville. The latter was carrying a stable lamp which the Baron made him extinguish.

"No lights," he said. "Somebody would see it moving about on the cliff and start gossiping about it. Have the servants gone to bed?"

"Yes," said Rufus d'Estiers. "And Clarice?"

"She must be upstairs. We haven't seen anything of her," said Rolleville.

"As a matter of fact, she's a little out of sorts today," said the Baron. "Let's be getting off."

D'Ormont and Rolleville took the handles of the stretcher. They crossed the park and then a field to the lane which led from the village to the priest's staircase. The starless sky was black with heavy clouds; and in the darkness the little procession, practically feeling its way, stumbled over ruts and banks. Curses kept slipping out; the Baron d'Etigues angrily hushed them.

"Will you stop that noise, confound you!" he muttered savagely. "Somebody will recognize our voices!"

"Who will recognize our voices, Godfrey? There's absolutely nobody about, for you took your precautions with regard to the coastguards," de Bennetot protested.

"Yes, they're safe enough. They're at the inn, guests of a man I can rely on. Nevertheless it's just possible that a patrol is making its round."

There came a depression in the plateau which the road followed. Then it rose again; and they made their way as best they might to the spot at which the staircase rose to the top of the cliff.

It had been hollowed out of the cliff many years before on the suggestion of a priest of Benouville, in order that the country people might descend to the beach. It was lighted by openings cut through the chalk. Through them there were magnificent views of the sea, whose waves were dashing against the rocks below, and into which one seemed to be on the point of plunging.

"It's going to be a difficult job, to get that stretcher down those steps," said Rolleville. "We'd better help you. At any rate we can light the staircase for you."

"No," said the Baron with decision. "It is wiser to separate. So back you get."

The three of them obeyed without further protest. The Baron lighted a bull's-eye lantern; and without any delay the two cousins set about the difficult task of getting the stretcher down the staircase.

It proved a long job. The steps were steep and the turnings in the cliff were sometimes so narrow that they were compelled to raise the stretcher right on end to get it round them. The little lamp afforded but a feeble light that illumined but a few steps at a time.

De Bennetot soon lost his temper, and to such a degree that with the natural brutality of a badly brought up boor he proposed simply to "chuck the whole thing down," that is to say, to push the unfortunate girl, litter and all, through one of the openings in the chalk.

At last they reached the beach, which was composed of a fine gravel, and stopped to recover their breath. A little way off two boats were drawn up side by side. The sea, quite calm, unruffled by the smallest wave, lapped against their keels. De Bennetot pointed out the hole he had made in the bottom of the smaller of the two, which for the time being was closed by a kind of stopper of straw. They set the stretcher on the three thwarts.

"Let's tie the whole lot together," said Godfrey d'Etigues.

De Bennetot made a very sensible objection; he said: "And if ever there's a search, and this boat and stretcher and girl are found tied together at the bottom of the sea, this stretcher will prove damned awkward evidence against us."

"We've got to go far enough out to make it impossible for anyone to recover anything ever," said the Baron. "Besides it's an old stretcher which hasn't been used for the last twenty years. I routed it out from a loft full of lumber. There's nothing to fear from that."

He spoke in a shaky, fearful voice that de Bennetot hardly recognized.

"What's the matter with you, Godfrey?" he asked.

"The matter with me? What should be the matter with me?" muttered the Baron more than a trifle indistinctly.

"Then?..."

"Then shove the boat down into the water... But first of all, according to the instructions of Beaumagnan, we've got to remove her gag and ask her if there is any last wish she wants carrying out. You'd better get it over."

"Me?" de Bennetot almost howled. "Me touch her? Me see her? I'd rather die!... Suppose you do it!"

"I couldn't... I'll be damned if I could," murmured the Baron huskily.

"But she's guilty... She committed those murders."

"Of course... Of course... At least it's probable that she did... The only thing is she looked such a gentle creature."

"Yes," said de Bennetot. "And she's so pretty—as beautiful as the Virgin."

With one accord they fell on their knees on the pebbles and started to pray aloud for the girl who was about to die and on whose behalf they called for "the intervention of the Virgin Mary."

Godfrey mingled verses from the burial service with prayers and de Bennetot punctuated them at intervals with fervent amens. This appeared to restore their courage a trifle, for they suddenly rose, burning to get the business over.

De Bennetot brought the great boulder he had ready, and tied it firmly to the iron ring. They pushed the boat down the beach into the still water. Then, together, they pushed the other boat down the beach and clambered into it. Godfrey took the two oars while de Bennetot tied the painter of the boat of the doomed woman to the last thwart of the boat they were in, then shipped the rudder.

So they rowed out to sea to the quiet accompaniment of dripping oars. Shadows darker than the night allowed them to make their slow way safely between lowering rocks towards the open sea. But, at the end of twenty minutes, their progress grew slower and slower; and they came to a stop.

"I can't go any further," said the Baron in a faint voice. "My arms have given out. It's your turn."

"I couldn't move her a yard," de Bennetot protested with manifest sincerity.

Godfrey made another attempt and gave it up.

"What's the use?" he said. "Surely we've got far enough out and to spare. What do you think?"

"Of course we have," said de Bennetot quickly—"especially since there's a breeze from the shore which will take the boat further out still."

"Then pull that straw out of the hole."

"You've got to do that," protested de Bennetot, to whom the act seemed the very act of murder.

"Enough of that nonsense!" growled the Baron savagely, "Get on with it!"

De Bennetot pulled on the painter. The other boat came slowly up alongside, its gunwale rubbing the gunwale of the boat they were in. He had only to lean over to lay his hand on the straw.

"I'm afraid G-G-Godfrey," he stammered. "By my eternal salvation, it is not I who do this, but you. Understand that."

Godfrey growled like a wild beast, sprang forward, thrust him aside, bent over the gunwale, and tore the bolt of straw out of the hole.

There came a gurgle of rising water; and it upset him to such a degree that, in a sudden revulsion of feeling, he wished to stop up the hole again.

He was too late, de Bennetot had slipped into his seat and taken up the oars. Recovering all his strength in an access of panic at that sinister sound, he pulled with such violence that a single stroke drove their boat several fathoms from the other.

"Stop!" shouted the Baron. "Stop! I wish to save her! Stop! Curse you!... It's you who are killing her, not me!... Murderer! I would have saved her!"

But de Bennetot, mad with terror, incapable of hearing or of understanding, was plying the oars with a fury that threatened to break them.

The corpse, for what else could one call this inert creature, helpless and doomed to death in that scuttled boat, remained alone. The sea must inevitably fill the boat in a few minutes, and it must sink beneath the waves.

Godfrey realized that. Therefore, making the best of it, he took the other pair of oars, and without caring whether anyone heard the splashes or not, the two confederates strove with the most desperate efforts to escape with the utmost possible speed from the scene of their crime. They dreaded to hear some faint cry of anguish or the terrible murmur of an object that sinks and over which the water closes forever.

The doomed boat floated almost without movement on the surface of the sea, on which the air, loaded with low clouds, appeared to weigh with an extraordinary heaviness.

D'Etigues and de Bennetot must have been halfway back to the shore. The sound of their flight was no longer heard. At that moment the boat heeled over to starboard; and in a kind of stupor of terror and agony that dazed her, the young woman thought that the end had come. She did not wince; she did not shiver. The acceptance of death produces a state of mind in which one seems already on the other side of the grave.

However she was faintly astonished not to feel the touch of icy water. At the moment it was the thing from which her delicate flesh most shrank. No; the boat was not plunging under. It seemed more likely rather to capsize because somebody had

THE SINKING BOAT

passed a leg over the gunwale. Somebody? But who? The Baron? His confederate?

She learned that it was neither the one nor the other, for a voice which she did not know murmured:

"You can stop being frightened. It's a friend who has come to rescue you."

This friend bent over her and without even knowing whether she heard or not, continued: "You have never seen me... my name is Ralph... Ralph d'Andresy... It's all right now... I've stopped the hole with a stocking rolled round one of the rowlocks. It's a makeshift; but it will work all right—especially since we are going to get rid of this great boulder."

With his knife he cut the ropes which fastened the young woman to the stretcher, cut loose the boulder, and succeeded in heaving it overboard.

Then drawing aside the folds of the rug which enveloped her, he said:

"You can't think how delighted I am things have turned out so much better than I expected. Here you are, safe! The water has not even had time to reach you. What luck we've had! You're feeling all right?"

She whispered so low that he hardly heard it:

"No... My ankle... Their ropes twisted my foot and cut into it."

"That will soon be all right," he said. "The important thing is to get back to the shore. Your two executioners will have certainly landed by now and must be scrambling up the staircase as hard as they can climb. So we have nothing to fear from them."

He got to work quickly. He took the two oars, which de Bennetot had not taken the trouble to remove—unless perhaps he had thought that if the boat were found it would look less suspicious if the oars were in it—and began to row towards the shore, telling her how he had come to her help in the nick of time, in a cheerful, careless voice, as if nothing more extraordinary had happened than happens at an ordinary picnic.

"Let me introduce myself in a rather more formal way, though I'm not particularly presentable at the moment, since I am only dressed in my shirt, one stocking, and a knife hanging from a string from my neck," he said. "I am Ralph d'Andresy, at your service—since chance willed it. And a very simple chance it was... I overheard a conversation... I learned that there was a plot in action against a certain lady. So I took the liberty of forestalling it. I hurried down to the beach, undressed, and when the two cousins came out of the entrance of the tunnel I slipped into the water. All I had to do then was to hide behind your boat and catch hold of the stern when they started to tow it out to sea. And that was what I did do. Neither of them had the slightest idea that they were taking out with their victim a champion swimmer who had made up his mind to save her. But I'll tell you more about it later when you're in a state to understand. I've got an idea that at the moment I'm babbling away to the empty air."

He paused.

"I'm feeling very ill," she murmured. "I'm utterly worn out."

"I can tell you what to do," he said quickly. "Lose consciousness. Nothing is so restful as to lose consciousness."

She seemed to follow his advice, for after a little moan or two, she began to breathe quietly and regularly. He covered her up with the rug and fell to rowing again.

"It's better as it is," he said to himself. "I can act exactly as I like without having to explain what I'm doing."

The fact that there was no one to listen to him did not prevent him from indulging in a sustained monologue, with all the satisfaction of a man who is exceedingly pleased with himself and everything he does. The boat moved quickly towards the shore. The dark mass of the cliffs loomed ahead.

THE SINKING BOAT

When the keel of the boat ground its way into the pebbles, he jumped out of it, then lifted the unconscious young woman, with an ease which demonstrated the uncommon strength of his muscles, and carried her to the foot of the cliff.

"Boxing champion also," said he—"to say nothing of the Greco-Roman style. I don't mind telling you, since you cannot hear me, that I found these useful accomplishments in my inheritance from father... and a jolly lot of others! But enough of this trifling. Rest here, under this rock, where you're safe from the treacherous waves... I shall be back presently. I expect you will be very keen on taking vengeance on those two cousins. That makes it necessary that the boat should not be found and that they should believe you thoroughly and completely drowned. So do not be impatient."

Without wasting any more time he put this plan into execution. Once more he rowed out the boat to the open sea, pulled out the rowlock and his stocking out of the hole, and, sure that it would sink, took to the water again. As soon as he reached the shore, he put on his clothes which he had hidden in a cranny in the cliff.

He went back to the young woman and said: "Come, the next job is to climb to the top of the cliff; and it's not the easiest job in the world."

Little by little she came out of her swoon and he saw faintly the glimmer of her open eyes.

With his help she tried to stand upright, but uttered a cry of pain, and would have fallen but for his arm. He lowered her to the ground, took off her shoe, and found that her stocking was all bloody. It was in no way a serious injury, but uncommonly painful. He used his handkerchief as a temporary bandage. They had to be getting on their way; and he hoisted her on to his shoulder and began the ascent of the staircase.

Three hundred and fifty steps! If Godfrey d'Etigues and Oscar de Bennetot had had great difficulty in carrying, the two of them, the young woman down, what an immense effort was demanded by the ascent, and that from a young man! Four times he had to stop, streaming with sweat, feeling that he would never be able to go on. Nevertheless he went on, all the while with a cheerfulness no fatigue could dash. At the third halt, having sat down with the girl on his knee, he found that she was laughing faintly at his jokes and unflagging spirit. At last he finished the ascent with her charming form hugged tightly to him, his hands and his arms assuring him of its supple firmness.

When he reached the top he gave himself but the shortest rest, for a fresh breeze had risen and was clearing the sky. Fortunately they had no great distance to go to find security; and with a last brisk effort he carried her across a field into a lonely barn which he had had in mind all the while. He carried her up the ladder into the loft, laid her on a heap of straw, covered her with the rug, told her that she was safe and need fear nothing and that he would soon be back. Then he closed the trapdoor, unhooked the ladder, hid it under straw, and hurried to the sleeping inn. With catlike quietness he filled a basket with some cold meat, cheese, bread, a bottle of wine, a bottle of water, and a lantern. He was soon back at the barn, climbed up into the loft with his basket, drew up the ladder, and shut the trapdoor.

"Twelve hour's sleep and safety!" he said in a tone of satisfaction. "No one will disturb us here. At noon tomorrow I'll get a carriage for you and take you wherever you like."

Here they were then, shut up together after the most tragic and marvellous adventure that one could imagine. How far away it all seemed now—all those dreadful scenes of the day! The tribunal of enquiry, the inexorable judges, the sinister executioners, Beaumagnan, Godfrey d'Etigues, the condemnation, the descent down to the sea, the boat sinking in the darkness, what nightmares already dim! They had come to an end in an intimate comradeship of victim and rescuer.

By the light of the lantern hanging from a beam he gave the young woman food and drink and dressed her wound with infinite gentleness. Protected by him, far from the snares and hatred of her enemies, Josephine Balsamo lay back in utter trustfulness. She shut her eyes and fell asleep.

The lamp illumined clearly her beautiful face, flushed by the fever of so many emotions. Ralph knelt down in front of her and contemplated her at length. Finding the heat of the barn oppressive, she had unfastened the top of her bodice; and he could see her admirably shaped shoulders and the purity of the line where they joined the neck.

He bethought himself of that black mark of which Beaumagnan had spoken, and which was plain to see in the miniature. How could he have resisted the temptation to make sure if it were really there on the bosom of the woman he had saved from death? Gently he drew down the top of her frock. Low down on her right shoulder a beauty spot, black as one of those *mouches* which coquettes used formerly to stick at the corner of their lips, marked the white and silky skin and rose and fell with the even rhythm of her breathing.

"Who are you? Who are you?" he murmured, greatly troubled. "From what world do you come?"

He too, like the others, was conscious of an inexplicable discomfort; like them felt the mysterious impression that emanated from this strange creature, accentuated by those curious details of her life and by her astonishing beauty. And he could not help questioning her as if she were able to answer on behalf of the woman who had, those long years, before been the model of the miniature.

Her lips formed words which he did not understand. And he was so near to them and the breath they breathed forth was so sweet that, trembling like a leaf, he brushed them with his own.

She sighed. Her eyes opened. At the sight of Ralph on his knees before her she blushed and at the same time smiled; and this smile still wreathed her lips when her heavy eyelids had come down again over her eyes and she had sunk back into her slumber.

Ralph was distracted; quivering with passionate admiration, Clarice utterly forgotten, he murmured the most exalted phrases and clasped his hands as before an idol to which he was addressing a hymn of the most ardent and frenzied adoration.

"Oh, how beautiful you are!... I did not think there was so much beauty in the world... Do not go on smiling... I can quite understand that men desire to make you weep—your smile is so troubling... One would like to efface it so that no one might ever see it again. Ah, do not smile at anyone but me, I implore you!"

Then in a lower voice and even more passionately he continued:

"Josephine Balsamo. How sweet your name is! And how much more mysterious it makes you! Did Beaumagnan call you a witch?... He was wrong. You're an enchantress... You have emerged from the darkness and you're the light—the light of the sun!... Josephine Balsamo... Enchantress... Magician!... What a world opens before me!... What a wealth of happiness I see... My life began at the very moment at which I took you in my arms. I have no other memories but the memory of you... All my hope is in you... Heavens how beautiful you are!... It is enough to make one weep with despair."

He uttered these impassioned words, leaning over her, his mouth close to her mouth; but the kiss he had stolen was the only caress he allowed himself. There was not only a voluptuousness in the smile of Josephine Balsamo, but also such a modesty that he felt a profound respect for her; and his exaltation ended in the words of genuine gravity, full of juvenile devotion.

"I will help you... The rest of the world shall be able to do nothing against you... If you desire to reach, in spite of them, the goal at which they are aiming, I promise you that you shall succeed... Far from you or near you, I shall always be your defender and savior. Trust in my devotion."

At last he went to sleep, murmuring promises and oaths which had become rather incoherent; and it was a profound and dreamless sleep like the sleep of children who have to restore their overdriven young organizations.

The church clock struck eleven. He counted the strokes with a growing surprise.

"Eleven o'clock in the morning! Is it really possible?" he cried.

The light was filtering in through the chinks in the shutters and through openings under the old thatched roof. On the right, even, a ray of sunlight fell on the floor.

"Where are you?" he said in a dazed voice. "I do not see you."

The lamp had been extinguished. He sprang to the shutters and pulled them open. A flood of light filled the loft; but it did not reveal Josephine Balsamo.

He sprang upon the trusses of hay and in a childish fury flung them aside. No one. Josephine Balsamo had disappeared. He hurried down from the loft, hunted through the park, fairly ransacked the plateau and the road. In vain. In spite of the injury to her foot which had, the night before, made it impossible for her to set it on the ground. She had left their hiding place, crossed the park and the plateau and got away...

He returned to the barn to make a minute inspection of it. He did not have to seek long. He saw on the floor a rectangular piece of cardboard.

He picked it up. It was the photograph of the Countess of Cagliostro. On the back of it, written in pencil, were these two lines:

"My rescuer has all my gratitude, but he must not try to see me again."

V

ONE OF THE SEVEN BRANCHES

There are certain stories the hero of which passes through the most extravagant adventures and on the very edge of the dénouement awakes to find that it has all been the mirage of a dream.

When Ralph found his bicycle behind the bank where he had hidden it two nights before, he suddenly had the idea that he had been tossed about in a series of dreams, pleasant, picturesque, terrifying, and, above all, wholly deceptive. He did not cherish the hypothesis for any length of time. The photograph which he had in his possession, and even more perhaps the intoxicating kiss that he had snatched from the lips of Josephine Balsamo, set everything on the firm ground of reality. That at any rate was a certainty from which there was no getting away.

At this moment for the first time—he admitted it with a touch of quickly passing remorse—his thoughts returned to Clarice d'Etigues and to the delightful hours of the morning before.

But at Ralph's age these ingratitudes and these sentimental contradictions are easily dealt with. It appears that one is divided into two beings, the one of whom will continue to love in a kind of unconsciousness, with a love that is to play its part in the future, while the other abandons himself with frenzy to all the transports of the new passion. The image of Clarice rose before him, troubled and grief-stricken, as if at the back of the little chapel, lighted by flickering candles beside which he would from time to time go and pray. But the Countess of Cagliostro had at once become the unique divinity of his adoration, a despotic and a jealous divinity, who would not suffer one to rob her of the least thought, or the least secret.

Ralph d'Andresy—so we will continue to call the young man who, later, under the name of Arsène Lupin became so illustrious—Ralph d'Andresy had never loved. As a matter of fact he had been prevented from doing so by lack of time rather than by lack of opportunity. Burning with ambition, but not knowing in what sphere and by what means his dreams of glory, of fortune, and of power would be realized, he spent his energy in every direction in order to be ready to answer on the instant the call of destiny. His intelligence, his ingenuity, his will, his agility, the strength of his muscles, his suppleness, and his endurance, he cultivated all his gifts to the extreme limit, always astonished to discover that this limit ever receded further before the violence of his efforts.

With all this, however it was necessary to live, for he had no resources. An orphan, alone in the world, without friends or relations, without a profession, somehow or other he managed to live. How? It was a matter about which he could only give somewhat hazy explanations which he himself did not examine too closely. One lives as best one can. One deals with one's needs and one's appetite as circumstances permit. And there again he was astonished to perceive the richness of his aptitudes and the favorable opportunities that Fortune always seemed to bring him.

"The luck is on my side," he told himself. "Forward then. What will be will; and I have an idea that it will be magnificent."

It was at this point that he crossed the path of Josephine Balsamo. He perceived at once that, to win her, he would freely spend all the energy he had accumulated. His ambitions? He knew their goal for the future—Josephine Balsamo. Of a sudden he learned the reason of his existence and the significance of his preparations—Josephine Balsamo.

And for him Josephine Balsamo had nothing in common with the "infernal creature" whom Beaumagnan had endeavored to raise before the troubled imagination of his friends. All that vision of bloodshed, those accoutrements of crime, those trappings of the sorceress, vanished like a nightmare in face of the charming photograph in which he contemplated the limpid eyes and pure lips of the young woman.

"I shall find you!" he swore, covering it with kisses. "And you shall love me as I love you. To me you shall be the most submissive and the most adored of mistresses. If you have loved, you shall forget those you have loved; you shall pursue them with your hate. I shall read your mysterious life as one reads an open book. Your power of divination, the miracles you work, your incredible youth, everything which troubles and frightens the rest of the world, shall be so many ingenious devices at which we shall laugh together. Josephine Balsamo, you shall be mine!"

It was an oath he was resolved to keep; but he fully realized its extravagance and the audacity at the moment. In the bottom of his heart, he was still frightened of Josephine Balsamo, and he was not so far from feeling a certain irritation against her, like a child who wishes to be the equal but finds himself the obedient inferior of someone stronger than himself.

For two days he confined himself to the little bedroom which he occupied on the ground-floor of the inn, the window of which looked out on a courtyard planted with apple trees. They were days of meditation and waiting. On the afternoon of the third he took a long ride through the plain of Normandy, that is to say to the places where it was possible that he would meet Josephine Balsamo. He thought it quite unlikely that the young woman, still badly shaken by her horrible experiences, would return to her abode in Paris. Alive, it was necessary that those who had murdered her should believe her dead. Moreover not only to avenge herself on them but also to reach before them the goal that they were seeking, it was necessary that she should not leave the field of battle. And that field of battle was the region which they call the Caux country; and in it all the ends of intrigue seemed to be united. In that case why should he not suddenly see her charming figure round the corner of this or that road, or on the outskirts of this or that wood?

When he came back that evening he found on his dressing-table a bunch of spring flowers, periwinkles, narcissi, primroses, and wild strawberry blossoms. He asked the landlord how they came there. No one had been seen in his room.

"It is she!" he thought, kissing the flowers that she had just gathered.

For four consecutive days he posted himself under cover at the back of the courtyard. When he heard the sound of a footstep nearby, his heart jumped. Always he was disappointed. It caused him keen suffering. But at five o'clock on the fourth day, among the trees and bushes which covered the slope down the courtyard, he heard the rustling of a gown. Among them he saw a gown. He was on the point of darting forward, when he stopped short, overwhelmed by a sudden access of rage. He saw that it was Clarice d'Etigues.

She had in her hand a bunch of flowers exactly like the other one. She crossed the courtyard lightly to the window of his bedroom and putting her hand through it set those flowers on his dressing-table.

When she retraced her steps, he had a clear view of her face and was struck by its paleness. Her cheeks had lost their fresh coloring and her sunken eyes were witness to the bitterness of her grief and her hours of sleeplessness.

"You will make me suffer bitterly," she had said.

She had not foreseen however, that those sufferings would begin so soon and that the very day which had seen their love at its zenith, would be a day of farewell and of inexplicable desertion.

He remembered the prediction and raging at her for the injury he was doing her, furious at his disappointment, that it had been Clarice who had brought the flowers and not she for whom he was waiting, he suffered her to go away without a word.

However it was to Clarice—to Clarice who thus herself destroyed her last chance of happiness—that he owed the precious information which he needed to find his way in the darkness in which he was moving. An hour later he discovered that a letter was fastened to the bouquet. He tore it open and read:

"Is it already finished, dearest? No: it cannot be. There is no real reason for my tears surely?... It is impossible that you should have already had enough of your Clarice?

"Darling tonight they are all going away by train; and they will not come back till very late tomorrow. You will come, won't you? You will not leave me to weep again?"

Poor, mournful lines!... Ralph was not softened by them. He considered this journey of which she told him and remembered that accusation of Beaumagnan: "Learning from me that we were soon about to examine from cellar to roof a mansion near Dieppe, she betook herself there hastily—"

Was not this the goal of the expedition? And would he not find there an opportunity of joining in the struggle and drawing from it all the advantage that circumstances might offer?

That very evening at seven o'clock, dressed like a fisherman from the coast in blue flannel trousers, a thick woolen sweater, and a woolen cap pulled down over his ears, unrecognizable under the layer of ochre which reddened his face, he got into the same train as the Baron d'Etigues and Oscar de Bennetot, like them changed twice, and got out at a little village where he spent the night.

Next morning d'Ormont, Rolleville, and Rufus d'Estiers came in a carriage to fetch their two friends. Ralph followed them.

At the end of ten kilometers the carriage stopped before a long, dilapidated mansion called the Château de Gueures. When he came to the open gates, Ralph discovered that a whole host of workmen were swarming in the gardens and park, digging up the paths and the lawns, or scraping the basin of a pool which was fed by a small stream of which they had closed the sluice-gates. It was ten o'clock. On the terrace the contractors welcomed the five associates.

Ralph entered without being noticed, mingled with the workmen, and questioned them. From them he learned that the château had just been bought by the Marquis de Rolleville and that the work of restoration had begun that morning.

"Yes, Monsieur. Instructions have been given that any man who in the course of his digging finds coins, metal objects, copper, iron, and so forth, is to hand them over and he will be rewarded."

It was quite clear that all this turning things upside down had no other object than the discovery of something. Ralph asked himself what they were trying to find.

He strolled round the park, made a tour of the mansion, hunting through the cellars with especial care, without discovering anything of a nature to solve the problem, the data of which he did not know. It is all very well to seek but it is necessary to know what you are seeking.

At half-past eleven he had arrived at no result of any kind; and the necessity of doing something was impressing itself on his mind more and more strongly. Every delay gave the others greater and greater chances; and he risked finding himself confronted by the accomplished fact.

At that moment the five friends were standing on a long terrace behind the mansion, a terrace which looked down on the park and the lake. A small balustrade ran along the edge of it, broken at regular intervals by twelve brick pillars which served as pedestals for old stone vases, nearly everyone of which was broken.

A gang of workmen armed with picks set about demolishing the wall. Ralph watched them do it thoughtfully, his hands in his pockets and a cigarette between his lips, without bothering himself about the fact that his presence on that spot might appear a trifle strange.

Godfrey d'Etigues rolled a cigarette; and then having no matches, he walked up to Ralph and asked him for a light.

Ralph held out his cigarette and while the Baron was lighting his, a complete plan formed itself in his mind, a spontaneous, very simple plan, of which the least details rose before him in their logical sequence.

He pulled off his cap and displayed his carefully brushed curls which were not at all those of an ordinary fisherman. The Baron d'Etigues gazed at him earnestly, and, suddenly enlightened, fell into a fury.

"You again! And disguised! What is this new intrigue and how dare you follow me here? I've already told you in the clearest possible terms that a marriage between my daughter and you is impossible."

Ralph caught his arm and said imperiously:

"We don't want a scandal! That would do neither of us any good. Bring your friends to me."

Godfrey tried to shake him off.

"Bring your friends!" Ralph repeated in a yet more imperious voice. "I am going to render you a service. What are you looking for? Something antique, isn't it?"

"Yes," said the Baron impressed against his will by Ralph's earnestness. "We're looking for a candlestick."

"A candlestick with seven branches, of course that's what it is! I know its hiding-place. Later I shall be able to give you other information which will be useful to you in the work you have taken in hand. Then we'll talk about Mademoiselle d'Etigues. Today there is no question of her. Call your friends!"

Godfrey hesitated; but Ralph's confident promises impressed him. He called to his friend and they came at once.

"I know this young man," he said in a grudging voice. "And according to him we shall perhaps succeed in finding—"

Ralph cut him short.

"There's no perhaps about it, Monsieur," he said impatiently. "I belong to this part of the country. And when I was a boy, I used to play in this château with the children of an old gardener who was the caretaker of it. One day he pointed out to us a ring affixed to the wall of one of the cellars and said: 'That's a hiding-place that is. I've often been told of how they put valuables into it—gold candlesticks and clocks and jewelry.'"

These revelations made the Baron and his friends open their eyes. De Bennetot however raised an objection.

He said: "But we've already searched the cellars."

"Not thoroughly," Ralph declared. "I'm going to show you."

They made for the cellars by the quickest way, a staircase at the end of the left wing which descended to the basement from the outside of the building. Two large doors opened on to three or four steps, after which came a series of vaulted chambers.

"The third on the left," said Ralph, who, in the course of the tour he had made through them, had studied the ground. "Here... this one."

He made them all precede him, through a door so low that they had to stoop to enter it, into a dark cellar.

"You can't see an inch before your face," grumbled Rufus d'Estiers.

"That's true," said Ralph. "But here are some matches and I saw a candle-end on one of those steps into the cellars. Half a minute—I'll run for it."

He shut the door of the cellar, turned the key quietly, took it out of the door, and called out to his prisoners:

"Mind you light all the seven branches of the candlestick. You will find it under the last slab carefully wrapped up in spiders' webs!"

Before he got outside the building he heard the five of them hammering furiously at the door. He was sure that, worm-eaten and shaky, it would hold out but a very few minutes. But that was all the time he wanted.

He rushed up on to the terrace. A workman was demolishing the fourth of the little brick pillars. Ralph took his pick from him, saying:

"Hand it over, mate. The proprietor has just told me what to do."

"Shall I help you?" said the workman.

"There's no need, thanks."

Ralph hurried to the ninth pillar, and knocked the vase off it with a stroke of his pick. Then he attacked the top of the pillar, which was covered with cracked cement, which fell to pieces under his blows. Under the cement cap the pillar was hollow, and the hollow had been filled with earth and pebbles. Ralph started to clear them out quickly with the point of his pick. And about a foot down it turned up a piece of corroded metal. A glance showed him that it was veritably a branch of one of those great candlesticks one sees on the altars of many churches.

A group of workmen had gathered round him and at seeing this piece of metal which Ralph picked up and waved in the air, they cheered. It was the first discovery that had been made since they began work.

Doubtless Ralph would have kept his head and gone quietly off, pretending that he was going to find the five friends to give them this metal stem; but at that very moment there was a loud shouting at the corner of the building, and Rolleville, followed by the rest of the five, came bucketing round it, bellowing:

"Thief! Arrest him! Thief!"

Ralph dived through the group of workmen and took to his heels. It was absurd, like the rest of his conduct for the last few minutes, for if he had wished to win the confidence of the Baron and his friends he should not have shut them up in a cellar and robbed them of the object of their search. But since he was really fighting for Josephine Balsamo, he had no other idea in his head but that of offering her sooner or later the trophy he had just acquired.

Since the main road to the gates was blocked by workmen, he ran round the lake, knocked down two men who tried to bar his way and followed, at a distance of thirty yards, by a veritable horde of pursuers howling like mad men, ran into a small kitchen garden, surrounded on every side by a wall of a most discouraging height.

"Confound it!" he muttered. "I'm well shut in! I'm going to be the stag at bay, hang it!... What a mull I've made of it!"

Above the left wall of the kitchen garden rose the village church and the graveyard ran right into the interior of the garden in the shape of a small enclosed space, which formerly served as a burial ground of the lords of Gueures. Tall yew trees hung over its wall. As he ran round this enclosure a small door in the wall was half opened, an arm was stretched out to bar his way, a little hand seized him by the arm; and the astonished Ralph was drawn into a dark arch way by a woman who shut the door in the face of his pursuers, and turned the key in the lock.

He divined rather than saw Josephine Balsamo.

"Come on!" she said, plunging into the middle of the yews.

Another door was opened in the opposite wall of the little close; it let them into the village churchyard.

By the apse of the church stood an old-fashioned barouche of the kind one hardly ever sees nowadays anywhere except in the country. Harnessed to it were two thin, badly groomed horses. On the box sat a gray-bearded coachman whose bent back stuck out under his blue blouse.

Ralph and the Countess jumped into the carriage. No one had seen them. She said to the coachman:

"Take the road to Luneray and Doudeville. Be quick!"

The church was at the end of the village; and by taking the road to Luneray, they avoided passing any of the cottages. A long stretch of road rose in a steepish hill to the plateau. The two lean steeds developed the speed of first-class trotters and went up the hill at an astonishing pace.

The interior of this shabby-looking barouche was spacious, comfortable, and protected from the eyes of the indiscreet by shutters of wooden trellis-work. Indeed it conveyed such an impression of intimacy that Ralph fell on his knees and gave vent freely to his amorous exaltation.

He was choking with joy. Whether the Countess was offended or not, he decided that this second meeting, taking place in such extraordinary circumstances and after the night of the rescue, established relations between them which permitted him to omit several stages and begin the conversation with a formal declaration of love.

He did so at once and in an airy fashion which would have disarmed the most prudish of women.

"You? Is it indeed you? But how dramatic! At the very moment at which the hunt was going to tear me to pieces, Josephine Balsamo springs from the shadows and rescues me in my turn. Ah, how happy I am! How I love you! I have loved you for years... for a hundred years! Yes, I've a hundred years of love in me... An old love as young as you. And as beautiful as you are lovely!... And you are so lovely!... One cannot look on you without being moved to the depths of one's being... It's a joy; but at the same time it fills one with despair to think that, whatever happens, one will never be able to grasp your beauty in all its fullness. Your expression, your smile, their deepest meanings will forever elude us."

He quivered and murmured: "Oh, your eyes rest on me! You do not turn them away! You're not angry with me then? You allow me to tell you of my love?"

"Suppose I bid you get out?" she said, opening the door.

"I should refuse."

"And if I were to call the coachman to my aid?"

"I should kill him."

"And if I got out myself?"

"I should continue the declaration of my love along the road."

She burst out laughing.

"You have an answer for everything," she said. "Stay where you are; but no more nonsense! Tell me what happened to you and why those men were pursuing you."

He had gained his end.

"Yes, I will tell you everything since you do not repulse me... Since you accept my love."

"But I accept nothing," she said, still laughing. "You pile declaration on declaration and you do not even know me."

"I don't know you?"

"You hardly saw me that night—just by the light of a lantern."

"And didn't I see you during the day before that night? Didn't I have time to admire you during that abominable ordeal at La Haie d'Etigues?"

She turned suddenly serious and gazed at him earnestly.

"Oh, you were present, were you?" she said quickly.

"I was there, all right," he said with triumphant cheerfulness. "I was there; and I know who you are. Daughter of Cagliostro,

I know you! You can drop your mask. The first Napoleon played with you... You betrayed Napoleon III, helped Bismarck, and drove the brave General Boulanger to suicide! You bathe in the fountain of youth. You are a hundred years old—and I love you."

Her brow was furrowed with a faint frown of troubled doubt.

"Ah, you were there... I guessed as much... The brutes! How they did make me suffer!... And you heard their hateful accusations?" she said slowly and thoughtfully.

"I heard a lot of stupid things," he exclaimed. "And I saw a band of fanatics who hate you as they hate everything that is beautiful. But all that was imbecile and silly. Don't let's think any more about it. For my part, I only wish to remember the delightful miracles which spring up before your feet like flowers. I wish to believe in your everlasting youth. I wish to believe that you would not have died if I had not rescued you. I wish to believe that my love is supernatural and that it was by enchantment that you issued just now from the trunk of a yew."

She shook her head gently, serene again.

"No: to visit the Château de Gueure I had already passed through that ancient door, the key of which was in the lock; and knowing that they were going to make a great search this morning I was on the watch," she said. "I saw them hunting you from the gate of that garden. You were coming to it. I slipped back and waited."

"A miracle, I tell you!" he declared. "And here is another. For weeks and months, perhaps for longer, they have searched in that park for a candlestick with seven branches. And to find it in a few minutes in the midst of all that crowd and under the very eyes of our opponents, it was only necessary for me to wish to please you."

She started and stared at him with amazed eyes: "What? What are you talking about?... You've found it?" she cried.

"The candlestick itself: no—only one of its seven branches. Here it is."

She almost snatched the bronze metal branch from him and examined it almost feverishly. It was round, fairly strong, slightly bent, and the metal of it was hidden by a thick layer of verdigris. One of its ends, a little blackened, had let into one of its faces a large violet stone, rounded *en cabochon*.

"Yes," she murmured, "yes: there is no possible doubt about it. The branch has been sawed off level with the main stem. You've no idea how grateful I am to you!"

In a few picturesque sentences he gave her an account of his exploit. She could not get over her astonishment.

"But what gave you the idea? Why that inspiration to demolish the ninth pillar rather than another? Was it mere chance?" she asked.

"Not at all," he declared. "It was a certainty. Eleven out of the twelve pillars had been built before the end of the seventeenth century—the ninth, later."

"How did you know?" she asked quickly.

"Because the bricks of the eleven others are of a size that has not been in use for the last two hundred years, while the bricks of number nine are those which are in use today. Therefore number nine was demolished and then rebuilt. Why, if not to hide this branch of the candlestick?"

She was silent for a good minute. Then she said slowly:

"It's extraordinary... I should never have believed it possible to succeed... And so quickly! There, where we had all failed... Yes: it really was a miracle."

"Love's miracle," said Ralph.

The carriage sped along with astonishing rapidity, keeping to cross-country lanes, it avoided the passage through villages. Uphill and down dale the ardor of those two little thin horses never flagged. On either side the country passed like images in a dream.

"Was Beaumagnan there?" asked the Countess.

"Luckily for him he was not," said Ralph with a darkling air.

"Why luckily?"

"If he had been, I should have strangled him," said Ralph between his teeth. "I hate the gloomy dog."

"Not so much as I do," she said bitterly.

"But you haven't always hated him," said he unable to hide his jealousy.

"Lies and calumnies," said Josephine Balsamo coldly, without raising her voice. "Beaumagnan is an impostor, an unbalanced creature, full of morbid pride; and it is because I rejected his love that he desired my death. That I said the other day; and he did not contradict me... He could not contradict me."

"But what joyful words!" exclaimed Ralph. "Then you never loved him? What a weight off my spirits! But, after all, the thing was impossible! Josephine Balsamo to fall in love with a Beaumagnan!"

He laughed aloud in his joy.

"But listen, I do not wish to call you that any longer," he went on. "Josephine is not a pretty name. Let me call you Josine. May I? That's it, I will call you Josine, as Napoleon and your mother Josephine Beauharnais called you Josine. That's settled, isn't it? You are Josine... my Josine."

"Respect first, please," she said smiling at his childishness. "I am not your Josine."

"Respect! But I'm overflowing with respect. What! We were shut up together... You were entirely defenseless... And I remained on my knees before you as before an idol. And I'm full of fear! I'm trembling! If you were to give me your hand to kiss I should not dare to do it!"

VI

DETECTIVES AND POLICEMEN

The journey was one long protestation of love. Perhaps the Countess of Cagliostro was right not to put Ralph to the test by holding out her hand for him to kiss. But in truth, though he had sworn an oath to win that charming young woman and was resolved to do so, he felt for her a respect which left him just enough courage to ply her with amorous words, and no more.

Did she hear him? For a while, yes—as one listens to a child telling you prettily how fond he is of you. Then she sank into a profound thoughtful silence which disconcerted him.

At last he cried:

"Speak to me, I implore you. I speak jokingly in order to be able to tell you things that I should not dare to tell you seriously. But, at heart, I'm afraid of you; and I do not know what I am saying. Answer me, I beg you. Say just a few words that will recall me to reality."

"Only a few words?" she said slowly.

"Yes, just a few."

"Well, then, here they are: Doudeville Station is quite near; and the railway is waiting for you."

He crossed his arms with an air of indignation.

"And you?" he said.

"I?"

"Yes. What is going to become of you all by yourself?"

"Goodness!" she said quickly. "I shall try to get on as I've been getting on up to now."

"That's impossible. You cannot do without me any longer. You have entered upon a struggle in which my help is indispensable. Beaumagnan, Godfrey d'Etigues, the Prince of Arcola are so many ruffians who will crush you."

"They believe me dead."

"That's all the more reason for letting me join forces with you. If you are dead how do you wish to act?"

"Don't let that worry you. I shall act without their seeing me," she said confidently.

"But how much more easily through me as your agent! No; I beg you—and now I am speaking very seriously—do not reject my aid. There are things which a woman cannot accomplish by herself. Owing to the mere fact that you, a woman, are seeking the same end as these men and are consequently at war with them, they have succeeded in forming the most ignoble plot against you. They brought such charges against you and supported them by proofs apparently so sound that for a moment I actually saw in you the sorceress and criminal whom Beaumagnan was overwhelming with his hatred and contempt. Do not be angry with me for that. As soon as you began to defend yourself against them, I saw my mistake. Beaumagnan and his confederates became nothing more than your hateful and cowardly executioners. You dominated them by your dignity; and today not a vestige of all their calumnies lingers in my memory. But you must accept my help. If I have ruffled your sensibilities by telling you that I love you, you will hear no more about that. All I ask for is to be allowed to devote myself to you, as one concentrates oneself to that which is most beautiful and purest."

She yielded to his earnest pressure. They drove on through Doudeville. A little further on, on the road to Yvetot, the carriage turned into a farmyard, along the edge of which ran a row of beeches which seemed to be stunting the apple trees with which it was planted, and came to a stop.

"Here we get out," said the Countess. "This place belongs to Mother Vasseur, an excellent woman who was once my cook. She keeps an inn a little way down the road. Sometimes when I want a rest I come and stay with her for a day or two. We will lunch here, Leonard, and be off again in an hour."

She and Ralph turned into the high road again. She walked with the light step of a young girl. She was wearing a tightly-fitting gray frock and a mauve hat, with velvet strings, and trimmed with bunches of violets. Ralph walked a little behind her in order to feast his eyes on her.

Round the first corner they found a small white house with a thatched roof; in front of it was a small flower-garden. They stepped right into the bar which ran the length of the house.

"A man's voice," said Ralph doubtfully, nodding towards the door of a room on the other side of the bar.

"That's the room in which Mother Vasseur always gives me my meals," said the Countess. "I expect some of the villagers are in it."

On her words the door of it opened and a woman well on in years, wearing an apron and sabots, came out of it.

At the sight of the Countess she appeared utterly flabbergasted, shut the door sharply behind her and stuttered something they could not understand.

"What's the matter?" said Josephine Balsamo in a tone of anxiety.

Mother Vasseur dropped into a chair and murmured more clearly:

"Be off!... Bolt!... Be quick!"

"But why? Explain?" said the Countess.

The old woman got control of herself and said:

"Detectives... They're hunting for you... They've searched your trunks... They're expecting the policemen from the town... Run away, or you're lost!"

The Countess tottered, and looking as if she were about to faint, leaned against the bar. Her eyes met Ralph's in a supplication. It was for all the world as if she thought that she was lost and begged him to help her.

Ralph was stupefied. He stammered:

"B-b-but what d-d-do the police matter to you? It isn't you they're looking for!... Why on earth—"

"Yes, yes! It is her!" said Mother Vasseur. "They are looking for her!... Save her!"

Without grasping the full significance of this astonishing scene, Ralph divined that here was something in the nature of a tragedy. He caught the Countess by the arm, drew her to the door, and thrust her through it.

But crossing the threshold first, she started back in affright and cried:

"The police! They have seen me!"

The two of them hastily stepped back into the house. Mother Vasseur was trembling in every limb; she muttered stupidly:

"The police... the detectives."

"Be quiet!" snapped Ralph in a low voice, keeping quite calm. "I'll answer for its being all right. How many detectives are there?"

"Two."

"And two policemen. Then it's no use trying force; and we're surrounded. Where are those trunks they've searched?"

"Upstairs."

"Where's the staircase to them?"

"Here," she said, pointing to the door on the right.

"Right. You stay here; and don't give yourself away. Once more I tell you, I'll answer for its turning out all right."

Again he took the Countess by the arm and drew her towards the door Mother Vasseur had pointed out. A very narrow staircase brought them to a bedroom under the sloping roof. About it were spread all the frocks and lingerie which the detectives had turned out of two trunks. As they came into it they heard the two detectives come out of the room in which they had been lunching, into the bar; and when Ralph, crossing the room on noiseless feet, peered out through the window under the eaves, he saw the two policemen dismount and tie the reins of their horses to the posts of the garden gate.

The Countess did not stir. Ralph noticed that her face, haggard with fear and anxiety, had perceptibly aged.

"Quick!" he said sharply. "You must change that frock. Put on another... a black one for choice."

He returned to the window; and while she changed watched the detectives and the policemen talking in the garden and tried to catch what they were saying. When she had changed, and she was quick about it, he caught up the grey frock she had just taken off and slipped into it. For all his strength, he was uncommonly slender, with a lissom figure. The frock fitted him to perfection; the long skirt of the period, when he had pulled it down hard, hid his feet passably; and he appeared to be so delighted with this disguise and so easy in his mind that the young woman began to recover her confidence.

The voices of the police in the garden rose higher, and they could hear what they were saying.

"Listen," he said.

The four men were standing at the garden gate. One of the policemen said in the rough drawling voice of the countrymen:

"Are you quite sure that she stayed here occasionally?"

"Quite sure. And the proof of it is that there are two trunks of hers which she has left in storage here. One of them has her name painted on it—Madam Pellegrini. Besides, Mother Vasseur is a respectable woman, isn't she?" said one of the detectives.

DETECTIVES AND POLICEMEN

"There isn't a more respectable woman than Mother Vasseur in this part of the country," said the policeman.

"Well, Mother Vasseur declares that this Madam Pellegrini has been in the habit of coming from time to time to stay with her for a day or two."

"Between two burglaries, you bet!"

"Exactly."

"Then it would be a feather in our caps to capture this Madam Pellegrini?"

"It would indeed—larceny—swindling—receiving stolen goods—the whole bag of tricks in fact—and a swarm of confederates," said one of the detectives.

"Have they got a description of her?" asked the policeman.

"Yes and no," replied the detective.

"Yes and no?"

"They have two portraits of her which are entirely different. One is the portrait of a young woman, the other of an old one. As to her age, it is set as between thirty and sixty."

They laughed; then the rough voice of the country policeman went on: "But you're on her track?"

"Again yes and no. A fortnight ago she was working at Rouen and Dieppe. There we lost track of her. We found it again on the main line and lost it again. Did she go straight on to le Havre or turn off towards Fécamp? It is impossible to say. She has completely disappeared and left us floundering," said the detective.

"And what made you come here?"

"Just a chance. A railway porter who brought trunks here on a truck remembered that the name of Pellegrini was painted on one of them, and that it had been hidden under a label which came unstuck."

"Have you questioned any other travelers who stay at the inn?" asked the country policeman.

"Oh, precious few people stay here."

"What about the lady we caught sight of just now as we rode up to the inn?"

"A lady?"

"Yes, a lady. She just came out of this door and went straight in again. It rather looked as if she wanted to avoid us."

"A lady? In this inn? It isn't possible!"

"A lady in gray. She was too far off for us to be able to recognize her face again. But we saw her gray dress; and she is wearing a hat with flowers in it."

"The devil she is!" cried the detective. "We must look into this!"

They said no more, but there came the ominous clumping of large police boots along the flagged path of the garden.

During this conversation Ralph and the young woman had listened without uttering a word, staring at one another. As these new facts came to his ears, Ralph's face had grown darker and darker. She made no attempt to rebut them.

"They're coming... They're coming," she said in a hushed voice.

"Yes. They're coming; and we must be doing, or else they'll come upstairs and find you here," he said calmly.

As he spoke he snatched up her hat from the toilet table, put it on his head, pulled down the brim a little and tied the strings under his chin to hide yet more of his face. Then he gave her his final instructions.

"I'm going to clear the way for you," he said. "As soon as it is clear, you will walk quietly along the road to the farmyard where your carriage is waiting. Get into it, and see that Leonard has the reins in his hands."

"But what about you?" she said.

"I'll be with you in twenty minutes."

"But suppose they arrest you?"

"They won't arrest me, or you either," he said confidently. "But no hurry, mind you. Don't run down the road. Keep cool."

He stepped to the window and leaned out of it. The four men were on the point of entering the house. He slipped over the sill and dropped into the garden, uttered a cry as if he had just caught sight of them, and dashed off at full speed.

They yelled with one voice.

"Hi! The woman in gray!... It's her!... Halt! Or I'll fire!"

He crossed the road in one stride, jumped into the ploughed field on the other side of it, raced across it, and sideways up a slope to a farm. Then came another slope, then some fields; then he ran into a lane which skirted another farm and had a thick, quickset hedge on both sides of it.

He stopped short. He had outdistanced his heavily-booted pursuers considerably. He was out of their sight behind that thick hedge. In a jiffy he pulled off the hat, stripped off the frock, and thrust them well down into the bottom of the overgrown ditch. Then he put on his fisherman's cap, lit a cigarette, stuck his hands in his pockets, and went back the way he had come.

At the corner of the farm two breathless, bucketting detectives nearly ran into him.

"Hullo, fisherman! Have you met a woman—a woman in gray?"

"Yes... A woman who was running, you mean?... A regular madwoman," said Ralph.

"That's her!... Which way did she go?"

"She went into the farm."

"How?"

"Through the back gate."

"How long ago?"

"Not more than a couple of minutes."

The two men ran on. Ralph continued his descent of the slope, gave the policemen, who were struggling up it, a friendly greeting, walked briskly down to the ploughed field and across it, struck the road a little below the inn, close to the corner.

A hundred yards round it were the beeches and apple trees of the farmyard where the carriage awaited him.

Leonard was on the box, whip in hand. Josephine Balsamo, inside the carriage, held the door open.

Ralph said to Leonard: "Drive along the road to Yvetot."

"What?" cried the Countess. "But it takes us past the inn!"

"The essential thing is that they should not guess that we came out of this place. If we go round the corner toward Yvetot, they will not know where we came from. Just a gentle trot, Leonard... about the pace of a hearse returning empty from a funeral."

Leonard shook the reins, the horses trotted quietly round the corner along the road, past the inn. On its threshold stood Mother Vasseur. She just threw out her right hand sideways in a gesture of greeting and farewell and turned and went inside.

"That sets her mind at rest, poor old thing," said the Countess. "Look!"

Against the skyline, up by the farm, stood the four policemen, conferring. From the liveliness of their gestures it was clear that they were not of the same opinion. They had drawn the farm blank and were debating what to do next.

"That's all right," said Ralph. "The carriage is the last thing they'll connect with your flight, for they believe that you're somewhere on the other side of that hill. In fact, they'd simply laugh if anybody told them you were in it."

"They're going to question Mother Vasseur pretty severely," said the Countess.

"She'll have to get out of it as best she can. We can't help her," he said with decision.

When they had passed out of sight of the policemen, he bade Leonard drive faster.

"I'm afraid the poor beasts will not go much further. How long have they been going already?" said Ralph.

"Since this morning, when we left Dieppe. I spent the night there."

"And where are we going to?" he asked.

"The banks of the Seine."

"Goodness! Between forty-five and fifty miles in a day, at this pace! But it's a marvel!"

She did not say anything.

Between the two front windows of the carriage there was a strip of glass in which he could see her. She had put on a darker frock and a light toque from which a fairly thick veil hung down over her face. She pushed up the veil and took from the shelf fixed under the strip of glass a small leather bag which contained an old, gold hand-glass, and other toilet appurtenances, small, stoppered bottles, rouge, and brushes.

She took the hand-glass from it and gazed at her tired face in it for some time.

Then she poured some drops on it from a tiny crystal bottle and rubbed the wetted surface with a scrap of silk. Once more she looked at herself in the glass.

At first Ralph did not understand; he only observed the somewhat bitter and melancholy expression of a woman gazing at herself when she is not at her best.

Ten minutes, a quarter of an hour, passed in this silence and in the manifestly intense effort of that gaze in which all her thought and will were concentrated. The smile appeared first, hesitating, timid, like a ray of winter sunlight. Presently it became bolder and revealed its action by little details which presented themselves in turn to the astonished eyes of Ralph. The corner of the mouth lost its droop. The skin filled again with color. The flesh appeared to grow firm again. The cheeks and the chin recovered their pure outline; and all the grace of youth once more illumined the beautiful and tender face of Josephine Balsamo.

The miracle was accomplished.

"Miracle?" said Ralph to himself. "Not a bit of it. Or rather, to be exact, a miracle of the will. The influence of a clear and tenacious thought which refuses to accept decay, and which reestablishes discipline where disorder and surrender reign. As for the rest the mirror, the little bottle, the wonderful elixir—just a comedy."

He took the hand-glass, which she had set down beside her, and examined it. It was evidently the hand-glass described during the meeting of the conspirators at La Haie d'Etigues, that which the Countess of Cagliostro had used in the presence of the Empress Eugenie. The frame was engine-turned, the plate of silver at the back was all dented with blows.

On the handle was a count's coronet, a date, 1783, and the list of the four enigmas.

Urged by a veritable, painful need to wound her, he said with a sneer: "Your father indeed left you a precious mirror. Thanks to its talismanic power one recovers from the most disagreeable emotions."

"It's a fact that I lost my head," she said quietly. "That doesn't happen to me often. I've kept it in far more serious situations than that one."

"Oh come—more serious?" he said in a tone of incredulous irony.

She did not protest; and for a long while they did not exchange another word. The horses continued to trot with the same even brisk rhythm. The great plains of Caux, always alike and always different, unfolded vast vistas set with farms and woods. The Countess had lowered her veil. Ralph felt that this woman, who had been so close to him two hours before, to whom he had so joyfully offered his devotion, was drawing slowly and slowly away from him, becoming more and more a stranger. There was no longer any contact between them. That mysterious soul was sinking back into the dark depths in which it belonged; what he had seen of it was so desperately different from what he had dreamed.

The soul of a thief... a furtive restless soul, hostile to the light of day. Was it indeed possible? How could he admit that this face of a simple, innocent girl, that those eyes, clear as the waters of a virgin spring, were a mirage and a lie?

He had sunk to such a depth of disillusionment that, as they passed through the little village of Yvetot, he thought of nothing but flight. But he lacked the energy to fly; and that redoubled his anger. The memory of Clarice d'Etigues rose in his mind; and in a kind of revengefulness, he summoned up before it the clear image of the gentle young girl whose selfless abandonment had been so noble.

But Josephine Balsamo did not loose her prey. However tarnished she might appear to him, however deformed the idol might have grown, she was there! An intoxicating fragrance emanated from her. He was touching her. With a movement he could take her hand and kiss that perfumed flesh. She was all the passion, all the desire, all the voluptuousness, all the troubling mystery of woman; and once more the memory of Clarice vanished from his mind.

"Josine—Josine," he murmured so low that she did not hear him.

Moreover, what was the use of bemoaning his love and his suffering? Would she restore to him the confidence he had lost and regain in his eyes the prestige which was hers no longer?

They were drawing near the Seine. On the top of the slope which runs down to the river at Caudebec they turned to the left, among the wooded hills which dominate the valley of Saint-Wandrille. They drove along the ruins of the celebrated abbey, followed the course of the water which bathes the foot of its walls, came in sight of the river, and took the road to Rouen.

A few minutes later the carriage stopped. They stepped out of it; and Leonard drove on again, leaving them on the outskirts of a little wood from which they looked across the river. A meadow covered with waving reeds ran between it and them.

Josephine Balsamo held out her hand:

"Goodbye, Ralph. A little further on you will find Mailleraie Station."

"But what about you?" he asked.

"I? My abode is close at hand."

"I don't see it."

"Yes, you do: that barge which you can just see between the branches."

"I'll take you to it."

A narrow embankment ran across the meadow through the middle of the reeds. The Countess took her way along it, followed by Ralph.

So they came to a piece of open ground, close by the barge, which was still hidden behind a curtain of willows. No one could see them or hear them. They were alone under the expanse of blue sky. And there there passed some of those minutes of which one keeps the memory for a lifetime and which influence the whole course of one's destiny.

"Goodbye," said Josephine Balsamo once more.

He hesitated before this hand stretched out to him in final farewell.

"Won't you shake hands with me?" she said.

"Yes... yes..." he murmured. "But why should we separate?"

"Because we no longer have anything to say to one another," she said sadly.

"Nothing indeed; and yet we never have said anything," said he.

He took her warm and supple little hand in his and said:

"What those men said?... Their accusations in the garden of that inn?... Was it true?"

He craved some explanation, lie though it might be, which should permit him to retain some doubt.

But with an air of surprise she answered: "What on earth does that matter to you?"

"What? Of course it matters to me!" he cried.

"One might really imagine that those revelations could have some effect on you," she said looking at him with just a suspicion of mockery in her expression.

"What on earth do you mean?" he said in astonished accents.

"Goodness! It's very simple. I mean to say that I could have understood your being shocked at the confirmation of the monstrous crimes of which Beaumagnan and the Baron d'Etigues so falsely and stupidly accused me; but there is no longer any question of them."

"But I haven't forgotten their accusations either," he said.

"Their accusations against the woman whose name I gave them, against the Marquise de Belmonte. But it is not a question of crimes at all. What does all that chance revealed to you a little while ago really matter to you?"

He was taken aback by this unexpected question. She looked him straight in the face, smiling, entirely at her ease, and went on a trifle ironically:

"Doubtless the Vicomte Ralph d'Andresy has had his sensibilities ruffled? The Vicomte Ralph d'Andresy must evidently have moral principles, and the delicate sentiments of a gentleman."

"And supposing he has?" said he. "When I experienced that disillusionment—"

"Steady on!" she said sharply. "You've let the cat out of the bag! You're disappointed. You ran after a beautiful dream and it all vanished, now that the woman appears to you exactly as she is. Answer frankly since we are honestly trying to get things clear. You're disappointed, aren't you?"

"Yes, I am," he said dryly.

They were silent. She gazed deep into his eyes and murmured:

"I'm a thief, am I not? That's what you mean, isn't it? A thief?"

"Yes."

She smiled and said: "And what about you?"

And as he started back she caught him firmly by the arm, tried to shake him, and cried imperiously:

"Yes, what about you, my young friend? What are you? The time has come for you to lay your cards on the table also. Who are you?"

"My name is Ralph d'Andresy."

"Rubbish! Your name is Arsène Lupin. Your father Theophrastus Lupin, who combined the occupation of professor of boxing and gymnastics with the more lucrative profession of crook, was convicted and imprisoned in the United States, and died there. Your mother resumed her maiden name and lived as a poor relation at the house of a distant cousin, the Duke of Dreux-Soubise, One day the Duchess discovered that jewels of the greatest historical value, nothing less, in fact, than the famous necklace of Queen Marie Antoinette, had disappeared. In spite of the most exhaustive attempts to discover it no one ever knew who was the author of this theft, executed with a diabolical daring and cleverness. But I, I do know. It was you. You were six years old."

Ralph listened, pale with anger and grinding his teeth.

He muttered. "My mother was unhappy and humiliated. I wished to set her free."

"By thieving?"

"I was six years old," he protested.

"Today you're twenty; your mother is dead; you're robust, intelligent, and overflowing with energy. How do you make a living?"

"I work!" he snapped.

"Yes: in other people's pockets."

She gave him no time to deny it.

"You needn't say anything, Ralph," she went on quickly. "I know your life down to the last details. And I could tell you things about yourself that would astonish you, things that happened this year, and things that happened years ago. For I've been following your career for a very long time and the things I should tell you would certainly not be a bit more pleasant hearing than the things you heard not so very long ago at the inn. Detectives? Policemen? Inquiries? Prosecutions?... You've been perfectly well acquainted with them, quite as well acquainted with them as I am, and you're not twenty! Is it really worthwhile for us to reproach one another? Hardly. Since I know your life and since chance has uncovered for you a corner of mine, let us throw a veil over both. The act of theft is not a pretty one. Let us turn away our eyes and say nothing about it."

He remained silent. A great weariness invaded him. All at once he saw existence in a gloomy and depressing light in which nothing any longer had color, nothing beauty or graciousness. He could have wept. She paused, frowning thoughtfully and rather sadly, then she said: "Well, for the last time, goodbye."

"N-n-no... N-n-no!" he stammered.

"But it must be goodbye, Ralph. I should only do you harm. Do not try to mingle your life with mine. You have ambition, energy, and such qualities that you can choose your path."

She paused and said in a lower voice: "The path I follow is not a good one, Ralph."

"Why do you follow it, Josine? That's exactly what frightens me."

"It's too late to find another," she murmured.

"Then it's too late for me too!"

"No: you're young. Save yourself. Fly from the fate with which you are threatened."

"But you, Josine... But you?"

"It's my life," she declared.

"A dreadful life, which simply causes you suffering," he asserted.

"If you think so, why do you wish to share it?"

"Because I love you."

"All the more reason to fly from me, my dear. Any love between us is damned beforehand. You would blush for me; and I should distrust you."

"I love you," he persisted.

"Today. But tomorrow? Obey the order I gave you on my photograph the very first night we met: 'Do not seek to see me again.' Now go."

"Yes," he said slowly. "Yes. You're right. But it's terrible to think that everything is at an end between us before even I have had the time to hope... and that you will forget me."

"One does not forget a person who has saved one's life twice."

"No: but you will forget that I love you."

She shook her head and said: "I shall not forget."

Then with a thrill of emotion in her tone she went on more quickly: "Your enthusiasm, your initiative... everything that is sincere and spontaneous in you... and other qualities that I have not yet had time to discover in you... all that touches me profoundly."

Their two hands were still clasped; their eyes still gazed into one another. Ralph was quivering with tenderness.

She sighed and said gently: "When one says goodbye forever, one is bound to return one another's gifts. Give me back my portrait, Ralph."

"No, no! Never!" he cried.

"Then I," she said with a smile which intoxicated him, "I shall be more honest than you and honestly give back to you the gift you gave me."

"But what gift?" he asked, for he could remember no gift.

"The first night... in the barn... while I was sleeping... you leaned over me; and I felt your lips."

She bent towards him, put her arms round his neck, drew his head towards her, and their mouths met.

"Oh, Josine!" he cried, lost. "Do what you like with me. I love you... I love!"

They walked along the bank of the Seine, the waving reeds below them. They brushed against the long narrow spears shaken by the breeze. They went towards happiness with no other thoughts in their hearts but those which make lovers, walking hand in hand, tremble.

"One word, Ralph," she said, suddenly stopping short. "I feel that with you I shall be violent and exacting. Is there another woman in your life?"

"Not one," he said firmly.

"A lie already!" she said bitterly.

"A lie?"

"What about Clarice d'Etigues? You used to meet her in the fields. You were seen together."

He was a trifle ruffled, and he said sharply: "That's an old story... The merest flirtation."

"You swear it?"

"I swear it."

"All the better," she said with a somber air. "All the better for her. And let her never come between us! If she does—"

He drew her along, protesting: "I love you only, Josine! I have never loved anyone but you. My life begins today."

VII

THE DELIGHTS OF CAPUA

The *Nonchalante* was a barge in no way distinguished from any other barge. It was fairly old; its paint had faded; but it was well polished and kept very clean by a bargeman of the name Delâtre and his wife. From the outside there was very little to see of the *Nonchalante*'s cargo, a few cases, some old baskets, and three or four casks. But if you had slipped down the ladder into the hold, you would have seen at a glance that she carried absolutely nothing whatever. The whole of the inside had been divided into three rooms of moderate size, uncommonly comfortable and exceedingly well-kept—two staterooms opening into a saloon.

There Ralph and Josephine lived for a month. Monsieur and Madame Delâtre seemed to be morose; and they were certainly silent. Several times Ralph tried in vain to get into conversation with them. They acted as cook and butler. From time to time a small tug came to tow the *Nonchalante* up a reach of the Seine.

The whole course of the charming river in this way unrolled itself before their eyes in delightful landscapes through which they wandered, Ralph's arm round Josephine's waist... the Brotonne Forest, the ruins of Jumièges, Saint George's Abbey, the hills of Bouille, Rouen, Pont-de-l'Arche.

They were weeks of intense happiness. During those delightful hours Ralph expended a wealth of gaiety and enthusiasm. The wonderful views, the beautiful Gothic churches, the sunsets and the moonlight, everything served him as pretexts for impassioned declarations of his love. Josine, more silent, smiled as in a happy dream. Everyday drew her closer to her lover. If at the beginning she had acted from a mere caprice, she now found herself under the yoke of the law of love which quickened her pulses and taught her the danger and the pain of loving too much.

Of the past, of her secret life, never a word. Once however they did exchange a few sentences on this subject. As Ralph was chaffing her about what he called the miracle of her eternal youth, she said:

"A miracle? I don't understand what people mean by a miracle. For example, the other day we drove sixty miles... You cried out that it was a miracle. But if you'd kept your eyes a little wider open, you would have perceived that that distance was covered not by two horses but by four, for Leonard took the pair which had been drawing it out of the carriage and harnessed another pair in their places in that farmyard at Doudeville, where a relay was waiting for us."

"You have me there!" exclaimed the young man cheerfully.

"Another example," she went on: "No one in the world knows that your name is Lupin. But I assure you that that very night you rescued me from death, I knew you as Arsène Lupin and nothing else. A miracle? Not a bit of it. You know that everything that concerns Cagliostro interests me extremely; and when fourteen years ago I heard talk of the disappearance of the Queen's necklace from the house of the Duchess of Dreux-Soubise, I made the most minute enquiry into the circumstances. That brought me first of all to little Ralph d'Andresy and then to the son of Theophrastus Lupin. Later

I found traces of your handiwork in several jobs. I knew where I was."

Ralph reflected thoughtfully for a good half-minute; then he said very seriously:

"At that date Josine, darling, either you were twelve years old, and it certainly is miraculous that a little girl of that age should have succeeded in an enquiry in which the rest of the world failed, or you were as old as you are today, which is even more miraculous, O daughter of Cagliostro!"

She frowned. His jesting did not seem at all to her taste. She said even more seriously than he:

"We won't talk about that, Ralph—if you don't mind."

"I'm sorry," said Ralph, a little annoyed at having been discovered to be Lupin and desiring to score off her in turn. "Nothing in the world interests me more strongly than the problem of your age and the different exploits you have performed during the last hundred years. I've got some ideas of my own on the matter which are really worthy of consideration."

"Keep them to yourself," she said sharply.

"Wouldn't you like me to tell you about them?"

She gazed at him, curious in spite of her reluctance to discuss the matter. He took advantage of her hesitation to continue in a faintly mocking tone:

"My train of reasoning rests on two axioms: the first is, as you have pointed out, there are no miracles; the second is that you are your mother's daughter."

She smiled and murmured: "It certainly begins well."

"You are your mother's daughter," Ralph repeated. "That means that there was in the first place a Countess of Cagliostro. At the age of twenty-five or thirty, she dazzled all the Paris of the end of the Second Empire with her beauty and excited the liveliest curiosity at the Court of Napoleon III. With the aid of the young man she called her brother—it doesn't matter whether he was her brother, her friend, or her lover—

she had worked up the story of her relationship to Cagliostro and prepared the forged documents of which the police made use when they gave Napoleon III the information about the daughter of Josephine Beauharnais and that great thaumaturge. Expelled from France, she went to Italy, then to Germany, then disappeared—to come to life again twenty-two years later in the person of her adorable daughter, her exact image, the second Countess of Cagliostro, here present. Do we agree so far?"

Josine did not answer; she gazed at him with in expressive eyes in an impassive face.

He went on: "Between the mother and the daughter the resemblance was perfect—so exact that the affair began, quite naturally, all over again. Why should there be two Countesses? There will only be one, a single one, the unique and genuine Countess, she who has inherited the secrets of her father, Joseph Balsamo, the Count of Cagliostro. And when Beaumagnan sets about making his enquiry, it inevitably happens that he discover the documents which have already sent the police of Napoleon astray, and the series of portraits and miniatures which bear witness to the identity of the ever youthful woman and carries her origin back to the virgin of Luini to whom chance has given her such an astonishing resemblance.

"Moreover there is a living witness: the Prince of Arcola. The Prince of Arcola in the old days knew the Countess of Cagliostro. He conducted her to Modena. He saw her at Versailles. When he saw her a few years ago the exclamation escapes from him: 'It is she! And not a day older than she was!'

"Thereupon you overwhelm him with a world of proofs. You repeat the actual words exchanged at Modena between him and your mother, the actual words which you read in the very minute diary which your mother kept even of her least important doings and sayings. There is the complete explanation of the affair. And it is extraordinarily simple. A mother and a daughter who are exactly like one another and whose image recalls a picture of Luini.

"There is besides the Marquise de Belmonte. But I expect that the resemblance of that lady to you is fairly vague and that the strong prepossession and deranged brain of Beaumagnan were necessary to mix the two of you up. To sum up, there is nothing dramatic about it. It is merely an amusing and admirably managed intrigue. That's my account of the business."

He was silent. It appeared to him that Josine had lost some of her color and that she was frowning. She must be annoyed in her turn; and it made him laugh.

"I've hit the right nail on the head? What?" he said cheerfully.

She shrank away from him, saying coldly: "My past is my business and my age concerns nobody but myself. You can believe exactly what you like about them."

He caught hold of her and kissed her furiously.

"I believe that you are four hundred years old, Josephine Balsamo, and that there is nothing more delightful to kiss than a centenarian. When I think that you have perhaps known Robespierre and perhaps Louis XVI—"

They did not discuss the matter again, for Ralph was so clearly aware of Josephine's irritation at the slightest indiscreet attempt to probe her secret, that he did not dare to question her again. Besides, did he not know the exact truth?

Certainly he knew it and not a doubt remained in his mind. Nevertheless the young woman retained a mysterious prestige, which impressed him in spite of himself and rather annoyed him. He thought, seeing her withdrawn and aloof, of those Gods of Olympus who enveloped themselves in a thick mist. So round Josephine there were on every side impassable spaces in the midst of which she disappeared from his sight. Why also did she refuse to discuss the candlestick with seven branches and the enterprise of Beaumagnan? Was not that the affair which had brought them together and in a way associated them in a common task of conquest and vengeance?

At the end of the third week Leonard reappeared. Again Ralph saw the barouche with the little lean horses in it; and the Countess drove away in it.

She did not return till the evening. Leonard carried on to the barge two bundles wrapped in napkins which he slipped into a cupboard, of whose existence Ralph had been ignorant.

That night Ralph, having succeeded in opening the cupboard, examined the two bundles. They contained admirable lace and valuable vestments.

The next day there was another expedition. The result, was sixteenth-century tapestry.

On those days Ralph was exceedingly bored. Therefore at Mantes, finding himself once more alone, he hired a bicycle and for some hours rode about the country. After having lunched at an inn, he saw on the outskirts of a small country town a great mansion, the garden of which was swarming with people. He went to it. They were selling by auction some beautiful furniture and plate.

Idly he strolled round the house. The garden at the end of one of the wings was empty and against the wall was a thick shrubbery. Without considering what impulse urged him to the act, Ralph, seeing a ladder hanging against the garden wall, set it up against the house, climbed it, and slipped a leg over the sill of an open window.

There came a faint cry from inside the room; and he saw the startled face of Josephine. She recovered herself on the instant and said in a perfectly composed voice:

"Oh, it's you, Ralph, is it? I was just admiring a collection of beautifully bound little books. Wonders! And of an extraordinary rarity!"

That was all they said. Ralph examined the books and slipped three Elzevirs into his pocket while the Countess without Ralph's perceiving it, helped herself to some coins from a glass case.

They went down the main staircase and took their departure. In all that crowd no one took any notice of them. Three hundred yards down the road the carriage was waiting for them.

After that, at Pointoise, at Saint Germain, at Paris, where the *Nonchalante*, moored to the quay in front of the prefecture of police, continued to serve them as an abode, they "operated" together. Together but in such a fashion that neither could see the other's actions. "Let us turn our eyes away and say nothing about it," Josephine Balsamo had said. A supreme modesty which spared them the sight of a mean action.

If the reserved nature and the enigmatic soul of the Countess de Cagliostro found a perfectly natural expression in the accomplishment of these tasks, the impulsive nature of Ralph little by little gained the upper hand; and every time the operation finished in bursts of laughter. Success provoked in him veritable fits of hilarity.

"Since I've turned my back on the path of virtue, I may just as well take it lightly as not, and certainly not in the funereal way in which you do, Josine," he said airily.

At every new essay he discovered in himself unexpected talents and resources of which he had never dreamt. Sometimes, in a shop, on a racecourse, at the theater, his companion heard a gentle murmur of joy and saw a watch in her lover's hands, or a new pin in his cravat—and always the same coolness, always the serenity of an innocent man whom no danger can threaten.

But that did not prevent him taking the manifold precautions demanded by Josephine. They only left the barge in the dress of barge-folk. In a neighboring street, the old barouche with a single horse harnessed to it was waiting for them. In it they changed their clothes. Josephine always hid her face under a beautiful, flowered lace veil.

All these facts and a great many others fully informed Ralph about the real life of his mistress. He had no doubt whatever that she was at the head of a well organized band of confederates, with whom she held communication by means of Leonard. But also he had no doubt that she was prosecuting her search for the Candlestick with Seven Branches and keeping a close watch on the actions of Beaumagnan and his friends.

A double life, which often awoke in Ralph a dull irritation against Josephine, as she herself had foreseen. Forgetting his own actions, he was angry with her for acting in a manner which was not in accord with the ideas which in spite of everything, he retained about that matter of honesty. A mistress who was a thief and leader of a band of thieves shocked him. Now and again there was a collision between them with regard to quite insignificant matters. Their two personalities, so definite and so powerful, came into conflict.

So, when some trifle brought them into conflict, for all that they were confronting common enemies, they learned how much a love like theirs can, at certain moments, contain of rancor, pride, and hostility.

The incident which brought to an end what Ralph called the delights of Capua was an unexpected meeting one evening with Beaumagnan, the Baron d'Etigues, and Oscar de Bennetot. They saw the three friends go into the Theater of Varieties.

"Let's follow them," said Ralph.

The Countess hesitated. He insisted.

"What?" he cried. "When such an opportunity presents itself, aren't we going to profit by it?"

"What's the use?" she asked.

"What's the use?" he answered quickly. "But what a funny question! Are you afraid of my finding myself face to face with Beaumagnan?"

"No: but—"

"Look here, Josine: you do as you like. But I'm going after them."

Both of them went into the theater and established themselves at the back of a box. As they did so, in another box, quite close to the stage, they just had time to perceive before the attendant drew down the screen, the figures of Beaumagnan and his two acolytes.

A problem presented itself to them. Why should Beaumagnan, a churchman and apparently a man of rather ascetic habits, be found straying into a theater of the boulevards, in which they were playing a revue adorned with a very scantily dressed chorus, which could not be of the least interest to him? It was quite evident that there must be a reason of considerable importance and most probably, seeing who were with him, connected with the affair of the Candlestick, to bring him to such a place. To discover that reason was to catch up Beaumagnan in a single stride at the point he had reached in his investigations.

Ralph pointed out these facts to Josephine. She appeared to take no interest whatever in them; and her indifference made it clear to him that she had no intention whatever of taking him into partnership and that she had definitely decided that she did not desire his assistance in this mysterious affair.

"Very well," he said to her firmly. "Where there is a lack of trust, let each go his own way and each for himself. We shall see who collars the prize."

On the stage the girls of the chorus were dancing while the chief characters passed in front of them. The leading lady, a very pretty girl with very few clothes on, was taking the part of the spirit of a waterfall and she justified her name by the cascades of false jewels which streamed all round her. Round her forehead was a bandeau set with jewel of many colors, and her hair was lighted up with electric lamps.

During the first two acts the screen in front of the stage box remained down so that no one could see who were its occupants. But, during the interval after the second act, Ralph who had strolled round to the door of that box discovered that it was a little way open. He peeped in. The box was empty. He enquired of the attendant and learned that the three gentlemen had left the theater in the middle of the first act.

He went back to Josephine and said: "There's nothing to be done here. They've cleared out."

At that moment the curtain rose again. The leading lady once more appeared on the stage. Her hair drawn a little further back made it easier to see the bandeau which she was still wearing. He saw that it was a broad gold ribbon, in which were set large jewels *en cabochon*, of different colors. There were seven of them.

"Seven!" thought Ralph. "That explains why Beaumagnan came here."

While Josephine was in the ladies' cloakroom, he learned from one of the attendants that the leading lady of the revue, Bridget Rousselin, lived in an old house in Montmartre and came every day with a faithful old servant by the name of Valentine, to the rehearsal of the revue they were putting on next.

Next morning at eleven Ralph left the *Nonchalante*. He lunched in a restaurant in Montmartre, and soon after twelve, strolling down a steep, winding street, he passed in front of a small narrow house with a courtyard in front enclosed by a wall, and next door to a house divided into unfurnished flats. The curtainless windows of the top flat made it quite clear that it was vacant.

Forthwith, with his usual quickness, he formed one of those plans, which, directly it was formed, he put into execution almost mechanically. The situation of the house was uncommonly convenient for his purpose; and he was delighted to think that in a very short time he would know something which Josephine did not know and which would enable him to tease her. At the same time he made up his mind, as a loyal partner, to give her the benefit of his discoveries.

He strolled up and down with the air of a man who was waiting for someone. Of a sudden, taking advantage of the fact that the janitor of the flats was busy mopping the pavement in front of the house, he slipped behind her back into it, ran up the stairs to the top, forced the door of the empty flat, opened one of the windows which looked down on the roof of the house next door, made sure that no one could see him, and slipped out on to the roof.

It was only a few steps to a half-open dormer window. He climbed through it into a garret full of broken furniture, from which one descended to the floor below through a trapdoor. He had some difficulty in raising it a little way noiselessly and looked down on to the second-floor landing. There was no ladder.

Below, on the first floor, two women were talking. Listening with all his ears he learned that Bridget Rousselin was lunching in her boudoir, and that her servant, apparently the only other person in the house, was dusting her bedroom and dressing room in the intervals of waiting on her.

Then Bridget Rousselin called out: "I've finished, Valentine. What a blessing it is that there's no rehearsal today! I'm going back to bed till I have to start for the theater!"

This day at home rather upset Ralph's plans, for he had been expecting to make a thorough search of the house at his ease during her absence at rehearsal. Nevertheless he did not lose patience; he just waited for the luck to turn.

Some minutes passed. Bridget was humming some of the music of the new revue. Then the front-door bell rang.

"That's odd, Valentine," she said. "I wasn't expecting anyone today. Go and see who it is."

THE DELIGHTS OF CAPUA

The maid went downstairs. There came the sound of the opening and shutting of the front door.

She came upstairs again and said: "It's a gentleman from the theater—the manager's secretary. He brought this letter."

"Thanks. You showed him into the drawing room?"

"Yes."

From the clearness with which he heard her voice Ralph gathered that Bridget had come out on to the first-floor landing. He heard her tear open the envelope.

Then she said: "That's funny. The manager wants me to send him the bandeau I wear in the show, by his secretary. He wants to get it copied, and he'll let me have it back at the theater tonight."

Ralph swore under his breath: "Hang it!" he thought. "That bandeau is the chief object of my search. Is this manager also on the trail of it? And is Bridget Rousselin going to send it along to him?"

Her next words set his mind at rest.

"But I can't do it," she said. "I've already promised those stones."

"That's a pity," said Valentine. "The manager will be annoyed."

"I can't help it. I've promised to sell them—and for a big price too," said the actress.

"Then what am I to say?" asked Valentine.

"I must write to him," said Bridget.

She went into her boudoir, wrote the note, and gave it to Valentine.

"By the way, do you know this secretary?" she said carelessly. "Have you seen him at the theater?"

"No, I haven't. He must be a new one," said Valentine.

"Tell him to tell the manager how sorry I am, and that I'll tell him all about it at the theater tonight."

Valentine went downstairs again; Bridget went to the piano and did two or three voice exercises. They must have drowned the noise of the shutting of the house door, for Ralph did not hear it. The minutes passed.

He felt somewhat uncomfortable. This business seemed to him rather queer—this secretary they did not know, this request for the jewels looked to him uncommonly like a trap of some sort.

Then he was reassured by the sound of footsteps on the stairs. They went to the door of the boudoir.

"Valentine," he said to himself. "There was nothing in my fancies. The man has gone."

But of a sudden the playing stopped short in the middle of a run. Evidently the actress jumped up so suddenly as to upset the piano stool, for it banged on the floor. She said in an uneasy voice:

"Who are you?... Oh, of course, you're Monsieur Lenoir's new secretary... But what is it you want?"

A man's voice answered: "Monsieur Lenoir gave me the strictest instructions to bring those jewels back with me; and I must insist on having them."

"But I have written to him!" exclaimed Bridget in a yet more uneasy voice... "My maid must have given you the letter... Why hasn't she come upstairs? Valentine!"

The door of the boudoir was banged violently. Ralph heard the noise of a struggle and cries of: "Help! Help!" Then silence.

The moment he had grasped the fact that Bridget Rousselin was in danger, he had tried to open wide the trapdoor, noiselessly. But it stuck; and he lost precious time in forcing it up. Then he dropped onto the landing, ran down to the first floor and found three doors, all closed, to choose from.

As chance had it the one he opened was the door of the boudoir. It was empty and two or three chairs had been knocked over. An inner door led to the dressing room. That was empty too. He stepped into the bedroom whither the actress had fled.

The curtains were drawn. In the dim light he saw a man kneeling over a woman prone on the carpet, gripping her throat with both hands, and swearing abominably.

"Hell! You won't shut your mouth, won't you? You won't hand over those jewels, won't you? I'll show you, curse you!"

Ralph flung himself upon him. He loosened his grip on the woman's throat and rolled over. Ralph's head banged against the fireplace with a violence that dazed him for a moment.

That was unfortunate; and in addition this murderous ruffian was heavier than he, powerfully built, with muscles of steel. It looked as if the slender and youthful Ralph had no chance whatever against him. But there was a sudden groan and the big man rolled over and lay inert, while Ralph rose lightly to his feet.

He said: "A pretty stroke, wasn't it, old boy? I got it from the posthumous instructions of a gentleman named Theophrastus Lupin—from a chapter which deals with Japanese methods. It transports you to a better world for a minute or two and renders you as harmless as a lamb."

Without the loss of a moment he took the curtain cords and bound together the wrists of his opponent.

He had moved the curtains and was working in a fair light. He turned the man over to see his face. A sharp cry of amazement burst from his lips; and he exclaimed:

"Leonard!... Leonard, begad!"

He had never had a really good view of Josephine's coachman. He had always seen him crouched on the box of the carriage, with his head between his shoulders, and so disguising his figure that Ralph believed him to be almost a hunchback and certainly a weakling. But there was no mistaking that bony face ending in that gray beard. It was beyond all doubting Leonard, Josephine's factotum and right hand man.

He bound his legs together, just to make sure; and then on the carpet beside him he saw a whistle. He picked it up and was just about to stick it back in Leonard's pocket when an idea came to him. He went to the window and peeped round the edge of the curtain. On the other side of the street, about twenty yards down it, stood the old carriage.

On the box sat a young man in livery. But inside the carriage there was surely another confederate. Ralph was sure of it; and now nothing in the world would have prevented him from carrying the matter through to the bitter end.

He turned his attention to Bridget, who was moaning faintly, picked her up, and laid her on the bed. The marks of the ruffian's fingers were very red on her throat; but he had been in time to prevent the worst. She was only suffering from shock and terror. She half-opened her eyes.

He poured some water from the carafe into the tooth-glass, raised her, and held it to her lips. She swallowed a little, with difficulty. It seemed to relieve her; and she began to cry.

"Never mind! You'll be all right presently," he said gently. "Shut your eyes and relax. Don't move till I come back. I'll relieve you of the presence of this gentleman. I'll take him into the next room and question him. You're quite safe. I'm a detective; and luckily I was on his track."

He was pretty sure that she would keep quiet and give him no trouble. Probably, in the reaction, she would fall into the profound sleep of those who have been tortured and badly frightened. He dragged Leonard into the boudoir and shut the bedroom door. Then he went downstairs.

A glance into the drawing room showed him Valentine, as he had expected, in exactly the same condition as he had left Leonard. He decided that she was best as she was. It left him a freer hand.

"It's all right, miss," he said in a reassuring voice. "I'll loose you presently. I'm a detective; and the first thing for me to do is to catch the rest of the gang."

He went down the passage to the front door. As he had expected, it was not latched. He opened it an inch or two and looked at the door of the courtyard. Leonard had left that unlatched also.

Ralph permitted himself a somewhat sardonic smile. Then he went upstairs, opened the window of the boudoir a little way, and blew the whistle.

One of two things would happen. Either the whistle would be a warning to the confederate that things had gone wrong; and she would decamp. Or it would be a signal that the coast was clear and that she could join Leonard in the search for the jewels and any other evidence there was to be found in Bridget Rousselin's house.

He waited with a very somber air, his eye on the door of the courtyard. He was extraordinarily disturbed, horrified indeed. It was one thing to relieve well-to-do persons of objects of luxury, of which they had no real need, and which they hadn't the sense to keep—quite another to be an accomplice in a cold blooded murder. Surely the woman he adored would never go to such lengths. As the horror of it grew clearer and clearer, his pulse quickened in a feverish anguish. Who would come through the door of the courtyard?

That door opened; on the threshold stood Josephine Balsamo!

Ralph gasped; and for the moment his eyes went blind.

Then he was filled with a bitter fury.

Josephine came quietly through the door, as carelessly as if she were merely paying a call on a friend, and walked across the courtyard. The moment Leonard whistled, the way was clear; she had only to go to him.

Ralph was furious but quite calm. He was ready to fight this second adversary as he had fought the first, and conquer her, but with very different weapons.

He took the further precaution of locking the door of the dressing room. Bridget Rousselin could not interrupt them, even if she found the strength to do so. There came the sound of a light footfall on the staircase. The door opened and Josephine entered.

Ralph had formed a very just estimate of Josephine's power of self-control. But he did expect that the unexpected scene which met her eyes and the sudden and unexpected sight of him would shake it. Nothing of the kind.

She stopped short, gazed round the room, took in the trussed-up Leonard and Ralph's indignant face in a glance that lasted perhaps a second and a half.

Then she pushed up her veil and said in the most casual voice: "What are you looking at me like that for, dear?"

He stared at her with all his eyes; he did not wish to lose a quiver of her eyelids, or the faintest twitch of her lips. He said slowly:

"Bridget Rousselin has been murdered."

"Bridget Rousselin—murdered?" she said under her breath.

"Yes. The actress we saw last night, the one who was wearing the bandeau of jewels. You're not going to tell me that you don't know who she is, for you're here, in her house, and you had instructed Leonard to let you know directly he had done the job."

Her self-control indeed went. With a horror-stricken face and starting eyes, she cried: "Leonard?... Leonard?... He has—"

"Yes," declared Ralph. "He's murdered Bridget Rousselin. I caught him in the very act of throttling her."

Her legs seemed to fail her; she sank trembling on to a chair and stammered:

"The b-blackguard... The b-b-blackguard... It's impossible!"

And on a rising inflection in which with each word the note of terror grew clearer and clearer, she cried:

"He's committed a murder?... A murder?... It's impossible!... He swore to me that he would never kill!... He swore it!... I can't believe it!"

Was she sincere, or was it all comedy? Had Leonard acted in a sudden access of madness, or in accordance with instructions which bade him murder if the ruse failed. Formidable questions to which Ralph could not give the answer.

She raised her head, saw the accusation in his eyes, jerked herself to her feet and with hands outstretched towards him cried: "Why are you looking at me like that, Ralph? Oh, you can't suspect me of a horrible crime like that! You can't!... You can't believe that I knew of it... That I ordered or permitted such an abominable crime!... Tell me you don't!"

Almost brutally he caught her by the shoulder and forced her onto the chair again. Then, crossing his arms, he took two or three paces up the room and back; then, catching her again by the shoulder and glaring into her eyes, he said slowly in the accents of an inexorable accuser and even enemy:

"Listen to me, Josine. If you don't, this very instant, make a clean breast of it and tell me the whole story of this business and all the secret machinations which complicate it, I'm going to treat you as my mortal enemy. I'm going to take you out of this house, by force if I have to, to the nearest police station and denounce you as the accomplice of Leonard in the murder of Bridget Rousselin. Then you can get out of it as best you can. Are you going to tell me, or are you not?"

VIII

TWO WILLS

War was declared, and at the moment chosen by Ralph, a moment at which all the circumstances were in his favor, and Josephine, taken by surprise, weakened before an onslaught of a violence and implacability she had never looked for.

It must not, however, be supposed that a woman of her stamp was going to accept defeat without a struggle. She tried to resist. She would not admit that a tender and charming lover like Ralph d'Andresy could, at a single stroke, stand forth as her master and impose on her the harsh constraint of his will. She had recourse to wheedling, then to tears and promises, to all a woman's wiles. He showed himself inexorable.

"Will you speak!" he roared. "I've had enough of this obscurity. You may take a delight in it. I don't. I like things perfectly clear."

"What things do you want me to throw light on?" she cried, exasperated. "My life?"

"Your life is your own affair," replied Ralph. "Keep your past dark, if you're afraid to unfold it before my eyes. I'm perfectly well aware that you will always be an enigma to me and everyone else, and that your innocent face will never throw any light on what is going on at the bottom of your soul. But what I want to know is that side of your life which touches mine.

We have a common end in view. Let me know the path you are following. If you don't, I run the risk of getting mixed up in some abominable crime, and that's the last thing I want."

He hammered his right fist into his left palm.

"Get that clear, Josine! I will not murder! Rob? Yes. Burgle? Yes. But murder? No! A thousand times no!"

"I don't wish to murder, either," she protested.

"Perhaps not. But you let other people murder for you."

"It's a lie!"

"Then speak out—explain."

She wrung her hands and with a groan protested: "I can't! I can't!"

"Why? What prevents you from telling me all you know about this business, the things Beaumagnan revealed to you?" he urged.

"I should prefer not to let you get mixed up in this affair, not to let you oppose that man," she said earnestly.

He burst out laughing. "You're frightened on my account, perhaps?" he jeered. "A fine excuse! Reassure yourself, Josine. I'm not afraid of Beaumagnan. There's another adversary I fear much more than him."

"Who's that?" she said quickly.

"You."

He repeated in harsher accents: "You, my dear. And that's the reason why I'm so keen on getting the thing clear. When I shall really see you clearly, I shall no longer fear you. Have you made up your mind?"

She shook her head and said slowly: "No, I haven't!"

Ralph burst out furiously: "That is to say, you don't trust me. It's a splendid affair; you wish to keep it entirely to yourself. Right. We'll be going. You will have a clearer view of the situation outside."

With that he caught her in his arms and swung her over his shoulder as he had done at their first meeting at the foot of the cliff and, so burdened, walked towards the door.

"Stop!" she said.

This feat of strength, accomplished with an incredible ease, finished her taming. She felt that she had better not provoke him further.

He set her down on her feet. She sank on to a chair and said: "What is it you want to know?"

"Everything. First of all the reason for your coming here and for that scoundrel's murdering Bridget Rousselin."

"The bandeau with the stones in it," she said.

"But they're worthless—imitation garnets, imitation topazes, opals, beryls—"

"Yes. But there are seven of them."

"What of it? What was the object of his murdering her? It was so simple to bide your time and ransack her rooms the first chance you got," he suggested.

"Evidently. But it looked as if other people were on the track of them."

"Other people?"

"Yes. Early this morning, acting on my instructions, Leonard made inquiries about this Bridget Rousselin, for last night I noticed the bandeau she was wearing; and he reported that people were prowling about this house."

"People? What people?" he said quickly.

"Emissaries of the Belmonte woman."

"The woman who is mixed up in the business?" he asked.

"Yes. You find her everywhere."

"Well, what of it? Was that a reason for murder?"

"He must have lost his head. And it was my fault for telling him that I must have the bandeau at any cost."

"Well, you see what it is: We're at the mercy of a brute who loses his head and murders senselessly, stupidly. It's time to make an end of it, look you. I'm much more strongly inclined to believe that the people who were prowling round this house this morning were emissaries of Beaumagnan. Now you're not of a force to measure yourself against Beaumagnan. Let me take over the management of the affair. If you want to succeed, it is through me, and through me only, that you will succeed."

Josine weakened. Ralph asserted his superiority in a tone of such conviction that she had, so to speak, a strong physical impression of it. She saw him greater than he was and more powerful, more richly endowed than any other man she had known, equipped with a more subtle spirit, keener eyes, more diverse methods of action. She bent before this implacable will, before this immense energy that no consideration could turn from its course.

"Very well. I will tell you everything," she said. "But why here?"

"Here—and nowhere else," said Ralph firmly, knowing well that if the Countess of Cagliostro was once really herself again, he would obtain nothing.

"Very well," she said again, in a tone of bitter resignation. "Very well. I give in, since our love is at stake, and you seem to take it so little into account."

Ralph experienced a sensation of profound pride. For the first time he was conscious of exercising a real ascendancy over others, and of the extraordinary power with which he imposed his decisions on them. Truly the Countess was not in complete command of her usual resources. The supposed murder of Bridget Rousselin had to a considerable degree undermined her power of resistance, and the spectacle of the trussed-up Leonard added to her nervous distress. But how swiftly he had seized his opportunity and profited by his advantage to establish by threats and terrorizing, by force and cunning, his definite victory!

Now, he was the master. He had forced Josephine Balsamo to surrender and at the same time disciplined his own love. Kisses, caresses, seductive wiles, the enchantment of passion, the obsession of desire, he no longer feared any of them, since he had gone to the very verge of a rupture.

He picked up the rug which lay in front of the fireplace and rendered Leonard deaf by throwing it over him. Then he went back to Josine and sat down facing her.

"Fire away," he said.

"Since you will have it," she said in a tone of resignation, "we'll go straight through with it and make an end of it as quickly as possible. I'll spare you the details and come to the main facts straight away. It won't take long, and it won't be complicated. Two and twenty years ago then, during the months which preceded the Franco-Prussian war, Cardinal de Bonnechose, Archbishop of Rouen and senator, making a confirmation tour through the Caux country, was caught in a terrible storm and had to take shelter in the Château de Gueures, which was at that time inhabited by its last owner, the Chevalier des Aubes. He dined there. That night, as he was about to go to the bedroom they had got ready for him, the Chevalier des Aubes, an old man of nearly eighty, decrepit, but in full possession of his faculties, asked for a private interview with him. This was at once granted and lasted a long time. Here is a resumé of the revelations to which the cardinal listened, a resumé which he himself drew up later, of which I shall not change a single word. I know it by heart:

"'Monseigneur,' the chevalier began, 'I shall not astonish you by saying that my early years were spent in the middle of the great revolutionary tumult. At the time of the Terror I was twelve years old. I was an orphan, and every day I accompanied my aunt des Aubes to the neighboring prison, where she distributed the little money she could spare and tended the sick. They imprisoned all kinds of unfortunates and tried and condemned them as the fancy took them. So it came about that I saw a good deal of a gentleman whose name no one knew, or why he had been arrested, or who had denounced him. The

TWO WILLS

attentions I paid him and my piety won his confidence. He grew fond of me, and on the evening of the day on which he had been tried and condemned, he said to me:

"'"At dawn tomorrow, my child, the gendarmes are coming to conduct me to the scaffold, and I shall die without anyone knowing who I am. That is exactly as I wish it to be. I shall not even tell you. But circumstances render it necessary that I should entrust certain secrets to you and demand that you should listen to them as if you were grown up and later deal with them with the loyalty and coolness of a man. The mission with which I charge you is of the highest importance. I feel confident that you will be able to rise to the height of such a task and to keep, whatever happens, a secret in which the most important interests are involved."

"'Thereupon he informed me that he was a priest and, as such, the depositary of incalculable riches, in the form of precious stones of such quality that in each the highest possible value was attained in the smallest possible bulk. As they were acquired these precious stones had been hidden in the most original hiding-place in the world. In a corner of the Caux country, on common land on which everyone is at liberty to set foot, stands one of those huge blocks of stone which used to serve, and still serves, to mark the boundary of certain properties, of fields, orchards, meadows, woods, and so forth. This block of granite, with only its top above the earth and surrounded by bushes, had two or three natural holes in the top of it, filled up with earth in which grew small plants and wild flowers. Through one of these openings from which they carefully removed and replaced the lump of soil which closed it, into this open-air strongbox, they let fall these magnificent precious stones.

"'The cavities in the stones had actually been filled with them, and since no other hiding-place had yet been chosen they had put the stones which had been acquired during the last few years into a sandalwood box which, a few days before his arrest, the priest had himself buried at the foot of the block of stone.

"'He gave me directions for finding the place and communicated to me a formula, composed of a unique word, which, in the case of my forgetting the directions, would give me the hiding-place beyond any possibility of error.

"'He then exacted a promise from me that, when peaceful times returned, that is to say, at a date which he accurately reckoned to be twenty years ahead, I should first go and make sure that everything was in its place, and that starting from that date I should be present at the high mass celebrated in the church of the village of Gueures every Easter Sunday.

"'One Easter Sunday I should see a man dressed in black beside the holy water font. As soon as I should tell this man in black my name, he would take me close to the altar and point to a copper candlestick with seven branches, the candles in which were only lighted on feast-days. In response to this action of his I was to confide to him the formula which revealed the hiding-place.

"'Those were the two signs by which we should recognize one another; and after exchanging them I was to lead him to the block of granite.

"'I swore upon my eternal salvation to follow blindly the instructions he had given me. Next day the worthy priest mounted the scaffold.

"'Although I was very young, monseigneur, when I took that oath, I have kept it religiously. On the death of my aunt des Aubes I enlisted as a drummer boy and went through all the wars of the Directoire and the Empire. On the fall of Napoleon, at the age of thirty, I was dismissed from the army, in which I had risen to the rank of colonel. My first step was to make my way to the hiding-place of the jewels. I easily found the block of granite. Then on the Easter Sunday of 1816, at Gueures church I saw on the altar the copper candlestick. That Sunday the man in black was not standing by the holy water font.

"'I went to that church the next Easter Sunday and every Easter Sunday since, for in the meantime I had bought the Château de Gueures and after the manner of a scrupulous soldier I kept watch at the post assigned to me. I waited.

"'I have been waiting fifty years, monseigneur. No one has come. Not only has no one come but I have never heard a word from anyone's lips which had the slightest connection with the affair. The block of granite is in its place. Every Easter Sunday the verger lights the candles in the seven branches of the candlestick. But the man in black has never come to the meeting-place.

"'What was I to do? To whom was I to address myself? Enter into communication with some ecclesiastical authority? Ask for an audience of the King of France? No. My mission was strictly defined. I had no right to interpret it in my own way.

"'I remained silent. But after how many debates in my own mind! After what anguish at the thought that I might die and carry to my grave a secret of this immense importance!

"'This evening, monseigneur, all my doubts and scruples have vanished. Your fortuitous coming to the château appears to me an undeniable manifestation of the Divine will. You are at once the spiritual and temporal power. As Archbishop you represent the Church. As senator you represent France. I run no risk of making a mistake in making a revelation to you of such interest both to the one and the other. Hence it is for you to make the choice, monseigneur. Take the matter in hand, make the necessary negotiations. And when you tell me into whose hands this sacred stone should be delivered, I will reveal its hiding-place!'

"Cardinal Bonnechose had listened to the story without interrupting. But at the end of it he told the chevalier frankly that he found it rather hard to credit. Thereupon the chevalier left the room and came back in a couple of minutes carrying a small sandalwood casket.

"'Here is the casket of which the dead priest told me,' he said. 'I found it buried in front of the block of granite; and I though it wiser to have it here. Take it away with you, monseigneur, and have the several hundred precious stones it contains valued. You will then be satisfied that the story I have told you is true, and that that worthy priest was right to talk about incalculable riches, since the block of granite contains—so he assured me—ten thousand stones as fine as these.'

"The insistence of the chevalier and this proof which he adduced, prevailed with the cardinal. He undertook to make the necessary investigations and to summon the old gentleman to him as soon as he had discovered the proper destination of the treasure.

"The interview ended with this promise. The Archbishop had the firmest intention of fulfilling it; but the events which followed delayed him. These events, as you know, were the declaration of war on Germany and the disasters which followed it. The heavy duties of his double task took up all his time. The Empire fell in ruin. France was invaded. Months passed.

"When Rouen was threatened, the cardinal, desirous of sending to England certain documents which he reckoned of great importance, decided to send with them the sandalwood casket. On the fourth of December, the eve of the entry of the Germans into Rouen, a confidential servant of the name of Jaubert drove off in a dogcart along the road to Havre, where he was to embark.

"Two days later the cardinal learned that the body of Jaubert had been found in the forest of Rouvray, in a ravine ten kilometers from Rouen. The case containing the documents was brought back to him. The horse, the dogcart, and the sandalwood casket had disappeared. Investigation made it clear that the unfortunate servant had fallen in with a squadron of German cavalry making a reconnaissance beyond Rouen and robbing and murdering the well-to-do inhabitants of that town, flying to Havre in their carriages.

"Then came another piece of bad luck. At the beginning of January the cardinal had word that the Chevalier des Aubes, brokenhearted at the defeat of his country, had not survived it. Before dying he had sent a message to the cardinal. It ran:

"'The word of the formula which reveals the position of the block of granite is carved on the inside of the lid of casket... I have buried the candlestick in my garden.'

"So nothing whatever was left. The casket had been stolen, nothing was left to prove the truth that the story of the Chevalier des Aubes contained a word of truth. No one had examined the stones. Were they real, or were they imitation? Did the sandalwood casket merely contain some stage jewels and colored pebbles?

"Little by little doubt invaded the mind of the cardinal, a doubt so tenacious that in the end he decided to keep silent about the matter. The narrative of the Chevalier des Aubes must be considered an old man's wanderings. It would be dangerous to spread abroad such trash. Therefore he would keep silence. But—"

"But?" repeated Ralph, whom such trash interested enormously.

"But, before finally making up his mind," Josephine went on, "he wrote out this memorandum concerning his visit to the Château de Gueures and the events which followed it, and either it got mislaid, or he forgot all about it; and some years after his death it was found in one of his theological books when his library was sold by auction."

"Who found it?" said Ralph sharply.

"Beaumagnan."

She had related this story, with her head a little bowed, in the rather monotonous voice of a schoolgirl reciting a lesson she has learned by heart. When now she raised her eyes, she was astonished by Ralph's expression.

"What on earth's the matter with you?" she said quickly, staring at him.

"I find all this immensely exciting," he said. "Consider, Josine: step by step, by the confidential information of three old men, who have passed on the torch from one to the other, we go back rather more than a century, and there we come into touch with a legend—what do I say? with a formidable secret rather—which goes back to the Middle Ages. The chain is unbroken. Every link is in its place. And as the last link in this chain behold Beaumagnan. What has Beaumagnan done? Must we declare him worthy of his role, or relieve him of it? Am I to ally myself with him or tear the torch from his hand?"

Ralph's exaltation made it quite clear to Josephine that he would not allow her to break off her narrative. She hesitated, however, for the most important words, perhaps—at any rate, the most serious—remained to be spoken, the words which assigned to her her role.

But he said sharply: "Go on, Josine. The path that lies before us is magnificent. We will tread it together and together we will enjoy the reward which is waiting for us at the end of it."

This was fairly reassuring; and she went on:

"Beaumagnan is explained in one word; and that word is 'ambition.' From the very beginning he made his religious vocation, which is real enough, the servant of his ambition, which is boundless; and the two of them guided him into the Society of Jesus, in which he holds a post of considerable importance. The discovery of the cardinal's memorandum made him lose his head. Immense vistas have opened before him. He succeeded in convincing some of his superiors that this treasure really exists, inflamed them with the lust for incalculable wealth, and persuaded them to put at his disposal all the influence which the Jesuits possess, to help him in this enterprise.

"Then he gathered round him a dozen country gentlemen, more or less honorable and more or less in debt, to whom he revealed only a part of the affair and whom he has trained to be a band of conspirators ready for any task. Each of them has his sphere of action, each his sphere of investigation; and he holds them by the money he lavishes on them.

"Two years of careful and minute investigation have produced results by no means negligible. First of all they have learned that the priest who was guillotined was Brother Nicolas, treasurer of Fécamp Abbey. Then, by dint of ransacking secret archives and old records, they have discovered a curious correspondence formerly carried on between all the monasteries in France; and it appears to be established that since a very remote time there was throughout the country a current of money, which was in the nature of a tithe paid by all the religious institutions, that flowed only into the monasteries of the Caux country. This seems to have constituted a common treasure, an inexhaustible reserve in view of possible attacks to be repelled, or crusades to be undertaken. A treasury council, composed of seven members, handled this wealth, but only one of them knew its hiding-place.

"The Revolution destroyed all the monasteries. But the treasure existed. Brother Nicolas was its last guardian."

A prolonged silence followed her narrative. Ralph's curiosity had not been disappointed; and he was deeply moved. He murmured with restrained enthusiasm:

"But how splendid it is! What a magnificent adventure! I have always been perfectly certain that the past has bequeathed to the present fabulous treasures, the search for which inevitably takes the form of solving an almost insoluble problem. How could it be otherwise? Unlike us, our ancestors had not at their disposal the strongrooms and cellars of the Bank of France. They were obliged to choose natural hiding-places in which they heaped up their gold and jewels, and the secret of which they passed on by means of some mnemonical formula which was, so to speak, the key of the lock. Let a catastrophe occur, the secret was lost, and so was the treasure so painfully accumulated."

His excitement was increasing, and he cried joyfully: "But this treasure shall not be lost, Josine; and it is one of the most fantastic of all of them. If Brother Nicolas spoke the truth—and everything goes to show that he did speak the truth—if the ten thousand precious stones were dropped into this strange strongbox, one can reckon this property left by the Middle Ages,[3] this result of the efforts of millions of monks, this gigantic offering of a whole Christian people during the great epoch of fanaticism, everything that is in the bowels of a boundary stone in a meadow in Normandy at something like a thousand million francs! It's wonderful!"

Abruptly he moved to the couch on which Josephine was sitting and sat down beside her as if he wished to cut short his declaiming and demanded in imperious accents:

"And what has your role been in this adventure, Josine? What is your contribution to it? Have you any special information from Cagliostro?"

"Only a few words," she said. "On the list of the four enigmas which he left and which is in my possession, he has written against this one and against The Fortune of The Kings of France this note: 'Between Rouen, le Havre, and Dieppe. (So Marie-Antoinette declared.).'"

"Yes—yes—the Caux country... the estuary of the ancient river on the banks of which the Kings of France and the monks so prospered," Ralph murmured thoughtfully. "It is undoubtedly there that they have hidden the savings of ten centuries of rule and ten centuries of religion... The two coffers are there—not far from one another naturally—and it is there that I shall find them."

Then, turning towards Josine, he added: "So you were hunting for them, too?"

"Yes, but without any precise data."

"And another woman was looking for them as well as you?" he said, looking into the depths of her eyes. "The woman who murdered Beaumagnan's two confederates."

"Yes. The Marquise de Belmonte, who is, I suppose, another descendant of Cagliostro," she said.

"And you found nothing?"

"Nothing till the day on which I met Beaumagnan."

"Who wished to avenge the murder of his two friends, what?"

"Yes."

"And little by little Beaumagnan told you everything he knew?" he continued.

"Yes."

"Of his own accord?"

"Of his own accord."

"That is to say, you guessed he was aiming at the same goal as you, and you took advantage of the love with which you inspired him to lead him on to confide in you?"

"Yes," she said frankly.

"It was a big game you were playing."

"As it turned out, I was staking my life. In making up his mind to kill me he was undoubtedly actuated by the desire to rid himself of the love which was a torture to him, since I did not respond to it. And over and above that he was terrified at having revealed these secrets to me. I had suddenly become the enemy who might reach the goal before he did. The day he saw the mistake he had made I was doomed."

"Yet his revelations were, after all, nothing but some historical data, and vague at that," he objected.

"That's all they were," she admitted.

"And the branch of the candlestick which I got out of the little pillar was the first piece of definite evidence that came to light?"

"The very first."

"At least I suppose it was. For there is nothing to show that, after your rupture, he did not advance a step or two himself," suggested Ralph.

"A step or two?" she exclaimed in a tone of dismay.

"Certainly, one step," he declared. "Last night Beaumagnan went to the theater. Why, if not for the reason that Bridget Rousselin wore across her forehead a bandeau set with seven jewels. He wished to learn what it meant; and it was undoubtedly he who had her house watched this morning."

"Admitting that it is so, there is no way of our knowing it," she objected.

"Oh, yes; there is," he said.

"How? Who from?" she said quickly.

"Bridget Rousselin."

"Bridget Rousselin?" she cried.

"Certainly. We've got to question her."

"Question that woman?"

"Yes, that woman."

"Then—then—she's—she's alive!"

"Well, yes; she is."

He rose again, pivoted on his heels once or twice in a sketchy little dance that was half cancan, half jig, and said:

"I beg you, Countess of Cagliostro, not to look at me with such furious eyes. If I hadn't given you a bit of a shock with a view to weaken your power of resistance, you would not have whispered a word of that interesting story; and where should we be now? One day or other Beaumagnan would have scooped up the thousand millions and left poor little Josephine biting her nails. So come now! A sweet smile instead of that horrid scowl."

"You had the audacity... You dared... And all those threats... All that pressure to make me speak... It was a farce! I'll never forgive you—never!"

"Oh, yes you will," he said in a cheerful, mocking tone. "You'll forgive me all right—when you've recovered from that little wound to your vanity. All this has nothing to do with our love, you know. It counts for nothing between people devoted to one another, like us. One day one scratches, next day the other... until perfect concord is attained on every point."

"Always supposing a rupture does not take place first," she said between her teeth.

"A rupture? A rupture merely because I've relieved you of a few little secrets?"

But Josephine still looked so flabbergasted that he had to laugh outright, and fairly dancing up and down, like a delighted child, he went on:

"Lord, madam is annoyed!... And just because I've tried one of her own little tricks on her!... Really you ought not to lose your temper about a little thing like that... It makes me laugh."

She was no longer paying any attention to him. She pulled the rug off Leonard, pulled the handkerchief out of his mouth, and cut through his bonds.

Leonard leaped at Ralph, like a wild beast unchained.

"Don't touch him!" she cried.

Leonard stopped short, shaking his fist in Ralph's face.

"Behold the myrmidon!" said Ralph, laughing again. "Jumping up like a jack-in-the-box!"

Beside himself, the man foamed at the mouth and cried: "We shall meet again, my lad—we shall meet again—and if it isn't for a hundred years—"

"You also reckon in centuries—like your mistress," said Ralph.

"Go," said Josephine, pushing Leonard towards the door. "Go. You will bring back the carriage."

They exchanged a few words quickly, in a language Ralph did not understand; and the man went.

Then she turned to Ralph and said in a bitter voice: "And now?"

"Now?"

"Yes. What do you intend to do?"

"My intentions are perfectly honorable—angelic in fact—"

"Enough of this fooling! What do you mean to do? How do you propose to act?" she said sharply.

Of a sudden serious, he said: "I promise to act very differently from you who are always full of suspicion. I shall be what you have never been, a loyal friend who would blush to injure you."

"That is to say?"

"That is to say I'm going to put the indispensable questions to Bridget Rousselin, and to put them so that you can hear her answers. Does that suit you?"

"Yes," she said, but in a tone that showed that she was still irritated.

"In that case, stay here. It won't take long. There's no time to lose."

"No time to lose?"

"No. Listen and you'll understand. Don't stir."

Thereupon, leaving open the two doors of communication so that every word could be heard clearly, he went to the bed on which Bridget was lying.

The young actress smiled at him. In spite of her fear and of the fact that she had not caught a sound of what had been going on, she had at the sight of her deliverer a sense of security and confidence very comforting.

"I shan't tire you," he said. "I want to ask you a few questions. Are you in condition to answer them?"

"Certainly."

"Ah well, you have been the victim of a madman of sorts whom the police have been watching and whom they're going to shut up. So there is no longer any danger. But I want you to clear up a point if you can."

"What is it?"

"What is this bandeau set with jewels? Who did you get it from?" he said.

He perceived that she hesitated. However she said: "They are stones I found in an old casket."

"A wooden casket?" he asked quickly.

"Yes—all smashed and not even locked. It was hidden under a heap of straw in a loft in the little house in the country my mother lived in."

"Where?"

"At Lillebonne, between Rouen and le Havre."

"I know. And where did the casket come from?" he asked.

"I don't know. I never asked my mother."

"You found the stones in the box just as they are now?"

"No. They were set in large silver rings," she said.

"And those rings?"

"I had them last night in my makeup box at the theater; and a gentleman who came behind to compliment me on my acting caught sight of them and took a fancy to them."

"Was he alone?"

"No. He had two friends with him. It seems he is a collector; and I let him have the rings then and there and promised to take the stones to him today at three o'clock that he might restore them to their original settings. He is going to give me a good price for them."

"Have these rings inscriptions on the inside?" he asked.

"Yes: words in old-fashioned writing. But I never bothered about them."

Ralph considered. Then he said in a very serious voice: "I advise you to keep this business a dead secret. If you don't, it may have very unpleasant results, not for you, but for your mother. It's uncommonly odd that she should have rings, of no great value in themselves perhaps, but of extraordinary historical interest, hidden in her house."

Bridget was alarmed and cried: "I'm quite ready to give them up!"

"There's no point in that. Take care of the stones. I'm going to demand, in your name the restitution of the rings. Where does this gentleman live?"

"Rue de Vangirard."

"What's his name?"

"Beaumagnan."

"Good. And one last word of advice," said Ralph. "Leave this house. It is too isolated. And for some time—say for a month—go and live with your maid at an hotel. And don't receive strange visitors. Is it agreed?"

"Yes."

He left her, shutting the door behind him; and they went downstairs. Josephine waited for him in the street while he released Valentine.

When he came out, Josephine slipped her arm through his. She seemed greatly disturbed and to have forgotten her anger and desire for revenge.

"Do I rightly understand that you're going to his house?" she said anxiously.

"Beaumagnan's? Yes."

"But it's madness!"

"Why?"

"Go to Beaumagnan's at a time when you know that the other two are with him?" she cried.

"Two and one are three," he said cheerfully.

"For goodness' sake, don't go!"

"Why ever not? Do you suppose they'll eat me?" he said scornfully.

"Beaumagnan will stick at nothing," she protested.

"Is he a cannibal?"

"There's nothing to laugh at, dear."

"Don't cry, my Josine."

He felt that her fear for him was genuine, and that in a fresh access of tenderness, she was forgetting their disagreement.

"Don't go, dear," she repeated. "I know Beaumagnan's flat. Those ruffians will attack you; and there's no chance of anyone being able to help you."

"All the better, for in that case no one will be able to help them either," he said calmly.

"You will make a joke of it, Ralph. Nevertheless—"

He squeezed her arm; and said in a reassuring tone:

"Now, listen to me, Josine. I come into a colossal affair long after everyone else and find yourself confronted by two powerful organizations, yours and Beaumagnan's. Both of them, very naturally, refuse to welcome me, the third person to share the loot, so that either I've got to play a big game or remain negligible. Let me then deal with our enemy Beaumagnan as I've dealt with my little friend Josine. You must admit that I managed her fairly well and that I have more than one string to my bow."

Once more he offended her. She drew her arm out of his; walked on side by side in silence.

In his heart of hearts he asked himself whether his most relentless foe was not this gentle, pretty lady, whom he so passionately loved and by whom he was loved so passionately.

IX

THE TARPEIAN ROCK

"Does Monsieur Beaumagnan live here?"

The shutter of the peephole in the door had been drawn back; and the face of an old servant was pressed against the bars across it.

"He lives here. But he is not seeing anyone," that servant said grumpily.

"Go and tell him that a gentleman has come from Mademoiselle Bridget Rousselin," said Ralph imperiously.

The rooms of Beaumagnan were on the ground floor of a two-storied house. There was no janitor, no bell. There was an iron knocker to knock at the massive door, which was pierced by this peephole like a prison cell.

The servant went. Ralph waited more than five minutes. That a man should call, when they expected the young actress in person, was puzzling the three confederates.

The servant came back and said, still grumpily: "My master would be obliged if you would send in your card, sir."

Ralph gave him his card.

There was another wait, then the noise of bolts being drawn back and the unhooking of a chain, and Ralph was led across a hall with a polished floor, like a convent parlor, the walls of which looked uncommonly damp.

They passed two or three doors and came to a room with double doors. The outer of these was padded with leather so that no sound could come through it. The old servant opened it, ushered Ralph into the room and shut the two doors, leaving him face to face with his three enemies. He could hardly regard them as anything else, for two of the three watched him enter with the air of boxers on guard and ready to lead.

"It is him! It is indeed!" cried Godfrey d'Etigues flushing with anger. "It's our man of the Château de Gueures! The young fellow who stole the branch of the candlestick! Of all the infernal impudence! What have you come for today? If it's the hand of my daughter—"

Ralph laughed softly and said: "Upon my soul you don't seem able to think of anything else, sir. My feelings for Mademoiselle Clarice are the same as ever; and in my heart I still cherish the same respectful hope. But the object of my visit today is no more matrimonial than it was at Gueures."

"Then what the devil is your object?" stormed the Baron.

"That day at Gueures it was to lock you up in a cellar. Today—"

Beaumagnan had to step forward hastily to prevent the Baron from throwing himself on this intruder.

"Stay where you are, Godfrey! Sit down!" he cried. "Let the young gentleman tell us what he has come for."

He himself sat down at his desk. Ralph dropped on to a chair.

Before speaking he studied leisurely the faces of his opponents. He perceived that they had changed since their meeting at La Haie d'Etigues. The Baron in particular had aged. His cheeks had grown hollow and at moments his eyes had a hunted expression which impressed Ralph painfully. The fixed idea, the pangs of remorse can alone produce that feverish, restless air which he observed both in the Baron and in Beaumagnan. They could not keep their hands still.

Beaumagnan however kept control of himself. If he was haunted by the memory of Josephine's death, it was at rarer intervals than the Baron. It had worn him less, had less thrown him off his balance. It was only by fits and starts and at critical moments that it unmanned him.

Ralph thought to himself: "If I'm going to bring this off, I must produce such a critical moment. One or other of us has got to give ground."

"What is it you want, young man?" said Beaumagnan. "The name of Mademoiselle Rousselin has procured you admittance into my flat. With what intention—"

"With the intention of continuing the conversation you had with her at the theater last night," Ralph replied boldly.

The attack was indeed direct; but Beaumagnan did not flinch.

"I'm of the opinion that that conversation can only be continued with her, and I was expecting no one but her," he said drily.

"Mademoiselle Rousselin has a good reason for not coming," said Ralph.

"A very good reason?" asked Beaumagnan in a politely sceptical tone.

"Yes. She has been the victim of a murderous assault."

"Eh, what? Someone has tried to murder her? What for?" cried Beaumagnan.

"To take the seven stones from her as you gentlemen took the seven rings," said Ralph coldly. The Baron and Oscar de Bennetot jumped from their chairs. Beaumagnan showed better control of himself; but he stared with astonished eyes at this quiet young man whose inexplicable intervention assumed an air of arrogant defiance. But after all this adversary looked to be of no great importance; and he let that thought appear in the careless tone in which he countered.

THE TARPEIAN ROCK

"This is the second time you have interfered in matters which are no business of yours, young man. And you have interfered in a manner which will undoubtedly compel us to give you a well-merited lesson. The first time, at Gueures, after leading my friends into a trap, you took possession of an object which belonged to us; and that in ordinary language is known as larceny. Today your aggression is even more impudent, since you come and insult us to our faces, without the least excuse, knowing perfectly well that we did not steal those rings, but that they were handed over to us. Do you mind telling us what you mean by it?"

"You know quite well that there has been no larceny, nor aggression on my part," said Ralph firmly. "I have only acted in a manner entirely natural in one who is aiming at the same goal as you yourselves."

"Indeed, you are aiming at the same goal as we are, are you?" said Beaumagnan in a slightly sneering tone. "And what may that goal be?"

"The discovery of the ten thousand precious stones hidden in the block of granite."

Beaumagnan was indeed taken aback; and clumsily enough he showed it plainly by his air of astonished consternation and his gaping silence.

Thereupon Ralph drove his attack home, saying: "Doesn't it follow that since the four of us are seeking the incalculable treasure of the old monasteries, when our paths cross we come into collision? That's what must happen."

The treasure of the monasteries! The block of granite! The ten thousand precious stones! To Beaumagnan each phrase was the stroke of a hammer. Here was another rival to be dealt with! The Countess of Cagliostro out of the way, at once another competitor enters the race for the millions!

Godfrey d'Etigues and de Bennetot exchanged ferocious glances and expanded their chests in the manner of athletes about to plunge into a contest. Beaumagnan stiffened in his chair in his effort to recover his coolness. He felt that he would need it all.

"Legends!" he cried scornfully, striving to keep his voice steady and pick up the dropped thread of his ideas. "Old women's gossip! Nursery tales! Is that what you waste your time on?"

"No more than you," said Ralph in a pleasant tone, not wishing Beaumagnan to recover his balance but rather to upset him get more thoroughly. "Everything you do has some connection or other with this treasure. And not more than the Cardinal de Bonnechose did. I suppose his memorandum was old women's gossip. Not more than the dozen friends, of whom you are the leader and inspirer, do."

"Goodness, how well informed you are!" said Beaumagnan ironically.

"Better informed a great deal than you imagine," said Ralph quietly.

"And from whom did you get this precious information?" said Beaumagnan with a sneer.

"From a woman."

"A woman?" Beaumagnan repeated: and there was a sudden note of anxiety in his voice.

"From Josephine Balsamo, Countess of Cagliostro."

There came a groan from the Baron, a muttered oath from de Bennetot; and Beaumagnan cried in a tone of amazed dismay:

"Josephine Balsamo! Then you knew her!"

Ralph saw his way clearly. Just to drop the name of Josephine in the discussion had been enough to throw his enemies into the worst confusion, and in that confusion he was resolved to keep them. Indeed, so great was that confusion that Beaumagnan had committed the irremediable error of speaking of her as if she were no longer alive. Ralph smiled at him, a disquieting smile.

"D-D-Did you know her? When did you know her? Where? What did she tell you?" stammered Beaumagnan.

"I knew her at the beginning of last winter, as you did, monsieur," said Ralph, pressing his offensive. "And I enjoyed her acquaintance all through the winter till the very moment that I had the pleasure of meeting the daughter of the Baron d'Etigues. I saw her nearly everyday."

"You lie, sir!" cried Beaumagnan. "She couldn't have seen you everyday! She would have mentioned your name. I was a sufficiently close friend of hers for her not to have kept a secret of that kind from me."

"She kept that one," said Ralph drily.

"It's a slander!" Beaumagnan almost shouted. "You are trying to make us believe that an impossible intimacy existed between you and her. One may bring many accusations against Josephine Balsamo perhaps: accusations of coquetry, trickery but not this one—not of an act of debauchery."

"Love is not an act of debauchery," said Ralph calmly.

"What do you mean? Love! Josephine Balsamo loved you?"

"Yes," said Ralph.

Beaumagnan was beside himself. He sprang up and shook his fist in Ralph's face. In their turn his friends had to calm him; but he was still trembling with rage; beads of sweat stood out on his forehead.

"I hold him in the hollow of my hand all right," Ralph thought to himself. "In the matter of the crime and remorse he's as firm as a rock. But he is still being tortured by his passion for Josephine, and through that I shall do what I like with him."

For a good minute no one said anything. Beaumagnan mopped his brow. Then, making up his mind that this enemy, for all his delicate appearance, was not one to be rid of easily, he went on: "We're getting away from the point. Your personal feelings for the Countess of Cagliostro have nothing whatever to do with the matter in hand. I return therefore to my original question: what is it you want from us?"

"It's perfectly simple," said Ralph. "I can tell you in a few words. With regard to this religious treasure of the middle ages, which you personally want to recover for the treasury of the Society of Jesus, this is how we stand. These offerings flowed through channels in all the provinces into the seven principal abbeys of the Caux country, and constituted a common fund, managed by seven chosen administrators, of whom one only knew the hiding-place of the treasure. Each abbey possessed an episcopal or pastoral ring, which it handed down from generation to generation to its own delegate. As a symbol of its mission, the Council of Seven was represented by a candlestick with seven branches, each branch of which was set, a relic of the Hebraic liturgy and the temple of Moses, with a stone of the same kind and color as the stone in the ring to which it corresponded. For example, the branch I found at Gueures is set with a red stone, an imitation garnet, which was the representative stone of one of the abbeys; and we also know that Brother Nicolas, last administrator in chief of the abbeys of the Caus country, was a monk of Fécamp abbey. Are we in agreement so far?"

"Yes."

"Then it is enough to know the names of the seven abbeys to know the seven places in which a search has a prospect of success. Now seven names are inscribed on the inside of the rings which Bridget Rousselin handed over to you at the theater last night, and it is those seven rings I ask to examine."

"What?" cried Beaumagnan. "After we've been searching all these years, you come along and claim to reach at the first shot the same stage as we have?"

"Exactly," said Ralph with a cheerful grin.

"And if I refuse?"

"Excuse me, but do you refuse? I shall only tell you, in the event of your definite refusal."

"Of course I refuse!" cried Beaumagnan. "Your demand is absolutely senseless! I refuse categorically!"

"Then I shall denounce you."

Beaumagnan was astounded. He looked at Ralph as if he were dealing with a madman.

"You'll denounce me? What's this new game?"

"I shall denounce all three of you."

"All three of us?" said Beaumagnan with a chuckle. "And what are you going to accuse us of, my young friend?"

"The murder of Josephine Balsamo, Countess of Cagliostro!"

There was no word of protest, no gesture of revolt. Godfrey d'Etigues and Oscar de Bennetot seemed to sink into paralyzed heaps on their chairs. Beaumagnan turned livid and his chuckle ended in a horrible grimace.

He rose, dashed to the door, locked it, and put the key in his pocket. It had the effect of putting a little life into his associates. They sat upright again.

Ralph had the audacity to make a joke of it: "My dear sir," he said, "when a conscript joins his regiment they put him on a horse without stirrups till he learns to stick on."

"What do you mean?"

"I mean that I have sworn never to carry a revolver till I find myself confronted by a situation which I can not handle just with the help of my brain," said Ralph. "So you are warned. I haven't any stirrups; that is to say I haven't any revolver. You are three, all armed; and I am alone. Therefore—"

"Therefore, we've had enough of talk," said Beaumagnan in a threatening tone. "It's time for facts. You accuse us of having murdered the Countess of Cagliostro?"

"I do."

"And you have proofs to support this monstrous accusation?"

"I have."

"What are they?"

"A few weeks ago I was wandering about the estate of La Haie d'Etigues, hoping to have the good fortune of meeting Mademoiselle d'Etigues, when I saw a carriage driven by one of your friends. This carriage went into the park. I slipped in after it. A woman, Josephine Balsamo, was carried into the chamber in the old tower, in which you were all gathered together; and you formed yourselves into a tribunal of sorts. Her trial was conducted as dishonorably and unfairly as it could be. You acted as public prosecutor, monsieur, and you carried your treachery and vanity to the point of letting it be believed that this woman had been your mistress. As for these two gentlemen, they played the part of executioners."

"The proof! The proof!" snarled Beaumagnan, whose face had become unrecognizable.

"I was present, lying in the embrasure of the window, just above your head."

"It's impossible!" stammered Beaumagnan. "If it was true, you would have made some attempt to intervene and save her!"

"Save her from what?" asked Ralph who naturally did not wish to reveal anything about the rescue of Josephine. "I believed, as did the rest of your confederates, that you had condemned her to confinement in an English madhouse. So I went away when they did. I hurried to Etretat. I hired a boat and rowed about waiting for the English yacht of which you had spoken, intending to frighten the captain into releasing the unfortunate woman. It was a vain attempt and cost her her life. The English yacht never came. It was only later that I understood the dastardly trick you had played and was able to reconstitute the actual crime, in all its horror, the descent of the priest's staircase, the scuttled boat, and the drowning."

Listening in obvious terror, the three men had drawn their chairs closer together. De Bennetot quietly pushed aside the table which was between him and Ralph. Ralph observed the distorted features of Godfrey d'Etigues and the snarl that bared his teeth. Beaumagnan had but to give the signal, and he would have drawn his revolver and blown the imprudent young man's brains out.

But it was this very imprudence, quite inexplicable, that stayed Beaumagnan.

With a terrible air he said: "I repeat, monsieur, that you had no right to act as you have done and meddle with things that don't concern you. But I refuse to lie and deny the facts. Only... only I ask myself, since you have surprised such a secret, how you dare come here and provoke us. It's madness!"

"Why so, monsieur?" said Ralph simply.

"Because your life is in our hands."

Ralph shrugged his shoulders and said: "My life isn't in the slightest danger."

"Nevertheless there are three of us and not at all in the mood to disregard a matter which so closely touches our security."

"I run no more risk among you three than if it was your interest to act as my defenders," said Ralph calmly.

"Are you absolutely certain of that?"

"Absolutely, since you didn't kill me the moment you heard my story."

"And if I did decide to kill you?"

"An hour later you would all three be arrested."

"Nonsense!"

"It is as I have the honor of telling you. It's a quarter past four. One of my friends is walking up and down in front of the Prefecture of Police. It's a quarter past four. If I haven't rejoined him by a quarter to five, he informs the chief commissioner of your crime."

"Stuff and nonsense!" cried Beaumagnan, who appeared to recover confidence. "I am a well-known man. As soon as he mentions my name, they'll laugh at him!"

"They'll listen to him."

"In the meanwhile," said Beaumagnan, turning to Godfrey d'Etigues.

The order for the execution was on the point of being given. Ralph experienced the joy of genuine peril. In a few seconds the act, the execution of which he had retarded by his extraordinary coolness, would be committed.

"There's one more thing I should like to say," he said quietly.

"Speak!" growled Beaumagnan. "But on condition that it is a definite proof against us. We've had enough of accusations. With regard to the matter of the Countess and the view that justice may take of it, I'll attend to that. But I want a proof which proves to me that I'm not wasting my time discussing the matter with you. A proof at once—if not—"

He rose from his chair. Ralph rose too and faced him with imperious gripping eyes.

"Proof or death—that's what you mean, isn't it?" he said.

"Yes."

"Well, my answer is: the seven rings! At once! If not—"

"If not?"

"My friend hands over to the chief commissioner the letter which you wrote to the Baron d'Etigues, instructing him how to capture Josephine Balsamo and ordering him to murder her."

Beaumagnan pretended to be surprised: "A letter? Instructions to murder?" he said.

Ralph went into details; he said: "Yes, a letter in a kind of code, in which you get at the real meaning by ignoring a number of interposed sentences."

"Oh, that scrawl—I remember—yes," said Beaumagnan carelessly.

"A scrawl which constitutes the irrefutable proof you asked for," said Ralph coldly.

"Of course—of course—I admit it," said Beaumagnan ironically. "Only I'm not a schoolboy; and I take precautions.

That letter was given back to me by the Baron at the beginning of the meeting. I burned it."

"You burned the copy that was given to you. I took the precaution of keeping the original myself. I found it in the secret drawer of the Baron's rolltop desk. It is the original that my friend will hand over to the police."

The ring that had formed round Ralph broke. The savage faces of the Baron and his cousins no longer expressed anything but fear and anguish. Ralph gathered that the duel was at an end, and that without any real struggle—just a few feints and thrusts and parries. He had handled the affair with such skill and by his adroitness manoeuvred Beaumagnan into such a tragic situation, that, in the condition of mind in which he found himself, he could no longer get a clear view of the facts or discern his adversary's weak points. For after all, with regard to this letter of which Ralph declared he had the original: on what did that assertion rest? On nothing whatever. So that it had finally come about that Beaumagnan, after having demanded of Ralph an irrefutable proof before giving way, had by a singular anomaly, under the young man's adroit pressure, remained quite content with his bare assertion.

He gave ground quite suddenly without any effort to make terms. He opened a drawer, took out the seven rings, and said simply: "What assurance have I that you will not use that letter against us?"

"You have my word, monsieur," said Ralph. "Besides, where we are concerned circumstances never repeat themselves exactly—next time you will find a way of getting the upper hand."

"You may be sure of that, young man," said Beaumagnan; and he ground his teeth.

Ralph seized the rings with a trembling hand. Each of them had indeed a name engraved on its inside. On a scrap of paper he wrote quickly down the names of the seven abbeys:

Fécamp, Saint-Wandrille, Jumièges, Valmont, Gruchet le Valasse, Montvilliers, Saint-Georges de Boscherville.

Beaumagnan rang the bell. But when the servant came he bade him wait in the hall, and turning to Ralph, he said:

"Just one thing more: I'll make you an offer. You know the task we have set ourselves. You know exactly the point to which our efforts have brought us, and that the end is not so very far off?"

"That is my opinion," said Ralph.

"Well, do you feel disposed—I'm not going to beat about the bush—to cast in your lot with us?"

"On the same terms as your friends?"

"No. On same terms as myself."

The offer was bona fide; Ralph felt that it was; he was flattered by the tribute. Perhaps he would have accepted it, if it had not been for Josephine. But any alliance between her and Beaumagnan was out of the question.

"Thank you," he said gravely. "But for reasons into which I cannot enter, I must refuse."

"You are an enemy then?"

"No, monsieur, a competitor."

"No: an enemy," Beaumagnan insisted. "And as such liable—"

"Liable to be treated as was the Countess of Cagliostro," Ralph interjected.

"You've said it, monsieur. You know that the greatness of our end excuses the means which we are sometimes compelled to employ. If we employ them in your case, you will have yourself to thank for it."

"I shall," said Ralph.

Beaumagnan opened the door and said to the servant: "Show this gentleman out."

Ralph bowed to his three enemies and went across the hall. The servant opened the door with the peephole in it.

"Half a minute, my man," said Ralph.

He went lightly back to the door of the study, opened it to find the three confederates conferring, and with his hand on the handle of the door, and the path of escape clear, said in the most amiable accents:

"With regard to that famous compromising letter, I think I ought to tell you that I did not really take a copy of it, and that consequently my friend does not hold the original. And do you really think that that story about his walking up and down in front of the Prefecture, ready to dash in, if I don't turn up at a quarter to five, sounds probable? Goodbye, gentlemen. Sleep well. I'm looking forward to our next meeting."

He slammed the door in Beaumagnan's face and gained the street before he got it open.

He had won the second battle.

At the end of the street Josephine was waiting for him in a cab.

"Drive to Saint Lazare station, main line departure platform," he said to the cabman.

He jumped into the cab, quivering with delight, and said in the accents of a conqueror: "Here you are, darling—the seven indispensable names. Here's the list of them. Take it."

"And now?" she said.

"Well, there they are—the second victory in one day and what a victory! Goodness how easy it is to get the better of people! A little audacity, a clear head, careful reasoning, and a firm resolve to go as straight as an arrow to your goal, and obstacles clear out of your way of themselves. Beaumagnan is a smart chap, isn't he? Well, he crumpled up just as you did, my pretty Josine. Your pupil does you honor, doesn't he? Two first-class masters, Beaumagnan and Cagliostro's daughter smashed and pulverized in one day by a collegian! What do you think of that, Josine?"

He paused in his paean to say: "You're not angry with me for rubbing it in like this?"

"No, no," she said, smiling at him.

"And you're not angry about that little business at Bridget Rousselin's?"

"Don't you ask too much of me," she warned him. "It's better not to wound my pride. I've plenty of it and I'm vindictive. But after all one can't go on being angry with you for long. There's something peculiar about you which disarms one."

"Beaumagnan isn't disarmed, I'll be hanged if he is," he said thoughtfully.

"Beaumagnan is a man," she said.

"Well, I will make war on men; and I really believe that that's what I'm cut out for, for conquest, for the extraordinary and the fabulous. I feel that there is no situation from which I cannot emerge with honor. And it is tempting to fight when one is sure of victory, isn't it, Josine?"

Along the narrow streets on the left bank of the Seine the cab made its way at a good pace. They crossed the river.

"And from today I shall be victorious, Josine! I have all the trumps in my hand. In a few hours I reach Lillebonne. I unearth the Widow Rousselin, and, whether she like it or not, I examine the sandalwood casket on which the keyword is carved; and there we are. With that word and with the names of the seven abbeys, it will indeed be odd if I don't carry off the cup!"

Josephine laughed at his enthusiasm. He was exultant. He told her about his duel with Beaumagnan, kissed her, cocked snooks at the people they passed, opened the window and jeered at the cabman because his horse trotted like a snail.

"Make him gallop, old idiot! What? You have the honor of driving in your chariot the god of Fortune and the queen of beauty and your steed doesn't gallop!"

THE TARPEIAN ROCK 153

The cab went along the Avenue de l'Opera. It took the shortcut through the Rue des Petit-Champs and the Rue des Capucines. In the Rue Caumartin the horse did break into a gallop.

"Splendid!" cried Ralph. "Twelve to five; and we're nearly there. Of course it's understood that you come with me to Lillebonne?"

"Whatever for? There's no point in it. It's sufficient for one of us to go," she replied.

"As you like," said Ralph. "You trust me and you know that I shall not betray that trust and that we are allies—the victory of the one is the victory of the other."

But just as they came to the corner of the Rue Auber, the door of a courtyard on their left was thrown open, and without slowing up the cab ran through it.

Three men appeared at either door, Ralph was gripped and roughly dragged away before he could even make a show of resistance.

He heard Josephine, who had remained in the cab, say: "Saint Lazare Station! And be quick about it!"

The six men rushed him into the house, shoved him into a badly lighted room, and locked its massive door on him.

The exaltation which Ralph had been enjoying did not immediately abate. He went on laughing and joking, but in a growing fury and in tones that changed as it grew.

"Bravo, Josephine!... But what a masterstroke!... What a shot! Right in the middle of the bull's-eye and when I was least expecting it... How funny she must have found my songs of triumph! 'I am cut out for conquest, for the extraordinary and the fabulous!' Idiot that I was! When one is capable of such blunders, one should keep one's mouth shut. What a smash!"

He flung himself on the door. What was the use? It was the door of a cell. He tried to jump up to the little window which let in that dim light. There was no way of reaching it.

Then a noise caught his ear; and he perceived that a loophole had been cut in the corner of the wall, just under the ceiling, and that the barrel of a rifle was pointing at him, and that it followed his every movement.

All his anger turned on the invisible marksman; and he abused him freely.

"Hog! Guttersnipe! Come out of that hole, and I'll show you! A nice job yours is! Go and tell your mistress that she's hardly on the way to heaven yet, and that before long—"

He stopped short. It was a stupid waste of words. Then, passing suddenly from the height of fury to a quiet resignation, he lay down on a bed in an alcove which was fitted up as a dressing-room.

"You can kill me if you like," he said. "But don't stop me going to sleep."

Really he never dreamed of going to sleep. The first thing was to consider his situation quietly and draw from it conclusions which promised to be uncommonly disagreeable. In fact, they could be summed up in a few words. Josephine Balsamo had substituted herself for him, with the intention of reaping the fruits of his victory.

But what an organization she must have to be able to act so successfully in so little time! Ralph had no doubt that Leonard, accompanied by a confederate, had followed them to Beaumagnan's house and while he was in it had arranged with her the trap into which he had so simply fallen. This house must have been specially fitted up for such a purpose.

What could he do at his age against such enemies? On the one hand, Beaumagnan, with a whole world of correspondents and associates behind him; on the other hand, Josephine Balsamo, with so powerful and so well organized a gang.

He made a resolution. He said to himself: "Whether later I enter upon the straight path, as I hope to do, or whether, as is more probable, I keep on the path of adventure, I will equip myself with this indispensable organization! Woe to those who work by themselves! It is only leader of gangs who attain their ends. I mastered Josephine. Nevertheless, it is she who tonight will lay hands on the precious casket, while Ralph is groaning in his prison cell."

He had reached this point in his meditations when he found that an inexplicable torpor was invading him. It was accompanied by a feeling of general discomfort. He struggled against this unusual drowsiness, but his brain became clouded very quickly. At the same time he felt sick, and his stomach began to ache.

By a strong effort he shook off his drowsiness and walked across the room. But the heaviness increased. Of a sudden he threw himself down on the bed, a prey to a horrible thought. He remembered that in the cab Josephine had taken from her pocket a little gold sweetmeat box which she always carried, and as she ate two or three chocolates had, with an apparently mechanical gesture, offered him one.

"She has poisoned me!" he murmured, breaking into a cold sweat. "That sweet she gave me was poisoned!" He had no time to consider the truth of this suggestion. In an access of giddiness he seemed to topple into a great hole, and sank into oblivion.

Such a strong belief that he was dying had taken possession of him that, when he opened his eyes, he was not sure that he was alive. He took several deep and rather painful breaths, pinched himself, and spoke out loud. He was alive. The distant noises of the street confirmed him in his belief.

"Certainly I'm not dead," he said to himself. "But what a high opinion I've got of the woman I love! On account of a wretched narcotic she administered to me, as she had every right to do, I accuse her of poisoning me."

He could not tell how long he had been asleep—one day, or two, or more? His head was heavy; his mind was wandering; and his limbs were aching with a violent cramp. At the bottom of the wall he saw a basket of food which must have been let down through the loophole. No rifle was visible.

He was hungry and thirsty. He ate and drank. Such was his lassitude that he did not take the trouble to consider what might be the consequences of that meal. A narcotic? Poison? What did it matter? A passing sleep, or the sleep eternal, it made no difference to him. He went back to bed and fell asleep again for hours, for nights, for days.

In the end he came out of this deep slumber to become aware of certain sensations, much in the fashion in which one perceives gleams of light at the end of a tunnel. They were rather agreeable sensations. They were doubtless dreams, dreams of a pleasant rocking, accompanied by a continuous, rhythmical sound. At last he opened his eyes; then he perceived a framed picture, the canvas of which was covered with perpetually changing landscapes, shining or dark, full of sunlight or bathed in a golden mist.

Now he had only to stretch out his hand to find food. He began to enjoy the flavor of it more and more. He washed it down with a wine of a very delicate aroma. It seemed to him that, as he drank it, energy flowed into him. His eyes grew clear; the picture frame became an open window through which he saw a procession of hills and spires of village churches.

He found himself in quite another room, a small room, in which he had lived before, with his clothes and his books about him.

A stepladder rose at one side of it. Why did he not go up it since he had the strength? It merely needed an effort of will. He made the effort and mounted it. His head rose into the open air. A river flowed on his left and right. He murmured:

"The deck of the *Nonchalante*... The Seine... the Deux-Amants country."

He walked aft. Josine was there, sitting in a wicker work chair. There was really no transition between the combative rancor and revolt he had felt and the access of passion and desire which shook him at the sight of her. Had he, indeed, really felt any rancor and revulsion? Everything was drowned in an immense need to clasp her in his arms.

Enemy? Thief? Criminal if you like. But, after all, only a woman—above all, woman. And what a woman!

Dressed, as usual, in a simple frock, she was wearing that delicate veil which softened the luster of her hair and gave her so close a resemblance to the Virgin of Bernardino Luini. Her neck, of a warm creaminess, was bare. Her slender hands lay clasped in her lap. She was gazing at the abrupt slope of the Deux-Amants. And nothing could appear sweeter and more innocent than that face on which rested that perpetual, profound, and mysterious, smile.

Ralph was almost touching her at the moment at which she perceived him. She flushed slightly and lowered her eyelids, and she seemed not to dare to let her eyes rest on him through her long brown eyelashes. Never did a young girl display greater shyness and ingenuous timidity, less affectation and coquetry.

He was deeply touched by it. She feared this first meeting with him. Was he not going to abuse her, to throw himself on her, strike her, and heap abominable epithets on her? Or was he going to leave her with that scorn which is the worst of all things?

Ralph was trembling like a child. At the actual moment nothing counted with him but that which counts eternally with lovers—the kiss, the hands that clasp, the frenzy of glances that fail and of lips that faint with pleasure.

He fell on his knees before her.

X

THE MUTILATED HAND

The penalty of such loves is the silence to which they are condemned. Even when the mouths are speaking, the noise of the words they exchange does not break the heavy silence of the inner, solitary thoughts. Each follows his, or her, course of thought without ever penetrating into the very life of the other. A dispiriting intercourse from which Ralph, always so ready to expand, suffered more and more.

Josephine too must have been suffering from it, to judge from certain moments of extreme lassitude in which she seemed on the verge of those confidences that draw lovers closer than do embraces. Once she began to weep in Ralph's arms so bitterly that he looked for an access of surrender. But she recovered almost at once, and he felt her further away from him than ever.

"She cannot trust," he told himself. "She is one of those beings who dwell apart from their fellows in a solitude that has no bounds. She is a prisoner of the image she has formed of herself, has forced herself to form of herself; indeed, a prisoner of the enigma she has elaborated and which holds her in its invisible meshes. As the daughter of Cagliostro she has acquired the habit of the darkness, of the intricate, of plots, intrigues, and subterranean operations. To tell anyone the story of one of these machinations is to give him the thread which will guide him through the labyrinth. She is afraid and withdraws into herself."

By way of counter-stroke he kept silence himself and refrained from making any allusion to the adventure on which they had embarked, or to the problem of which they were seeking the solution. Had she obtained possession of the casket? Did she know the keyword? Had she plunged her hand into the hollow in that legendary block and emptied it of those thousands and thousands of precious stones?

On that matter, on every matter, silence.

Moreover, after they had passed Rouen, their intimacy slackened. Leonard, avoiding Ralph, reappeared again. The secret meetings began once more. The carriage and the untiring little horses everyday carried Josine away. Whither? On what enterprises? Ralph observed that three of the abbeys, Saint-Georges, Jumièges, and Saint-Wandrille, were close to the river. But then, if she were searching in this quarter, it must be that no solution had yet been found, and that she had simply failed.

This notion drove him abruptly to action. He sent to the inn near La Haie d'Etigues for his bicycle, and rode across the country to the outskirts of Lillebonne, in which Bridget Rousselin's mother was living. There he learned that a fortnight before—which was about the time that Josine had taken the train from Paris—the Widow Rousselin had shut her house and gone, so they said, to join her daughter in Paris. The evening before a lady had come to see her.

It was ten o'clock at night before Ralph got back to the barge which was moored to the southwest of the first curve beyond Rouen. A little while before reaching it he passed Josine's carriage, which the little horses, utterly exhausted, could scarcely drag along. When it came to the bank of the river Leonard jumped down from the box, opened the door, bent down, stood up with the inert body of the fainting Josine in his arms, and carried her to the barge. Ralph lent a hand, and the two of them carried her down to her cabin. The woman of the barge came to tend her.

"Look after her," said Leonard roughly. "She has only fainted. But you're all to stay on board, and don't you forget it!"

He went back to the carriage and drove off.

Josine was delirious most of the night, but Ralph could make no sense of her incoherent utterances. Next morning she had nearly recovered. Next evening Ralph went to the nearest village to buy a newspaper. He read among the local news:

'Yesterday afternoon, the police of Caudebec, on receiving information that a woodcutter had heard the screams of a woman appealing for help from an old limekiln on the outskirts of Maulevrier Forest, sent a sergeant and a constable to enquire into the matter. As these two representatives of the law approached the clearing in which the limekiln stands, they perceived over the fence two men who were dragging a woman towards a closed carriage beside which another woman was standing. Compelled to make the circuit of the fence, the police only reached the scene of action after the departure of the carriage. They at once started in pursuit of it, a pursuit which should have ended in the success of the police. But the horses drawing the carriage were so swift and the driver's knowledge of the lanes and byways of so extensive, that he succeeded in throwing them off his track in the network of roads to the north between Caudebec and Motteville. Moreover the night was coming on; and they have not yet succeeded in ascertaining in which direction this nice little gang escaped.'

"And they will not succeed," said Ralph to himself. "Nobody but me can reconstitute the facts since nobody but me knows the points of departure and arrival."

He formulated the following conclusions:

"One fact is certain: Mother Rousselin was in that old limekiln in charge of a confederate.

"Secondly, Josine and Leonard, who lured her away from Lillebonne and shut her up, go to see her everyday and try to extract some definite information from her. Yesterday the questioning was doubtless rather violent. Mother Rousselin yells; the police arrive. A desperate flight. They get away. Somewhere on their route they deposit their captive in another prison, already prepared for her; and once more they are safe. All these emotions brought about Josine's attack of nerves."

He studied an ordnance map of the route from Maulevrier Forest to the *Nonchalante*. The direct route was thirty kilometers; somewhere off that route, at some distance to the left or to the right Madam Rousselin was imprisoned. "Come," he said to himself, "the terrain of the conflict is marked out. It's about time that I made my entry on to the stage."

Next day he got to work, wandering along the Normandy roads, questioning the dwellers on them and trying to discover the points of the passage and the halting-places of "an old barouche drawn by two little horses." Logically and inevitably his quest must come to a successful end.

During those days the love of Ralph and Josephine Balsamo was at its keenest and most passionate. The young woman, knowing that the police were on her track, and remembering what she had heard at the Vasseur Inn, at Doudeville, did not dare to leave the *Nonchalante* and traverse the Caux country. So after every expedition Ralph found her on the barge, and they threw themselves into one another's arms with an exasperated desire to enjoy to the full the delights which, they foresaw, must soon come to an end.

Only such dolorous delights as two lovers on the verge of separation can have. Suspect delights that doubt poisoned. Either of them divined the secret designs of the other, and even as their lips met either knew that the other, for all their love, was acting as if they were at daggers drawn.

"I love you! I love you!" Ralph reiterated desperately while his inmost thought was how to find means of snatching Bridget's mother from the talons of his mistress.

Sometimes they gripped one another with the violence of two creatures veritably battling with one another. There was a brutality in their caresses, a threat in their eyes, hate in their hearts, and despair in their tenderness. One would have said that they were watching one another to discover the weak point at which to strike with the deadliest effect.

One night Ralph awoke with a sensation of extreme discomfort to find Josephine at his bedside, with a lamp in her hand, looking down on him. He shivered. Not that her charming face wore other than its usual smiling expression. But why did that smile seem to him so wicked and so cruel?

"What's the matter? What do you want?" he said sharply.

"Nothing—nothing," she said in careless accents, and she left him.

But she came back presently to show him a photograph.

"I found this in your pocketbook," she said. "I could hardly believe that you carried about with you another woman's photograph. Who is it?"

It was the photograph of Clarice d'Etigues. He hesitated, then said: "I don't know. It's a photo I picked up."

"Come: don't lie!" she said brusquely. "It's Clarice d'Etigues. Do you suppose I've never seen her? You were in love with her."

"No! Never!" he said firmly.

"You were in love with her, and she with you. I'm certain of it. And it is still going on."

He shrugged his shoulders, but as he was about to defend the young girl, Josephine broke in:

"I don't want to hear anything more about it. You're warned, and it's just as well. I'm not going out of my way to look for her, but if she ever crosses my path—all the worse for her."

"And all the worse for you, if you touch a hair of her head!" he exclaimed imprudently.

She paled. Her lips quivered, and laying her hand on his neck, she stammered: "You dare to take her part against me... against me!"

Her hand, very cold, contracted. He had the impression that she was going to strangle him and sprang out of bed. In her turn she was alarmed, thinking that he was going to strike her, and snatched from her bodice a little dagger with gleaming blade.

In these attitudes of attack they stared into one another's eyes, and it was so painful that Ralph murmured:

"Oh, Josine, what a pity it is that it should have come to this!"

No less moved, she sank into a chair, and he threw himself at her feet.

"Kiss me, Ralph—kiss me—and don't let's think anything more about it!" she murmured in a broken voice.

They clasped one another in a feverish embrace. But he observed that she still held the poniard, and a very slight movement would have driven it into his neck.

At eight o'clock the next morning he left the *Nonchalante*.

"I have nothing to hope from her," he told himself. "As for love: she loves me indeed, and sincerely; and she wishes, as I do, that this love was without reserves. But it cannot be. She has a hostile soul. She distrusts everything and everybody, and me above all."

At bottom he found her impenetrable. In spite of all his suspicions and, for that matter, of considerable evidence, even though the very spirit of evil dwelt in her, he refused to admit that she would go to the length of actual crime. He could not reconcile the idea of murder with that sweet face, which neither hate nor anger rendered less sweet. No: Josephine's hands were not stained with blood. But he thought of Leonard and never doubted that he was capable of putting Bridget's mother to the most terrible torture.

The short road from Rouen to Duclair, a little before the latter place, runs between the meadows on the bank of the Seine to the cliff which hangs over the stream. Caves have been hollowed in the actual chalk and serve the peasants as toolhouses and sometimes as lodgings for themselves. It came about that Ralph at last noticed that one of these caves was occupied by three men who were weaving baskets from the osiers of the neighboring stream. A small hedgeless vegetable garden lay in front of it.

A careful study of their habits and some suspicious details led him to suppose that father Corbu and his two sons, poachers and petty thieves with an uncommonly bad reputation, were affiliated with that band the members of which Josephine always had ready to her hand, and also to suppose that this cave of theirs was one of those refuges—inns, sheds, limekilns, and so forth, which Josephine had established all about the country.

He had to change his surmise into a certainty without attracting anyone's attention. He tried therefore to turn the enemy's position, and climbing on to the cliff, took his way from the river by a woodland path which dipped into a slight depression. At the bottom of the depression he crawled through the bushes and briars to a spot five or six feet above the cave.

He had brought food and drink with him and there he spent two days and two nights. Concealed by the bushes and the thick grass under them, he took an unobtrusive part in the life of the three men. On the second day a conversation he overheard proved uncommonly enlightening: the Corbu family had been in charge of Madam Rousselin and since the flight from Maulevrier Forest were actually keeping her at the end of their cave.

How was he to set her free? Or how, at any rate, was he to get near her and obtain from the unfortunate woman the information which she had doubtless refused Josephine? Carefully considering the habits of the Corbus, he formed and rejected several plans. But on the morning of the third day he saw the *Nonchalante* descend the river and come to her moorings at the foot of the cliff, about three-quarters of a mile from the cave.

At five o'clock in the evening two people came across the gangway and along the riverbank. In spite of her peasant's dress, he recognized Josephine by her walk. Leonard was her companion.

They stopped in front of the Corbus' cave and conversed with them as with persons on whom they had chanced by accident. Then, since there was no one on the road, they went sharply into the garden. Leonard disappeared into the interior of the cave. Josephine remained outside, sitting on an old and rickety chair, under the cover of a screen of shrubs.

Old Corbus hoed away at his garden. His sons went on with their basket-work.

"The questioning is going to begin again," murmured Ralph. "What a pity it is I cannot be present at it!"

He watched Josephine, whose face was almost entirely hidden under the drooping brim of a large, common straw hat, of the kind that peasants wear during the hot weather. She never stirred; she was leaning forward a little with her elbows on her knees.

The minutes slipped by and Ralph began to ask himself what he was doing there, when all at once he fancied he heard a groan close by, which was followed by smothered cries. Yes, they certainly came from close beside him. The sounds rose, indeed, from the middle of the thick grass which surrounded him. How was it possible?

He crawled to the point at which the noise seemed loudest, and it took him a very little time to understand what was happening. The edge of the cliff, in which the hollow ended, was covered with stones, and among these stones was a little heap of bricks hardly noticeable among the bushes and roots. It was the ruins of a chimney.

That explained the phenomenon which had surprised him. The cave of the Corbus must come to an end a long way in the rock; and there must be a passage running down to it which had formerly served as a chimney. Through this passage and the heap of bricks the sounds came.

There came two louder cries of agony. Ralph thought of Josephine. By turning round he could still see her at the end of the little garden. Still sitting, bent forward, her body motionless, she was carelessly pulling the petals off a capucine. Ralph supposed, or rather tried to suppose, that she had not heard those cries. Perhaps even she knew nothing about what was going on. In spite of that he trembled with indignation. Whether or no she actually had a part in the terrible questioning that the unfortunate woman was undergoing, was she any the less to blame? And all the obstinate doubts in his mind, by which she had profited up to then, ought they not to vanish in the face of the implacable reality? Everything that he had felt to her prejudice, everything that he had refused to know was true, since she must have definitely set Leonard to the task with which he was busy and of which she had been unable to endure the horrible spectacle.

Carefully but quickly Ralph pulled aside the bricks and scooped away the heap of earth. When he had finished the cries had ceased, but the sound of words came to his ears hardly louder than a whisper. He had, therefore, to continue his work and clear the upper part of the passage. Then, lying with his head well down in it, he could hear distinctly. Two voices were speaking in turn—the voice of Leonard and a woman's voice,

THE MUTILATED HAND

without doubt the voice of Madam Rousselin. The unfortunate woman seemed to be at the end of her strength and a prey to indescribable terror.

"Yes... yes," she murmured, "I'm going to tell you, since I said I would. But I'm so worn out you must excuse me, good gentleman... Besides... All these things happened such a long time ago... Twenty-two years have passed since..."

"Stop babbling and come to the point!" growled Leonard.

"Yes," she replied. "I am coming to the point. It was at the time of the war with Prussia, twenty-two years ago... And as the Prussians were advancing on Rouen, where we were living, two gentlemen came to my poor husband, who was a carrier... gentlemen whom we had never seen before. They wished to get out of the country, with their trunks, like a great many other people at that time, you know. My husband accepted their offer and without wasting any more time, for they were in a hurry, set out with them in his carrier's cart. Unfortunately, owing to the fact that our other horses had been requisitioned, we had only one horse, and that one wasn't up to much. Besides, it was snowing... Seven miles out of Rouen he fell down and could not get up again... The gentlemen were shivering with fear, for the Prussians might turn up at any moment. It was then that a man from Rouen, who my husband knew quite well, a confidential servant of the Cardinal de Bonnechose—Monsieur Jaubert his name was—drove up in a dogcart... You can see what happened... They talked... The two gentlemen offered him a large sum for his horse... Jaubert refused. They begged him, and then they threatened him... And then they threw themselves on him like madmen, and in spite of the prayers of my husband, knocked him on the head... After that they looked into his dogcart, found in it a casket, which they took, harnessed Jaubert's horse to the carrier's cart, and went off leaving the poor man half dead."

"Quite dead," said Leonard more accurately.

"Yes: my husband learned that months later, when he was able to enter Rouen again."

"And didn't he inform the police about it?"

Madam Rousselin appeared to hesitate; then she said: "Yes... No doubt he ought to have done perhaps... Only—"

"Only they'd bought his silence, hadn't they?" sneered Leonard. "They opened the casket in front of him and found jewels in it and gave your husband his share of the loot."

"Yes—yes... the rings... the seven rings," she said. "But that wasn't his reason for keeping silence... The poor man was ill. He died a little while after he came back from Rouen."

"And that casket?"

"It was left in the empty cart so that my husband brought it back with the rings. I kept silence, as he had done. It was already an old story, and I was afraid of the scandal, too... They might have accused my husband. It was just as well to keep my mouth shut. I went away to Lillebonne with my daughter, and it was only when Bridget left me to go on the stage that she took the rings... which for my part I never wanted to touch... That's the whole story, Monsieur. Don't ask me anything else."

"What do you mean, the whole story?" said Leonard, and he sneered again.

"It's all I know," said the widow fearfully.

"But I've no interest in that precious story of yours. What we're quarreling about is another thing... As you very well know."

"What do you mean?"

"The letters carved on the inside of the casket, on the lid—that's the whole point of the business."

"Those half rubbed-out letters! I swear to you, good gentleman, I never even dreamed of trying to make them out."

"That's all right, and I'm quite willing to believe it," said Leonard. "But then we come again to the original point: what has become of the casket?"

THE MUTILATED HAND

"I've told you. It was taken from me—the evening before you came to Lillebonne with the lady, the lady who wore a thick veil."

"It was taken from you, was it? Who by?"

"By a person of my acquaintance."

"A person who was looking for it?" said Leonard sharply.

"No. That person saw it on the top of a cupboard in my sitting-room and fancied it as a curio," said the widow.

"What was that person's name—for the hundredth time—what was that person's name? That's what I want to know," stormed Leonard.

"I can't tell you that. It was someone who has been very kind to me, and to tell would only do harm great harm. I will not tell."

"But, you old fool, that person would be the first to tell you to speak!"

"Perhaps—perhaps. But how am I to know that? I cannot write... We see one another from time to time... Why, we were to meet next Tuesday, at two o'clock."

"Where?"

"It's impossible... I'd no right—"

"What? Have we got to begin all over again?" growled Leonard impatiently.

The widow cried in a voice of terror: "No, no! good gentleman! I beg you!"

The words ended in a cry of pain.

"Oh, the brute!... What is he doing to me? Oh! my poor hand!"

"Speak, then, curse you!"

"Yes, yes... I will!... I will!"

But she broke off short; her voice gave out. She was at the end of her strength. Leonard, however, went on pressing her and Ralph caught some words painfully uttered: "Yes... we're to meet on Tuesday... at the old lighthouse... But, no!... I have no right!... I would rather die!... You can do what you like!... I'd rather die!"

She was silent.

Leonard growled: "What's the matter with the pigheaded old beast now? She's not dead I hope. Oh, you old donkey, you shall speak! I'll give you ten minutes and then I'll make an end of it."

A door was opened and then shut. Doubtless he was going to inform Josephine of the admissions he had so far obtained and to get instructions from her as to the course the rest of the questioning was to take. Ralph pulled his head out of the chimney and saw him go to her and stand over her. He talked to her with excited gestures; she listened to him.

"The brutes!" Ralph execrated both of them, the one no less than the other. The groans of Madam Rousselin had moved him profoundly and he was trembling with rage and burning to act. Nothing in the world should prevent him from rescuing this woman.

As was his custom, he started to act the moment that the vision of the things that he must accomplish unfolded itself before him in logical sequence. In these cases hesitation is apt to spoil everything. Success depends on the audacity with which one forces one's way through obstacles that as yet one does not even know. He glanced at his adversaries. All five of them were some distance from the cave. Quickly he went down the chimney, this time feet foremost. It was his intention to make his way down the crumbling shaft as gently as possible. But almost on the instant he went down at full speed accompanied by most of its crumbling walls and arrived at the bottom with a bump and the crash of falling stones and bricks.

"Hang it all! If only they didn't hear it outside!" he said to himself.

He listened. No one was coming. The darkness was so great that he believed himself to be still on the hearth. But stretching out his arms he found that the chimney had landed him in a little chamber hollowed out of the end of the cave and so small that his hand immediately touched another hand which almost seemed to be on fire. His eyes grew used to the darkness; and he saw gleaming eyes fixed on him in a gray and haggard face contorted with terror. She was not bound or gagged. What use would it have been? Her weakness and terror rendered escape impossible.

He bent down and said to her: "Don't be frightened, I saved the life of your daughter, Bridget, who was also a victim of these people who are persecuting you on account of the casket and the rings. I've been on their track ever since they took you from Lillebonne. I'm going to save you too, but on condition that you never say a word about what has happened to anyone."

But what was the use of explanations that the unfortunate woman was incapable of understanding? Without wasting any more time, he picked her up and hoisted her on to his shoulder. Then he walked to the mouth of the cave and quietly opened the door which was not locked as he expected.

A little way off Leonard and Josephine were still talking, behind them, at the bottom of the garden the white road stretched away to the large village of Duclair; and on it were the carts of the countryfolk, coming and going.

Then, at what he judged to be a propitious moment, he threw the door open, walked quickly down the garden path and laid Madam Rousselin on the turf at the bottom of it.

At once, all about him there rose an outcry. The Corbus rushed forward along with Leonard, all four of them, spurred to a conflict by an unreasoning impulse. But what could they do? A carriage was coming along the road from the right, another from the left. To attack Ralph in the presence of all these witnesses and recover the unfortunate woman by force was to betray themselves and bring upon themselves the inevitable enquiry and the penalty of the law. They stopped short, exactly as Ralph had foreseen.

In the calmest manner in the world he called to two nuns, wearing large caps, one of whom was driving a little wagonette drawn by an old horse, and asked them to succor a poor woman whom he had found unconscious by the side of the road, her fingers crushed by some carriage.

The good sisters who were in charge of a refuge and small infirmary at Duclair were only too ready to do so. They installed Madam Rousselin in the wagonette and covered her with shawls. She had not recovered consciousness and was delirious, waving her mutilated hand, the thumb and first finger of which were swollen and bleeding.

The horse trotted quietly off.

Ralph remained motionless, thoroughly upset by the sight of that mutilated hand; and so upset was he that he did not notice the movements of Leonard and the three Corbus who had surrounded him and were about to attack him. When he did perceive them, the four of them had cut him off from the road and were trying to force him into the garden. No peasant was in sight; and the situation seemed so favorable to Leonard that he drew his knife.

"Put that up and leave us!" cried Josephine. "You Corbus too. None of that foolishness!"

She had not risen from her chair while all this had been going on, but now she rose among the bushes.

Leonard protested: "It isn't foolishness! The foolishness would be to let him go—now that we've once got him."

"Be off!" she commanded.

"But that woman—that woman will denounce us!"

"No she won't. It's not to Mother Rousselin's interest to speak. Now be off!" said Josephine.

THE MUTILATED HAND

Leonard and his friends moved away. She came close up to Ralph.

He looked at her at length, with a look which appeared to disquiet her to the point that to break the silence she had to say jestingly: "Each in turn, isn't it, Ralph? Between you and me success passes from one to the other. Today you have the upper hand. Tomorrow—but what's the matter with you? You do look funny! And your eyes are positively savage."

He said curtly: "Goodbye, Josine."

The color in her cheeks faded a little and she said: "Goodbye? You mean au revoir."

"No: goodbye."

"Then—then—you mean that you don't wish to see me again?"

"I don't wish to see you again," he said coldly.

She lowered her eyes. Her eyelids quivered. Her lips were smiling and at the same time infinitely dolorous.

"Why, Ralph?" she murmured.

"Because I've seen a thing that I cannot—that I can never forgive you," he said.

"What?"

"That poor woman's hand."

She looked as if she were going to faint and murmured, "Ah, I understand... Leonard hurt her. But I forbade him to do anything of the kind... I thought she had yielded merely to threats."

"You lie, Josine! You heard the woman's cries, just as you heard them in Maulevrier Forest. Leonard acts, but the will to evil, the intention to murder is yours, Josine. It was you who sent your accomplice to the little house in Montmartre with instructions to kill Bridget Rousselin if she resisted. It was you who sometime ago put the poisonous cachet among those which Beaumagnan would swallow. It was you who, during the years before that, destroyed Beaumagnan's two friends, Denis Saint-Hébert and George d'Isneauval."

"No, no! I won't let you say so!" she broke out. "It isn't true! And you know it isn't!"

He shrugged his shoulders and said slowly: "Yes: the legend of the other woman created to meet the necessity of the case... another woman who is your exact image and commits the crimes, while you, Josephine Balsamo, content yourself with less brutal adventures. I believe in that legend. I let myself get muddled up in all these stories of identical women, daughter, granddaughter, and great granddaughter of Cagliostro. But it's all over, Josine. If my eyes deliberately closed themselves formerly in order not to see things, the sight of that mangled hand has definitely opened them to the truth."

"You are acting on lies, Ralph! On wrong interpretations! I never knew the two men of whom you speak!"

He said wearily: "It may be so. It is not altogether impossible that I am making a mistake. But it is altogether impossible that I should henceforward see you through this fog of mystery in which you've hidden yourself. You are no longer mysterious to me, Josine. I see you as you are—that is to say as a criminal."

He paused and added in a lower voice: "As a sick woman even. If there is a lie anywhere, it's the lie of your beauty."

She was silent. In the shadow of her straw hat her face was still sweet. The accusations of her lover did not ruffle her. She was altogether seductive, altogether enchanting.

He was disturbed to the very depths of his being. Never had she appeared to him so beautiful and so desirable; and he asked himself if it were not folly to seize a freedom which he would curse on the morrow.

"My beauty is not a lie, Ralph," she declared. "And will come back to me because it is for you that I am beautiful."

"I shall never come back."

"Yes, you can no longer live without me. The *Nonchalante* is close by, I shall be waiting for you tomorrow."

"I shall never come back," said he, once more ready to bend the knee.

"In that case, why are you trembling? Why are you so pale?" she said stretching out her arms toward him.

He perceived that his salvation depended on his silence, that he must flee without answering, and never turn his head.

He thrust off the two hands which were grasping him, and went.

XI

THE OLD LIGHTHOUSE

All that night, Ralph pedaled away, as much to wear himself out with a salutary weariness as to throw the gang off his track. Next morning, utterly worn out he came to a stop at an hotel at Lillebonne.

He forbade them to awake him, locked and bolted his door, and slept for twenty-four hours. When he had dressed and breakfasted, all he thought of was mounting his bicycle and returning to the *Nonchalante*. The struggle against love had begun.

He was very unhappy, and having never suffered, having always followed his whims, he raged against a despair to which it would have been so easy for him to put an end.

"Why not yield?" he said to himself. "I can get there in two hours. And what is there to prevent me going off again a few days later when I shall have hardened myself against the parting?"

But he could not do so. The vision of that mutilated hand was a veritable obsession and ruled his actions. It obliged him to recall those other barbarous and hateful deeds which enabled him to see this one as their natural sequel.

Josephine had done this; then Josephine had murdered; Josephine did not shrink from murderous acts and found it quite simple and natural to kill and kill again when murder helped her enterprises. From murder Ralph shrank, with a physical repulsion, a revolt of every instinct. The idea that he might be drawn, in some access of madness, to shed blood, filled him with horror. And with this horror the most tragic of realities associated indissolubly the image of the woman he loved.

He stayed away, but at the cost of what efforts! In what groans did his impotent revolt die away! Josephine stretched out her lovely arms to him and offered her mouth to his kisses. How resist the appeal of that voluptuous creature?

Moved to the lowest depths of his egotism, for the first time he became aware of the immense suffering he must have inflicted on Clarice d'Etigues. Now he could imagine her tears, the overwhelming distress of her shattered life. Shaken by remorse, he addressed to her discourses full of tenderness in which he recalled the moving hours of their love.

He did more. Knowing that the young girl received her letters direct, he dared to write to her:

'Forgive me, dear Clarice. I have treated you like a scoundrel. Let us hope for a brighter future and think of me with all the indulgence of your generous heart. Once more, forgive me—forgive.

RALPH.'

"If only I were with her, how quickly I should forget all these horrible things!" he said to himself. "The essential thing is not to have innocent eyes and kissable lips but a loyal and serious spirit like that of Clarice."

Only it was the eyes and the ambiguous smile of Josephine that he adored; and when he thought of her caresses, it was little he cared that she had a spirit which was neither loyal nor innocent.

In the meantime he set about hunting for the old lighthouse of which Madam Rousselin had spoken. Since he knew that she lived at Lillebonne he had no doubt that that lighthouse was in the neighborhood of it and that was the reason he had gone in the direction he did when he left Josephine.

He was not mistaken. He had only to make enquiries to learn, firstly, that there was an old, abandoned lighthouse in the woods which surrounded the Château de Tancarville, and secondly that the owner of that lighthouse had entrusted the keys of it to the Widow Rousselin, who, on the Tuesday of every week, went to clean it. A simple nocturnal expedition put him in possession of those keys.

It was only two days from the day on which the unknown person who possessed the casket was certainly going to meet the Widow Rousselin; and since she, a prisoner or an invalid, had not been able to put off the engagement, everything was arranged in a manner that would enable him to profit by an interview which he reckoned so important. This prospect soothed him. The problem which had been worrying him for weeks and of which the solution seemed to have become a matter of days, again took possesion of his mind.

To leave nothing to chance, on the Monday evening he paid a visit to the meeting-place, and on the Tuesday, when, an hour before the meeting he briskly traversed the woods of Tancarville success appeared to him inevitable; and he was brimming with pride and pleasure.

Part of these woods, beyond the park, stretches as far as the Seine and covers the cliffs. The roads run through it from central crossroads, and one of them leads through ravines and over steep ridges towards the rugged promontory, on which rises, half visible, the abandoned lighthouse. During the week the spot is absolutely deserted. Sometimes on a Sunday picnickers take possession of it.

If you ascend to the top of it, you get a glorious view over the Tancarville canal and the river estuary. But the bottom of it was at that time buried in brush wood. On the ground floor is a single room, of a fair size, pierced by two windows, and furnished with two chairs. It opens on the land side on an enclosure full of nettles and weeds.

As he drew near it Ralph's pace slackened. He had a very natural impression that important events were about to happen and that they were not only thus meeting with an unknown and the definite conquest of a formidable secret, but that they were a continuation of the supreme battle in which the enemy would be definitely defeated.

And this enemy was the Countess of Cagliostro—the Countess who knew as well as he the admissions torn from the Widow Rousselin, and who, incapable of accepting defeat and disposing of unlimited means of investigation, must have easily found this old lighthouse, in which the last act of the drama was about to be played.

"And not only," said he under his breath, laughing at himself, "do I ask whether she will come to the meeting-place, but in reality I hope keenly that she will be there and that I shall see her again and that, both of us victors, we shall fall into one another's arms."

Through a gate in the little wall, the top of which was bristling with broken bottles, he went into the enclosure. There was no trace of anyone's passage through the weeds; but it was possible to cross the wall in another place and to climb in through one of the windows at the side.

His heart was beating. His fists were clenched. He was ready for the struggle, if a trap had been laid for him.

"But how silly I am!" he thought. "Why a trap?"

He turned the handle of the worm-eaten door and entered.

On the instant he felt that someone was in hiding in the recess beside the door. He had no time to turn upon the assailant. Scarcely did he become aware of him, by instinct rather than by actual vision than a noose that dragged him backwards tightened round his neck and a knee came with brutal violence against the small of his back. Suffocated and jolted, he was at the mercy of his opponent and came heavily to the ground.

"A good stroke, Leonard!" he muttered. "A pretty revenge!"

He was wrong. It was not Leonard. He caught sight of his assailant's profile and recognized Beaumagnan. Then while Beaumagnan was tying his hands, he rectified his error and admitted his surprise in the simple words:

"So—so—the candidate for the priesthood!"

The rope which encircled his neck had been run through a ring in the opposite wall just above one of the windows. Beaumagnan who was acting with jerky movements and apparently half mad, opened that window and half opened the shutter that opened out wards. Then, using the ring as a pulley-block, he pulled the rope and compelled Ralph to walk across the room. Ralph saw through the half-opened shutters the empty space, which, from the top of the steep slope on which the lighthouse had been built, fell among sloping boulders and great trunks of trees whose leafy tops shut out the horizon.

Beaumagnan twisted him round, set his back against the shutters, and tied him to them by the wrists and ankles. Ralph was now in this predicament: in the case of his trying to move forward, the rope round his neck, tightening through the slipknot would strangle him; if on the other hand the whim took Beaumagnan to get rid of his victim, he had only to give him a sharp push, the shutters would give way and Ralph, dangling over the abyss, would find himself being hanged.

"An excellent position for a serious conversation," he sneered.

Moreover his mind was made up. If it was Beaumagnan's intention to give him the choice between death and divulging the steps that he, Ralph, had been able to make towards a solution of the problem, he would speak without the slightest hesitation.

THE OLD LIGHTHOUSE

"I'm at your orders," he said. "Ask away."

"Be quiet!" snapped Beaumagnan, in raging accents. He stuck a pad of cotton wool over Ralph's mouth and fastened it in place by a handerchief tied round his head.

"A single sound—a single movement—and with one blow of my fist I'll knock you into the abyss!" he snarled.

He looked at him for a moment as if he were asking himself whether he had not better do it at once and be done with it.

But of a sudden he left him, crossed the room on tiptoe and stretching himself at full length on the threshold, looked through the door which was a little way open.

"Things are going badly," thought Ralph, uncommonly anxious. "They are going all the more badly because I don't understand at all what is really happening. How comes he to be here? Am I to suppose that he is the benefactor of the Widow Rousselin, that benefactor whom she did not wish to compromise?"

That hypothesis did not satisfy him.

"No: that isn't it. I have fallen into a trap not because it was set for me but because I was foolishly careless. It's plain that a beggar like Beaumagnan knows the whole Rousselin business, that he has learned of these meetings and the hour of these meetings; and then, knowing that the widow has been abducted, he watches and makes other people watch the neighborhood of Lillebonne and Tancarville. So it came about that they have discovered that I was on the spot and my goings and comings—and then the trap—and then—"

This time Ralph's conviction was profound, the conqueror of Beaumagnan at Paris, he had just lost the second engagement. Victorious in his turn, Beaumagnan had spread him out on a shutter like a bat nailed to a wall and was now looking out for the other person in order to seize him and tear the secret from him.

One point however remained obscure. Why this attitude of a wild beast ready to spring upon its prey? That was quite out of keeping with the probably quite peaceful meeting which was to take place between him and that unknown person. Beaumagnan had only to go out and wait for him outside and say:

"Madam Rousselin is ill and has sent me in her place. She would like to know the inscription engraved on the lid of the casket."

"Always supposing," thought Ralph, "that Beaumagnan hasn't reason to expect some other person to come—and that he does not distrust that person... and that he is not preparing for another attack."

It was sufficient for such a question to present itself to Ralph for him to perceive at once the exact solution. To suppose that Beaumagnan had laid a trap for him, Ralph, was only half the truth. The ambush was a double one. Who then could Beaumagnan be looking for in this fever of exasperation if not for Josephine Balsamo?

"That's it! That's it!" said Ralph to himself, the facts of the matter at last clear to him. "He has guessed that she is alive. Yes, the other day in Paris when we had that tussle he must have guessed this amazing fact. And that's another blunder I've made... for lack of experience. Should I have spoken like that and acted like that if Josephine Balsamo were not alive? What? I told this man I had read between the lines of his letter to Baron Godfrey, that I was present at the famous gathering at La Haie d'Etigues, and yet failed to understand what he really had in store for the Countess of Cagliostro! And was it likely that a young fellow like me, so thoroughly alive, would abandon that charming woman? Come then: if I was at the trial I was certainly at the priest's staircase. I was certainly present at the embarkation. I certainly rescued Josephine. And we loved one another not with a love which dated from last winter, as

I pretended, but with a love posterior to Josephine's supposed death!... That is what Beaumagnan said to himself."

Proof piled on proof. Events linked themselves together like the links of a chain. Entangled in the Rousselin affair and consequently sought for by Beaumagnan, Josephine had not failed to search the neighborhood of the lighthouse. Informed of this at once, Beaumagnan formed his ambuscade. Ralph had fallen into it; it was now the turn of Josephine!

One would have said that Fate wished to confirm immediately the ideas which had been running through Ralph's mind. He had scarcely reached this conclusion when there came the sound of a carriage coming up the road which runs along the canal under the cliff. On the instant, Ralph recognized the quick trot of Leonard's horses.

Beaumagnan, on his part, must have known what was happening, for he sprang up and listened.

The noise of hoofs ceased, then began again slower. The carriage was mounting the rocky lane, which winds up towards the plateau and from which runs the forest path, in which there is no room for a carriage, which ascends the steep slope to the old lighthouse.

In five minutes or less, Josephine would appear.

Every second of every one of those solemn minutes increased the agitation and frenzy of Beaumagnan. He muttered incoherent words. His mask of romantic actor grew uglier and uglier till his face became of a purely bestial hideousness. The instinct, the will to murder contorted his features; and all at once it became clear that this will, this savage instinct were inflamed against Ralph, against Josephine's lover.

Once more his feet began to pace mechanically the tiled floor. He was walking up and down without knowing it; he was going to kill without knowing it, like a drunken man. His arms outstretched themselves. His clenched fists moved forward like two battering rams that a slow, continuous, and irresistible force would have thrust against the young man's bosom. A few more steps, and Ralph would be dangling in the abyss. He shut his eyes. However, he was not in the slightest degree resigned and tried hard to retain a vestige of hope.

"The rope will break," he thought, "and there will be thick grass for me to fall on. Truly it is not the fate of Monsieur Arsène Lupin d'Andresy to be hung. If, at my age, I have no chance of getting out of such a hole as this, it must be that the gods have no intention of taking a real interest in me. In that case there is nothing to regret."

He thought of his father and of the instruction in gymnastics he had had from Theophrastus Lupin. He murmured the name of Clarice.

However, the blow did not come. Even as he felt him within striking distance, it seemed that his adversary stopped in his spring.

He opened his eyes. Beaumagnan, drawn up to his full height, was towering above him. But he did not move; his arms had fallen; and on his face, on which the thought of murder had impressed the most abominable expression, the decision seemed to be suspended.

Ralph listened and heard nothing. But perhaps Beaumagnan, whose senses had been rendered extraordinarily acute by his emotions, heard Josephine coming. As a matter of fact, he drew back a step or two and then with a rush took up his post in the recess to the right of the door.

Ralph had a good view of his face. It was hideous. He looked for all the world like a sportsman practising bringing his gun to his shoulder in order to get the stiffness out of his arms and bring it up quickly when the time came to shoot. So Beaumagnan's hands were moving in the gestures necessary to the crime. They kept opening for the strangling, moved to a suitable distance from one another, and closed their curved fingers like talons.

Ralph was panic-stricken. His impotence was terrible; it was a veritable martyrdom.

Though he was well aware that any movement was useless, he struggled to break his bonds. If only he had been able to call out to warn her! But the gag smothered his cries and the bonds cut into his flesh.

Outside the deep silence was broken by the sound of footsteps. The gate grated on its hinges, a petticoat rustled among the tall weeds, a foot crunched the pebbles.

Beaumagnan, flattened against the wall, raised his forearms; his hands, trembling like the hands of a skeleton shaken by the wind, seemed already to be closing round a neck and to be gripping it, all alive and throbbing.

Ralph moaned behind his gag.

And then the door opened and the scene was played.

It was played exactly in the manner in which Beaumagnan had planned and Ralph pictured to himself. The figure of Josephine Balsamo stepped over the threshold and on the instant was crushed down in Beaumagnan's rush. A feeble moan from her was drowned by a kind of furious baying which poured from the assassin's throat.

Ralph groaned. Never had he loved Josephine so dearly as at the moment in which he saw her in her death agony. Her faults? Her crimes? What did they matter? She was the most beautiful creature in the world and all that beauty, that adorable smile, that charming body, made for all the caresses, were about to be annihilated. No help was possible. No force could avail against the irresistible strength of this brute.

What saved Josephine was the excess of Beaumagnan's love which death alone could glut. At the last moment it was unable to complete its sinister task. At the end of his strength, racked by a despair which suddenly assumed the appearance of madness, Beaumagnan rolled on the ground tearing at his hair and banging his head on the tiles.

Ralph breathed again. Though appearances were against it and though Josephine did not move, he was sure she was not dead. As a matter of fact, slowly, coming out of the horrible nightmare, she raised herself, and after several violent fits of shuddering, at last stood upright, her usual well-balanced and calm self. She was dressed in a cloak with a cape to it and was wearing a toque from which hung a veil embroidered with large flowers. She let the cloak fall, revealing her bare shoulders, for her bodice had been torn in the struggle. As for the toque and veil, which had been badly rumpled, she threw them into a corner and her hair, freed from them, fell on each side of her forehead in heavy, even curls full of tawny lights. Her cheeks had more color in them than usual and her eyes were shining more brightly.

A long moment of silence followed. The two men gazed at her with distracted eyes, no longer as if she were an enemy, or sweetheart, or a victim, but simply as a radiant woman whose enchanting fascination charmed them. Ralph deeply moved, Beaumagnan motionless and prone, both of them admired her with the same fervor.

She raised to her lips a little metal whistle that Ralph knew well. Leonard must be on guard a little way off and would at once hurry to its call. But she changed her mind. Why call him when she remained the absolute mistress of the situation?

She went to Ralph, unknotted the handkerchief which kept the gag in its place, and said: "You did not come back, Ralph, as I thought you would. But you will come back, won't you?"

If he had been free, he would have clasped her to him furiously. But why did she not cut through his bonds? What secret design prevented that?

He said firmly: "No. It's all over."

She raised herself on to the top of her toes and glued her lips to his, murmuring: "All over—between us? You're mad, Ralph!"

Beaumagnan sprang to his feet and, beside himself at the sight of this unexpected caress, advanced on her. But, as he stretched out his hand to seize her arm, she turned on him; and suddenly the coolness she had maintained up to that moment gave place to the real feelings which filled her, the feelings of execration and furious rancor with which he inspired her.

She broke out with a violence of which Ralph had not believed her capable: "Don't touch me, you wretch! And don't suppose that I'm afraid of you. Today you're alone. And I saw quite clearly just now that you would never dare murder me. Your hands were trembling. My hands will not tremble, Beaumagnan, when your hour comes."

He recoiled before her imprecations and her threats; and she went on, in a fresh access of hate: "But your hour has not yet come. You have not suffered enough. You did not suffer because you believed me dead. Your punishment now shall be to know that I am alive and that I love! Yes; understand that: I love Ralph. I loved him first in order to avenge myself on you and tell you of it later. And I love him today for no reason at all, just because he is himself and I can no longer forget him. He hardly knew it; I hardly knew it myself. But for some days, ever since he fled from me, I have felt that he is my whole life. I did not know what love was; and that is what love is: it's this madness which burns me."

She was a prey to delirium just as the man she was torturing. Her amorous cries seemed to hurt her as much as they hurt Beaumagnan. But to see her like that filled Ralph rather with distaste than with joy. The flame of passion and admiration and love, which had flared up in him in the hour of her peril, died down for good and all. Her beauty and charm vanished like a mirage; and on her face, which nevertheless had in no way changed, he saw the ugly reflection of a cruel and diseased spirit.

She continued her furious onslaught on Beaumagnan, who stood jerking with jealous fury. And it was really uncommonly disconcerting to see these two creatures, who, at the very moment at which circumstances were about to furnish them with the keyword of the enigma which had puzzled them so long, forget everything in the outburst of their passion. The great secret of past ages, the discovery of the jewels, the legendary block of granite, the casket, the inscription, the Widow Rousselin, and the person actually on the way to reveal the truth to them—these were so many old wives' tales in which neither of them no took any interest. Love, like a furious torrent, swept everything away. Hatred and passion had plunged into the eternal conflict which tears the hearts of lovers.

Once more the fingers of Beaumagnan were curved like talons and his trembling hands were outstretched to strangle her. But she raged at him, blind and beside herself, and flung in his face the insult of her love.

"I love him, Beaumagnan!" she cried. "The fire which burns you and devours me, too, is a love like your love; with it is mingled the idea of death and murder. Yes, I would rather kill him than know that he was another's, or than know that he loves me no longer. But he does love me, Beaumagnan! He loves me! He loves me!"

An unexpected laugh burst from Beaumagnan's convulsed lips; his fury ended in a fit of sardonic hilarity.

"He loves you, Josephine? You're right: he loves you! He loves you as he loves all women. You're beautiful and he desires you. Another passes and he desires her, too. And you suffer as I do the tortures of hell. Confess it!"

"The tortures of hell, yes," she said, "the tortures of hell if I believe in his falseness. But it isn't so; and you're trying stupidly to—"

She stopped short. Beaumagnan was chuckling with such a malicious joy that she was afraid.

In a low voice and in a tone of sudden pain she said: "A proof! Give me a single proof... Not even a proof... A mere indication... Something that compels me to doubt... And I'll kill him like a dog!"

She drew from her bodice a small life-preserver, a ball of lead with a whalebone handle. Her eyes grew hard.

Beaumagnan answered: "What I bring you will not make you doubt; it will give you certainty."

"Speak... Give me a name."

"Clarice d'Etigues," he said.

She shrugged her shoulders and said confidently: "I know all about that; a flirtation of no importance."

"It was important enough to him since he asked her father's permission to marry her," sneered Beaumagnan.

"He asked what? But it's nonsense! It's impossible! I got to know all about it. They met one another two or three times in the country—not more."

"Better than that, they met in the young woman's set of rooms in the Château."

"You lie!" she cried.

"What you must mean is that her father is lying, for these facts were confided to me by Godfrey d'Etigues the night before last," he said in a tone of sinister triumph.

"And who did he get them from?"

"From Clarice herself."

"But it's absurd! A girl never admits a thing like that!"

"I tell you he got it out of her the day before yesterday."

"But what put him on to it? They have never seen one another again," she said.

"They write to one another."

"A proof, Beaumagnan! Give me a proof this instant!" she cried with a sudden fury.

"Will a letter satisfy you?"

"A letter?"

"Written by him to Clarice," said Beaumagnan.

"Written four months ago?"

"Written four days ago."

She clutched at her bosom and paled and said between her teeth: "Have you got it?"

"Here it is."

Ralph, who had listened to the last dozen sentences with extreme discomfort, trembled. He recognized the letter which he had sent from Lillebonne to Clarice d'Etigues.

Josephine took it from Beaumagnan and read it in a low voice, giving every syllable its full value:

'Forgive me, dear Clarice. I have treated you like a scoundrel. Let us hope for a brighter future and think of me with all the indulgence of your generous heart. Once more, forgive me—forgive.

RALPH.'

She hardly had the strength to finish the reading of this letter, which denied her and wounded her vanity in the cruelest fashion. She tottered. Her eyes sought those of Ralph. He understood that Clarice was condemned to death and in his heart of hearts he knew that never again would he feel anything but hate for Josephine Balsamo.

Beaumagnan said quietly, in explanation: "Godfrey intercepted this letter and sent it to me, asking my advice. The postmark on the envelope was Lillebonne; that's how I got on the track of both of you again."

Josephine said nothing. Her face displayed so profound a suffering that it might have touched one. The tears which rolled slowly down her cheeks might have awakened one's pity, if her grief had not so plainly been dominated by a bitter lust for vengeance. She was making her plans, devising the snare.

Shaking her head, she said to Ralph: "I warned you, Ralph."

"A man who is warned is worth two," he said in a joking tone.

"Don't make a joke of it!" she cried with savage impatience. "You know what I told you, that you had better be careful never to let her cross the path of our love."

"And you know what I told you," Ralph retorted with the same irritating air. "If ever you touch a single hair of her head—"

She trembled and said bitterly: "How can you laugh at my suffering like this? How can you take the part of another woman against me?... Against me!" Then she added in quieter, threatening accents: "All the worse for her."

"Don't worry about her," he said. "She's safe enough, since I'll protect her."

Beaumagnan watched them with a gloomy joy; their discord and all this hate that welled up in them warmed his heart. But Josephine recovered control of herself, reckoning, doubtless, that it was a waste of words to speak of a vengeance which would be hers in due time. At the moment other cares thrust this one from her mind, for, a little way off, someone blew a whistle gently.

The grief and fury vanished from her face and she said: "Did you hear that whistle, Beaumagnan? It's one of my men who are watching the path to the lighthouse. The person for whom we are waiting must be in sight, for I suppose that's what you are here for, too?"

Indeed, the presence of Beaumagnan at that place at that hour needed to be accounted for. How had he known of the meeting and the meeting-place? What special information had he with regard to the Rousselin business?

She cast a glance at Ralph. He, at any rate, bound hand and foot, could not hamper her plans or take part in the final battle. But Beaumagnan appeared to trouble her; and she went towards the door as if she wished to be the first to meet the person they expected, when, at the very instant at which she was going to it, quick footsteps were heard. She stepped backwards, therefore, with a movement that thrust Beaumagnan aside and cleared the door for the entrance of Leonard. He looked sharply from one to the other of the two men, then drew Josephine aside, and whispered in her ear.

She seemed astounded and murmured: "What do you mean? What on earth do you mean?"

She turned her head that they might not see her expression; but Ralph had an impression that it was one of extreme joy.

"Don't stir," she said. "The owner of the casket is here. Out with your revolver, Leonard. Be ready to shoot."

She turned on Beaumagnan, who was trying to open the door, and cried: "You must be mad! Stay where you are!"

But when he insisted she lost her temper and said: "What do you want to go out for? What are you up to? You must know this person and want to balk us and get away with the casket. Is that your game? Speak up!"

Beaumagnan did not loose the handle of the door. Josephine gripped his arm with her right hand and tried to hold him back. Perceiving that she would not succeed, she turned towards Leonard, and with her left hand pointed to Beaumagnan's left shoulder with a gesture which bade her henchman strike and strike quietly. In about a second he had drawn a dagger from his pocket and driven it into their enemy's left shoulder.

Beaumagnan groaned and cried: "The damned jade!" and dropped fainting to the floor.

She said calmly to Leonard: "Help me; and be quick about it."

The two of them dragged Beaumagnan into the recess. Leonard cut off the end of the rope which was round Ralph's neck, and the two of them bound together the wounded man's wrists and ankles. Then she looked at his shoulder and said: "That's nothing—two or three days in bed and he'll be all right again. Come on."

They went back to the door.

She had performed these actions quietly, without the slightest haste and, from the expression on her face, she might have been doing the most ordinary things in the world. Every gesture was quiet and easy; she gave her orders with no vestige of excitement. But there was a note of triumph in her voice that inspired Ralph with a growing uneasiness, and he was on the point of shouting to warn the person who, in his or her turn, was walking into the trap.

But what was the use? The measures of Josephine had been taken too carefully for his cry of warning to upset them. Besides he did not quite know what to do. All kinds of absurd notions were running through his mind. And then—then it was too late. A groan burst from his lips.

Clarice d'Etigues came through the door!

XII

MADNESS AND GENIUS

Up to that moment Ralph had been feeling but a moderate apprehension. The danger only threatened him and Josephine. For his part, he trusted to his cleverness and lucky star; and as for Josephine, he knew that she was quite capable of defending herself against Beaumagnan.

But Clarice! Confronted by Josephine Balsamo, Clarice was a mere victim at the mercy of the treachery and cruelty of an enemy. And from that moment his fear was mingled with a kind of physical horror, which actually made his hair stand upright on his head and gave him what is vulgarly called gooseflesh. The implacable face of Leonard also added to his fear. He remembered the Widow Rousselin and her crushed fingers.

Truly he had seen clearly ahead when, coming to the meeting-place an hour before, he guessed that the great battle was before him and that he would come to grips with Josephine. Up to now they had had mere skirmishes, mere affairs of outposts. Now it was a struggle to the death between all these opposing forces; and he was confronting them with his hands bound, a rope round his neck, and this additional enfeeblement with which the coming of Clarice afflicted him.

"I've a lot to learn yet," he said to himself with a groan. "I'm chiefly responsible for this horrible situation, and Clarice is once more my victim."

The young girl stood speechless before the threat of the revolver which Leonard leveled at her. She had come on light feet, as one comes to meet someone one is glad to see again, and had stumbled into the midst of this scene of violence and crime, while the man she loved stood before her bound and motionless.

She stammered: "What's the matter, Ralph? Why are you tied up like that?"

She stretched out her hands towards him, as much as to ask his help as to offer him hers. But what could either of them do? He noticed her worn features and the extreme lassitude of her bearing; and he could hardly refrain from tears at the thought of the painful confession her father had torn from her.

But, in spite of everything, he said with imperturbable assurance: "I've nothing to be frightened of, Clarice, no more have you. Absolutely nothing. I answer for everything."

She looked round at the others and was astonished to recognize Beaumagnan. She said timidly to Leonard: "What is it you want? This is rather terrifying. Who was it made me come here?"

"I did, Mademoiselle," said Josephine.

Clarice had already been struck by Josephine's beauty. A scrap of hope came to her at the thought that nothing but help and protection could come from so beautiful a creature.

"Who are you, Madam? I don't think I know you," she said timidly.

"I know you," said Josephine, whom the grace and sweetness of the young girl seemed to irritate, though she kept her anger under control. "You're the daughter of Baron d'Etigues. I know, too, that you're in love with Ralph d'Andresy."

Clarice blushed but did not deny it.

Josephine said to Leonard: "Go and shut the gate. Put the chain and padlock you brought on it, and set up that old notice-board with 'Private' on it."

"Am I to stay outside?" asked Leonard.

"Yes; I've no need of you at the moment," said Josephine with an air which terrified Ralph. "Stay outside. And see that no one interrupts us—on any account."

Leonard forced Clarice to sit down on one of the chairs and drew her arms behind her with the intention of tying her wrists to the back of it.

"There's no need to do that," said Josephine. "Leave us."

He did as she bade him.

She looked from one to another of her three victims in turn. All three disarmed and reduced to impotence, she was mistress of the field of battle and on pain of death could impose her inflexible decrees.

Ralph's eyes never left her; he was trying to discover her intentions and her plans. Her calmness impressed him more than anything. She showed none of that excitement and feverishness which would have, so to speak, disarticulated the conduct of any other woman in her place. There was not a trace of triumph in her attitude. There was rather a certain weariness, as if she had acted under the impulsion of inner forces, which she was not strong enough to discipline. For the first time he divined in her a careless fatalism, as a rule concealed by her smiling beauty, which was perhaps the very essence and explanation of her enigmatic nature.

She sat down on the other chair close to Clarice, and with her eyes on her face said slowly, with a certain dryness and monotony in her intonation: "Three months ago, Mademoiselle, a young woman was secretly abducted on getting out of a train and transported to the Château of La Haie d'Etigues, where there were gathered together, in a large isolated chamber, a dozen of the noblemen of the Caux country. Among them were Beaumagnan, whom you see here, and your father. I will not tell you everything which was said at this meeting and of all the ignominy that was heaped on that young woman by these people who pretended to be her judges. But it came about that after a pretense of a trial, that evening, when the rest of the guests had gone, your father and his cousin de Bennetot carried her to the bottom of the cliff, tied her down in the bottom of a boat with a hole in it and heavily loaded with a big boulder, rowed her out to sea, and there abandoned her."

Breathless with amazement Clarice stammered: "It isn't true! It isn't true!... My father would never do such a thing!... It isn't true!"

Without paying any heed to her indignant protest, Josephine quietly continued: "Without any of the conspirators being aware of it, there was a spectator at that meeting at the château. That spectator kept watch on the two murderers—there's no other name for them, is there?—followed them, clung to the scuttled boat, and when they abandoned it, rescued their victim. From where did that spectator come? Everything leads us to believe that he passed the previous night and morning in your room, received by you not as a fiancé, since your father refused to hear of his marrying you, but as a lover."

This accusation and this insult struck Clarice like the blows of a mallet. On the instant she was overwhelmed and incapable of resisting or even of defending herself. Pale and fainting, she lay back in her chair and groaned: "But what a thing to say!"

"But you said it yourself—to your father—the day before yesterday," said Josephine coldly. "Is there any need for me to go into the whole story and tell you what became of your lover? That very day Ralph d'Andresy abandoned you to follow the woman he had saved from a terrible death. He devoted himself to her, body and soul, won her heart, lived her life, and swore to her never to see you again. He took that oath in the most categorical fashion: 'I did not love her,' he said. 'It was a mere passing flirtation. It is all over.' Then following a passing misunderstanding between her and him, this woman discovered that he was writing to you, that he wrote the letter which I have here, in which he begged you to forgive him and gave you hopes of the future. You understand now that I have some right to treat you as an enemy?" She paused and added gloomily: "As a mortal enemy."

Clarice was silent. Terror took possession of her, and she considered with an increasing apprehension the gentle and terrifying countenance of the woman who had taken Ralph from her and declared herself her enemy.

Trembling with pity and careless of exciting the anger of Josephine, Ralph said solemnly: "If I have ever sworn a solemn oath that I am resolved to keep in the face of everything and everyone, Clarice, it is the oath I have sworn that not a hair of your head shall be touched. You have nothing to fear. Inside of ten minutes you shall leave here safe and sound—ten minutes, not more."

Josephine did not take up the challenge; she continued quietly: "That, then, is the position in which we stand to one another, clearly set forth. Let us get on to the facts; and I'll be quite brief. Your father, mademoiselle, Beaumagnan and their confederates, were engaged in a common enterprise; for my part, I am seeking the same end and Ralph is seeking it with passionate intensity. From that it comes about that we are waging an unceasing war against one another. Now, all of us have had relations with a woman of the name of Rousselin, who possessed an old casket which we had needed to succeed in that enterprise. She has parted with that casket to another person. We questioned her in the most pressing manner without getting from her the name of that person, who, it appears, had heaped benefits on her and whom she did not wish to compromise by any indiscreet statement. All that we could learn was—it's an old story, of which I propose to give you main facts, which you will follow with the greatest interest both from our point of view... and from your own."

Ralph began to discern the course that Josephine was taking and the end to which she must inevitably come.

It was so frightful that he said angrily: "No, no: not that! There are things which should never be revealed!"

She did not appear to hear him, and went on inexorably: "This is the story: Twenty-two years, ago, during the war between France and Prussia, two men, who were flying from the invaders and escaping under the guidance of old Rousselin, murdered a servant of the name of Jaubert in order to steal his horse. With that horse they were able to escape. Moreover, they carried away with them a casket that they had also stolen from their victim, which contained jewels of great value. Later old Rousselin, whom they had compelled to accompany them and to whom they had given his share of the booty some worthless rings, came back to his wife at Rouen and almost immediately died there. To such an extent had this murder and his involuntary complicity in it depressed him. Thereupon relations were established between the widow and the murderers, who feared that she might let the truth slip out; and it came about I take it, mademoiselle, that you now understand with whom we are concerned?"

Clarice was listening to this revelation with so painful an air of terror that Ralph exclaimed: "Silence, Josine! Not a word more! What you are doing is in the highest degree vile and absurd. What's the use of it?"

"The use of it?" she said sharply. "The time has come for the whole truth to be told. You have thrown us, her and me, into opposition. It is only fair that she and I should be on equal terms in our suffering."

"You're a perfect savage!" he murmured in a tone of despair.

But Josephine, turning again to Clarice, continued her explanation coldly: "Your father and his cousin de Bennetot kept an eye on the Widow Rousselin; and it is quite clear that she removed to Lillebonne by the instructions of Baron d'Etigues, for it must have been much easier to keep an eye on her there. Then, as the years went on, someone was found, more or less in the know, to carry out this task. This was you, Mademoiselle. The Widow Rousselin became so fond of you that, as far as she was concerned, there was no reason to fear any hostile action. For nothing in the world would she have betrayed the father of the little girl who from time to time came to play at her house. Evidently these visits were secret in order that no thread might link the present with the past, visits for which, sometimes, meetings in the neighborhood of the town were substituted—at the old lighthouse or elsewhere. It was in the course of one of these visits that you saw in her house at Lillebonne the casket that Ralph and I were seeking; and the whim took you to take it away with you to La Haie d'Etigues. When, then, Ralph and I learned from the Widow Rousselin that the casket was in the possession of a person whose name she would not give, that this person had heaped benefits on her, and that they were to meet on a given day at the old lighthouse, we decided at once that it would be enough for us to come there, instead of the Widow Rousselin, to discover part of the truth. And as seen as we saw you appear we became at once convinced that the two murderers were none else but de Bennetot and the Baron d'Etigues; that is to say, the two men who, at a later date, tried to murder me."

Clarice was weeping, her slender form shaken by great sobs. Ralph did not doubt that the crimes of her father were quite unknown to her, but also he did not doubt that these accusations of her enemy suddenly showed her in their true aspect a number of things which up to then had been obscure to her, and compelled her to consider her father a murderer. How heartrending it must be for her! Josephine had truly struck home. With what a frightful knowledge of evil was this executioner torturing her victim! With what a refinement a thousand times more cruel than the physical tortures inflicted on the Widow Rousselin by Leonard was Josine taking vengeance on the innocent Clarice!

"Yes," she went on in somber accents, "a murderer... His wealth, his château, his horses, all that he has are the fruits of crime. It is so, isn't it, Beaumagnan? You can also bear witness to this fact, since by means of it obtained your hold over him. Master of a secret that you discovered in some way or other—it does not matter how—you made him act exactly as you bade him and profited by the first crime he had committed and the fact that you could bring it home to him, to compel him to serve you and to murder those who were in your way. I know something about that! What a set of ruffians you are!"

Her eyes sought the eyes of Ralph. He had the impression that she was trying to excuse her own crimes by bringing to light the crimes of Beaumagnan and his confederates.

But he said sternly: "And now? Have you finished? Or are you going on tearing this unfortunate child to pieces? What more do you want?"

"I want her to speak," said Josephine.

"And if she speaks, will you let her go free?"

"Yes," she replied.

"Then question her," he said. "What is it you demand? The casket, the keyword inscribed on the inside of the lid? Is that what you want?"

But whether Clarice was willing to answer or not, whether she knew or did not know the truth she seemed incapable of speaking a word, or even of understanding the questions put to her.

Ralph pressed her: "Try to get the better of your grief, Clarice," he said. "It's the last trial; and all will be over. Answer, I beg you. There is nothing in what you are called on to tell which can possibly be against your conscience. You have taken no oath of secrecy. You are betraying no one. In that case—"

His gentle, imploring voice was making the young girl feel easier in mind. He became conscious of it and asked: "What has become of that casket? Did you take it to La Haie d'Etigues?"

"Yes," she murmured in a tone of exhaustion.

"Why?"

"It took my fancy—it was just a whim."

"Did your father see it?" he said quickly.

"Yes."

"The same day?"

"No. Some days later."

"Did he take it away from you?" he asked with a note of keener interest in his voice.

"Yes."

"What reason did he give for doing so?"

"None at all."

"But you had had time to examine it?"

"Yes."

"And you saw an inscription inside the lid, didn't you?"

"Yes."

"In old characters, wasn't it? Roughly carved?"

"Yes."

"Did you make it out?"

"Yes."

"Easily?"

"No; but I did make it out."

"And can you remember the inscription?"

She hesitated; then she said doubtfully: "Perhaps... I don't know... They were Latin words."

"Latin words? Try to remember them."

Clarice hesitated again; then she said: "But ought I to? If it's such an important secret, ought I to reveal it?"

"You may, Clarice. I assure you you may," he said earnestly. "You may, because the secret belongs to no one. No one in the world has any greater claim to know it than your father, or his friends, or myself. The secret belongs to the person who shall find it out, to the first passerby who shall be able to profit by it."

She yielded. What Ralph said must be right.

"Yes, yes; no doubt you're right. But I attached so little importance to that inscription that I can't remember exactly what it was... It was something to do with a stone and a queen."

"You must recall it, Clarice; you really must," he begged, for a sudden fresh overclouding of Josephine's face made him again anxious.

Slowly, her brow knitted in the effort to remember, correcting herself and contradicting herself, the young girl succeeded in saying:

"Here it is—I remember—this is exactly the sentence that I made out... five Latin words... in this order:

Ad lapidem currebat olim regina."

She had hardly got the last syllable out when Josephine bent sharply towards her and cried furiously: "It's a lie! That formula—we've known it for ages! Beaumagnan can bear witness to that. We knew it, didn't we, Beaumagnan? She's lying, Ralph! She's lying! The Cardinal mentions those five words in his memorandum; and he considered them of so little importance and so firmly refused to attach any meaning to them that I did not even tell you about them!... In days gone by the queen ran to the stone. But where is it, that stone? And who was the queen who ran to it? We've been trying to find out for the last twenty years. No, no! There's something else!"

Once again that terrible rage filled her, that rage which did not manifest itself in a raised voice of incoherent words but in an agitation altogether interior, which one divined from certain symptoms and above all from the unusual and abnormal cruelty of her words.

Bending over the young girl she cried: "You lie!... You lie!... There is one word which sums up the meaning of those five... What is it?... There's a keyword... A single keyword... What is it?"

Terrorized, Clarice lost the power of utterance.

"Think, Clarice," Ralph implored her. "Try to remember... Besides those five words, did you not see something else?"

"I don't know... I don't think so," moaned the young girl.

"Try to remember... You must remember. Your safety depends on it!" he cried.

But the very tone of his voice and his frightened tenderness for Clarice exasperated Josephine.

She gripped the young girl's arm and cried: "Speak! If you don't—"

Clarice stuttered incoherently. Josephine blew a shrill blast on her whistle.

Almost on the instant Leonard stood on the threshold of the door.

Josephine said, in terrible, inexorable accents: "Take her away, Leonard, and question her!"

Ralph jerked in his bonds and cried furiously: "You coward! You wretch! What are you going to do? Are you really the lowest of women? Leonard, if you touch that child, I swear by God that one day or another—"

"How frightened you are for her!" snarled Josephine. "How the idea of her suffering does upset you! You were certainly born to understand one another, you two... The daughter of a murderer and a thief! Yes, a thief!" she said, turning to Clarice. "This fine lover of yours is nothing but a thief! He has always made his living by theft. As a child, he was a thief! To give you flowers, to give you that little engagement ring you wear on your finger, he stole! He's a burglar and a swindler. Why, his very name, that pretty name of Andresy, was simply a theft. Ralph d'Andresy? I should think so! Arsène Lupin, that's his real name. Keep him, Clarice; he will become famous. Oh, I've seen him at work, this lover of yours! A master! A marvel of cunning! What a pretty couple you two will make if I don't take a hand in the game! What a child of destiny yours will be, son of Arsène Lupin, grandson of Baron Godfrey!"

This idea of their child added flames to her fury. The madness of evil was unchained.

"Get on, Leonard!" she cried.

"You savage beast!" shouted Ralph, beside himself. "What a horror! You have indeed torn off the mask! There's no longer any need for you to act your comedy! That's what you really are—an executioner!"

But there was no holding her; she was set in her barbarous desire to hurt and torture the young girl. With her own hands she pushed Clarice, whom Leonard was dragging towards the door.

"Coward! Monster!" Ralph yelled. "A hair of her head, look you—a single hair! It means death for the two of you! Loose her, you monsters!"

He strained so violently against his bonds that all the apparatus devised by Beaumagnan to hold him smashed. The worm-eaten shutter tore from its hinges and fell in pieces into the room behind him.

There was a moment of anxiety in the opposing camp.

But the ropes, though loosened, were strong and hampered him sufficiently to render him helpless. Nevertheless Leonard drew his revolver and pressed it against Clarice's temple.

"If he makes another step, a single movement, blow her brains out!" cried Josephine.

Ralph did not stir. He did not doubt that Leonard would carry out that order and that his slightest gesture meant instant death to Clarice. Then?... Then must he resign himself to her fate? Were there no means of saving her?

Josephine gazed somberly at him; then she said: "Come: you understand the situation and you're going to behave yourself."

"No," he replied, wholly master of himself. "No; but I'm considering."

"Considering what?" she sneered.

"I promised her that she should go free and that she had nothing to fear. I mean to keep my promise."

"You're a little late about it, aren't you?" she said and sneered again.

"No, Josephine: you're going to let her go."

She turned to Leonard and said: "What are you wasting time for? Be quick about it!"

"Stop!" said Ralph in a tone ringing with such a certainty of being obeyed that she hesitated.

"Stop and let her go," he repeated. "You hear, Josephine? I wish you to let her go. It isn't a matter of postponing the infamous thing you propose to do or of abandoning it. It's a matter of instantly letting Clarice d'Etigues go and opening that door for her to go through."

It must be that he was wholly sure of himself and that his will rested on truly extraordinary grounds for him to formulate it with so imperious a solemnity. Even Leonard himself was impressed and stood undecided; while Clarice, who had not grasped the full horror of their intention, appeared to take comfort.

Josephine, taken aback, murmured: "Words—just words. Some fresh ruse—"

"Facts," he declared, "or rather one fact which dominates everything and before which you will have to give way."

"What does that mean?" asked Josephine, more and more disturbed. "What is it you want?"

"I don't want—I demand."

"What?"

"The immediate liberty of Clarice. The liberty of leaving this place without either you or Leonard stirring a foot."

She burst out laughing and asked: "Is that all?"

"That's all."

"And in exchange you offer me?"

"The keyword of the enigma!"

She quivered and said: "You know it, then?"

"Yes."

The drama had suddenly undergone a complete change. From all the furious antagonism which flung them into conflict with one another, from the hatred and fury of love and jealousy, there seemed to come clear only their anxiety about the great enterprise. The obsession of vengeance passed into the background of Josephine's mind. The thousands and thousands of jewels were, as Ralph had willed, once more gleaming before her eyes.

Beaumagnan raised himself painfully into a sitting posture and was listening with all his ears.

Leaving Clarice to the care of her confederate, Josine stepped nearer to Ralph, and said: "Is it sufficient to know the keyword of the enigma?"

"No," he said with decision. "It is still necessary to interpret it. The meaning of the formula is hidden behind a veil; and the first thing to do is to pierce that veil."

"And have you done it?"

"Yes. I already had some ideas about the matter. Just now, all at once, the truth flashed on me."

She knew that he was not the man to joke at such a juncture.

"Tell me about it," she said, "and Clarice shall go."

"Let her go first and I'll tell you my idea. Of course I won't reveal it with a rope round my neck and my hands bound, but free and in no way hampered."

"But it's absurd!" she protested. "You revolutionize the whole situation. As it is it's absolutely in my power to do what I like."

"Not now," he declared. "Now you depend on me and it is for me to dictate the conditions."

She shrugged her shoulders and looked round the room somewhat helplessly, then she was obliged to say: "Swear to speak the exact truth. Swear it by the tomb of your mother."

He said calmly: "By the tomb of my mother I swear to you that twenty minutes after Clarice has crossed this threshold I will show you the exact place where that block of granite is, that is to say, the hiding-place of the treasure accumulated by the monks of the abbeys of France."

She tried to thrust off the incredible fascination that Ralph was of a sudden exercising over her with this fabulous offer, and cried in a tone of revolt: "No, no! It's a trap! You know nothing at all!"

"Not only do I know, but I'm not the only one to know," he said.

"Who else knows?"

"Beaumagnan and the Baron."

"Impossible!" she cried.

"Think a little," he said quietly. "The day before yesterday Beaumagnan was at La Haie d'Etigues. Why? Because the Baron had recovered the casket and they studied the inscription together. Then, if there are not only the five words mentioned by the Cardinal, if there is also the word, the magic word which sums them up and gives the key to the mystery, they have seen it and they know it."

"What does that matter?" she said, gazing at Beaumagnan. "I hold him safely enough."

"But you do not hold Godfrey d'Etigues; and perhaps at this very minute he is on the spot with his cousin, the two of them sent in advance by Beaumagnan to explore the spot and make preparations for carrying off the treasure. Do you understand the danger? Do you understand that the loss of a minute may mean the loss of the game?"

She held out fiercely, crying: "I win it if Clarice speaks."

"She will not speak—for the excellent reason that she has told you all she knows," he said in a tone that carried conviction.

"Be it so, but then do you speak yourself, since you have been so foolish as to make this disclosure. Why should I set her free? Why should I obey you? As long as Clarice is in the hands of Leonard, I have only to will to drag from you everything you know."

He shook his head. "No," he said. "That danger is passed; that storm is at a distance. Perhaps, as a matter of fact, you have only to will; but equally as a matter of fact, you can no longer will that. You have no longer the strength to will it."

And it was true; and he was certain of it. Hard, cruel, "infernal," as Beaumagnan had said, but nonetheless a woman and subject to failure of nerve, she committed her evil deeds rather on impulse than by a deliberate effort of will—in an access of madness and hysteria, which was followed by a kind of lassitude, by enfeeblement as much moral as physical. Ralph was sure that at that very moment she was suffering from such a reaction.

"Come, Josephine: be consistent," he said. "You have staked your life on this card, the conquest of boundless riches. Are you going to throw away the fruit of all your efforts when I offer you those riches?"

Her resistance was weakening. But she protested: "I don't trust you."

"That isn't true. You know quite well that I keep my promises. If you hesitate—but you do not hesitate. In your heart of hearts, you have made your decision; and it is the right one."

She remained thoughtful for a moment, then with a gesture which signified: "After all, I shall lay my hands on the girl again. My vengeance is only postponed," she said: "By the memory of your mother?"

"By the memory of my mother, by all that is left me of honesty and honor, I will throw complete light on the matter."

"So be it," she said. "But you and that girl will not exchange a single word apart."

"Not a word," he said readily. "Besides, I've nothing to say to her that anyone may not hear. Set her free—that's all I want."

She gave the order: "Loose the girl, Leonard, and take those ropes off him."

Leonard's face wore an expression of strong disapproval. But he was too well-disciplined to protest. He left Clarice and cut the bonds which still crippled Ralph.

Ralph's behavior was not of the most fitting considering the seriousness of the occasion. He stretched his legs, performed two or three exercises with his arms, and took several deep breaths.

"I like this better," he said cheerfully. "I've no vocation for playing at prisoners. To deliver the good and punish the evil, that's what really interests me. Tremble, Leonard."

He turned to Clarice and said: "I beg you to forgive me for all that has happened. It shall never occur again, you may be sure of it. Henceforth you're under my protection. Do you feel strong enough to get home?"

"Yes—yes," she said. "But what about you?"

"Oh, me—I do not run any risk. Your safety was the essential thing. But I'm afraid that you won't be able to walk far."

"I haven't far to walk. Yesterday my father brought me to stay with one of my friends; and he is to fetch me tomorrow."

"Is it near here?"

"Yes."

"Well, say no more about it. Any information you give will be used against you."

He conducted her to the door and told Leonard to unlock the padlock and open the gate.

When Leonard had done so, Ralph said to Clarice: "Be prudent, and fear nothing, absolutely nothing, either on your own account or on mine. We shall meet again when the right hour strikes; and it will not be long striking whatever be the obstacles which separate us now."

He shut the door after her. Clarice was saved.

Then he had the cheek to say: "What an adorable creature!"

In after days, when Arsène Lupin related this incident in his great struggle with Josephine Balsamo, he could not refrain from laughing.

"Yes," he would say. "I laugh now as I laughed at the moment; and I remember that for the first time I executed one of those little dances which have often served me since to mark most difficult victories... and that victory was devilishly difficult.

"In truth I was overjoyed. Clarice free, everything appeared to me to be accomplished. I lit a cigarette, and as Josephine planted herself before me to recall our bargain, I had the bad manners to blow a cloud of smoke right into her face."

"'Bounder!' she muttered.

"The epithet with which I retorted was really disgraceful. My excuse is that my tone was more roguish than coarse. And then—and then—have I any need of excuses? Have I any need to analyze the violent and contradictory feelings with which that woman inspired me? I do not pride myself on my psychology where she was concerned, or of having behaved like a gentleman to her. I loved her and at the same time detested her furiously. And after her attack on Clarice my disgust and contempt had become boundless. I no longer saw even the admirable mask of her beauty, but only that which lay beneath it; and it was a kind of carnivorous beast which suddenly appeared to me as I flung that abominable insult at her in the middle of my pirouette."

Arsène Lupin could laugh afterwards. Nevertheless it was a dangerous moment, and there is no doubt that for two pins either Josephine or Leonard would have blown his brains out.

She muttered through her closed teeth: "Oh, how I do hate you!"

"Not more than I hate you," he sneered.

"Bear in mind that Josephine Balsamo has not quite finished with that Clarice of yours," she retorted in a tone of sinister threatening.

"Nor has Ralph d'Andresy finished with her," he said quickly.

"Scoundrel!" she muttered. "You deserve—"

"A bullet through my head," he said, laughing. "It's out of the question."

"Don't you defy me too far, Ralph!"

"It's out of the question, I tell you," he repeated. "I am literally sacred. I am the gentleman who stands for a thousand millions. Destroy me and the thousand millions slip through your fingers, O daughter of Cagliostro! Every cell in my brain corresponds to a precious stone. A little bullet hole in it and you will call in vain on the spirit of your father! Not a sou for little Josine! I repeat, my darling, that I am taboo, as they say in Polynesia. Taboo from head to foot! Go down on your knees and kiss my hand. That's the best thing you can possibly do."

He opened the window which looked over the enclosure, took a deep breath, and said: "This place is perfectly suffocating. Leonard has a decidedly musty smell. Do you make a point of your executioner's keeping his hand on that revolver in his pocket?"

She stamped her foot and exclaimed: "Enough of this fooling! You laid down your conditions; you know mine."

"Your money or your life!"

"Speak, and speak at once!"

"What a hurry you're in!" he said in a mocking voice. "In the first place I fixed a delay of twenty minutes, to be quite sure that

Clarice should be out of reach of your claws; and it is not nearly twenty minutes since she went. Besides—"

"Besides what?"

"Besides, how can you expect me to solve in five seconds the problem that so many people have been nearly bursting themselves in their efforts to solve for years and years?"

She was immensely taken aback and cried fiercely: "What do you mean?"

"My meaning is quite simple. I want a little time for reflection."

"Reflection? What for?"

"To get the solution," he said coolly.

"What? You don't know it?"

"The keyword to the enigma? Of course I don't."

"Then you lied!"

"Don't let's get theatrical, Josephine," he said again in a tone of mockery.

"You lied, because you swore—"

"By the tomb of my poor mother," he said, smiling. "And I stick to it. But you must not get things mixed up. I did not swear that I knew the truth, I swore that I would tell you the truth."

"To tell it, you must know it."

"To know one must reflect, and you don't give me any time! Let's have a little silence, please! And first of all, let Leonard loose the butt of his revolver. It puts me off."

Even more than his jokes, the tone of insolent mockery in which he uttered them set Josephine's teeth on edge. She felt herself surpassed, and realizing the danger to her vanity she said:

"Take your time about it. I know you. You will keep your promise."

"Ah! You're going to try kindness on me! I never could resist kindness... Boy, writing materials! Fine handmade paper, a pen made out of a hummingbird's quill, the blood of a full-grown black woman, and a piece of candied peel, as the poet says."

He drew the pencil from his pocketbook and a visiting-card on which some words were already written in a particular order. He drew some lines to join these words to one another, then on the reverse he wrote the Latin formula:

"Ad lapidem currebat olim regina."

"Dog-Latin of the worst," he murmured. "I fancy that if I had been in the place of those good monks, I should have found better Latin and got quite as good a result. Nevertheless we must take it as we find it. So the queen rode at a gallop towards the block... The queen rode... Look at your watch, Josephine."

He was no longer laughing. For a minute or two perhaps, not more, his face was set in an expression of gravity, and his eyes, seemingly fixed on the void, showed an immense effort of meditation. He perceived, however, that Josine was regarding him with a look of admiration and boundless confidence, and he smiled on her with an absentminded air without breaking the thread of his ideas.

Motionless in his bonds, his face haggard with anxiety, Beaumagnan listened. Was it really a fact that the tremendous secret was about to be divulged?

Two or three more minutes passed in a dead silence. Then Josephine murmured: "What's the matter with you, Ralph? You look quite wrought up."

"Yes; I am," he said. "All this story of all this treasure hidden in a block of stone, in full view of everyone who comes near it, is in all conscience strange enough. But it's nothing, Josine, nothing at all compared with the idea which dominates the story. You cannot imagine how strange it is—and how beautiful! What poetry and what simplicity!"

MADNESS AND GENIUS

He was silent for a moment; then he declared sententiously: "Josine, the monks of the middle ages were duffers." He looked round on the three of them and added: "Goodness, yes; pious personages, but, I repeat it at the risk of shaking your faith, duffers! Just consider: if a great financier took it into his head to protect his strongbox by writing on it, 'You are forbidden to open it,' you would reckon him a duffer, wouldn't you? Well, the method that these monks chose to protect their treasure is very nearly as ingenuous."

"No—no—it is incredible!" she murmured. "You have guessed wrong! You're making a mistake!"

"Duffers too, all those who have sought for it and found nothing. Blind souls! Narrow minds! What? You, Leonard, Godfrey d'Etigues, Beaumagnan, their friends, the whole of the Society of Jesus, the Archbishop of Rouen, you had these five words under your eyes; and it was not enough! Why, hang it all, a board-school child solves problems as difficult as this!"

She raised the objection: "But, before everything, it was a matter of one word and not of five."

"But it's there; the word's there, confound it! When I told you a little while ago that the possession of the casket must have revealed the indispensable word to the Baron and Beaumagnan, I just wanted to frighten you and make you loose your hold on Clarice, for these gentlemen were simply puzzled. But the indispensable word is there, all right. It's there, mixed with the five Latin words. Instead of blanching as you all did in the face of this vague formula you ought, quite naively, to have read it, to have put the first five letters together, and to have studied the word composed of those five initials."

"But we thought of that," she said quickly. "It's the word ALCOR, isn't it?"

"Yes: the word ALCOR."

"Well, what about it?"

"What about it? But it contains everything, that word does! Do you know what it means?" he said impatiently.

"It's an Arabian word which means a 'test.'"

"And which the Arabs and all other people use to designate what?"

"A star."

"What star?"

"One of the stars in the constellation of the Great Bear. But that's of no importance. What relation could there be—"

Ralph's lips were wreathed with a smile of pity; and he said patiently: "Of course it's quite evident that the name of the star could not have any relation with the situation of a block of stone in the open country. One clings to this silly conclusion; and on that side all effort comes to an end. But it is exactly that which struck me when I got the word ALCOR from the five initials of the Latin inscription. Master of the magic word, the talismanic word, and having besides observed that the whole affair turned round the number seven—seven abbeys, seven monks, seven branches of the candlestick, seven stones of seven colors set in seven rings—at once, d'you hear? at once by a kind of reflex action of my mind I knew that the star ALCOR was part of the constellation of the Great Bear; and the problem was solved."

"Solved? How?"

"Hang it all. Because the constellation of the Great Bear is formed of exactly seven principal stars! Seven! Always the number seven! Do you begin to see the connection? Or am I to point out to you once more that if the Arabs chose and if the astronomers since accepted that designation of ALCOR, it is because this quite small star which is scarcely visible serves as a test, do you understand, as a test? To demonstrate that a certain person has good eyesight because they can see it with the naked eye. ALCOR is what you must see, what you must look for, the hidden thing, the concealed treasure, the invisible block of stone into which one slips the precious stones. It is the strongbox."

Josephine, in a fever of excitement at the nearness of the great revelation, murmured: "I don't understand."

Ralph pulled forward a chair into a position between Leonard and the window which he had opened with the very distinct intention of escaping the moment it became necessary, and sat down on it. As he spoke he was keeping a close watch on Leonard, who persistently kept his hand on the revolver in his pocket.

"Well, you're going to understand," he said. "It's as clear as the day, as spring water! Look."

He showed them the visiting card which he still held in his hand.

"Look. I've had this on me for weeks. From the beginning of our search I looked up in an atlas the exact position of the seven abbeys, of which I have written the names on this card. Here they are, all seven of them, in the different positions in which they stand in regard to one another. Therefore all I had to do just now, as soon as I knew the word, was to join the seven points by lines to reach this unexpected conclusion, Josephine, this marvellous, colossal, and yet very natural conclusion that the figure so formed exactly represents the Great Bear. Do you grasp this really astonishing truth? The seven abbeys of the Caux country, the seven primordial abbeys into which flowed the riches of Christian France, were placed in the same positions as the seven principal stars in the Great Bear. There is no mistake about this. You have only to take an atlas and join them by lines. It is the cabalistic design of the Great Bear.

"After that the truth at once became clear. At the very spot at which ALCOR is found in the Heavenly figure the block of stone will inevitably be found a little to the right below the abbey which corresponds to that star, that is to say a little to the right below the abbey of Jumièges, formerly the most powerful and richest of the abbeys of Normandy. It's a mathematical certainty. The block of stone is there and nowhere else. Thereupon two facts stand out uncommonly clear, in fact they stare you in the face: firstly that a little to the southeast of Jumièges, scarcely a league away from it, there is, at the hamlet of Mesnil-sous-Jumièges, quite close to the Seine, the ruins of the Manor of Agnes Sorel, the mistress of King Charles VII; secondly that the abbey communicated with that manor by a subterranean passage of which you can still see the entrance. The conclusion is that the legendary block of stone is near the Manor of Agnes Sorel, on the bank of the Seine, and the inscription doubtless means that the mistress of the King, his Queen of Love, ran towards this block of stone, of the precious contents of which she was ignorant, and sat down on it to watch the royal barque glide down the old river of Normandy.

"*Ad lapidem currebat olim regina.*"

A common, deep silence united Ralph and Josephine. The veil was raised. The light of day swept away the darkness. Between them it appeared that all hatred had ceased. There was a truce to the implacable conflicts which divided them and nothing remained but an immense astonishment at having so penetrated the forbidden regions of the mysterious past that time and space defended against human curiosity.

Sitting near Josephine, his eyes fixed on the picture which he had drawn, Ralph continued in a low voice with a restrained exaltation:

"Yes, those monks were very imprudent to trust such a secret to the guard of so transparent a word. But what ingenious and charming poets they were! What a delightful thought to associate Heaven itself with their earthly belongings! Masters of contemplation, great astronomers like their Chaldean ancestors they drew their inspiration from on high; the courses of the stars guided their existence; and they called on the constellations themselves to watch over their treasures. Who knows if the situation of their seven abbeys was not chosen at the beginning of things to reproduce on the soil of Normandy the gigantic figure of the Great Bear? Who knows—"

The lyric effusion of Ralph was truly justified; but he could not bring it to its proper end. If he was distrusting Leonard, he had forgotten Josephine. Suddenly she struck him on the head with her life preserver.

It was indeed the last thing he was looking for, although he knew that these treacherous attacks were a habit of hers. Stunned, he doubled up on his chair, then fell on his knees, then rolled over and lay prone.

He murmured in a shaky voice: "It's true, begad! I was no longer taboo." Then with the guttersnipe's chuckle which he doubtless inherited from his father, Theophrastus Lupin, he said again: "The damned jade! Not even respect for genius! You savage little beast, have you indeed a stone where your heart should be?... All the worse for you, Josephine. We would have shared the treasure. Now I'll keep the lot of it."

He lost consciousness.

XIII

THE STRONGBOX OF THE MONKS

It was but a passing paralysis such as a boxer suffers from a knockout blow. But when Ralph recovered consciousness he found without the slightest surprise that he was in the same situation as Beaumagnan, like him bound, and like him set with his back against the wall.

He was very little more surprised to see Josephine stretched on two chairs in front of the door, a victim of one of those nervous attacks which too violent emotions, too prolonged always brought on. The blow she had struck Ralph had thrown her into one of them. Leonard was tending her, holding a bottle of smelling-salts to her nostrils.

He must have summoned one of his confederates, for Ralph saw the young man enter whom he knew by the name of Dominique, the young man who had looked after the carriage in front of the house of Bridget Rousselin.

"Damn it!" said the newcomer on perceiving the two captives. "There seems to have been a squabble. Beaumagnan! d'Andresy! The chief does strike hard! Result a fainting fit. What?"

"Yes, but it's nearly over," growled Leonard.

"What are we to do?"

"Carry her to the carriage and drive her to the *Nonchalante*," growled Leonard.

"And what about me?"

"You're going to keep guard on these two," said Leonard nodding towards the prisoners.

"Hang it! They're awkward customers. I don't like the job," said Dominique, scowling at them.

Leonard took Josephine by the shoulders, Dominique by the ankles. They raised her and were carrying her out, when, opening her eyes, she said to them in a voice so low that she could not suppose that Ralph's hearing was fine enough to catch a syllable of what she said:

"No. I'll walk all right. You will stay here, Leonard. You're the best man to guard Ralph."

"Let me knock him on the head and be done with it," whispered Leonard. "This young fellow will bring us bad luck."

"I love him," she murmured.

"But he doesn't love you any longer."

"Yes. He will come back to me. Besides, whatever happens, I'm not going to let him go."

"Then what do you propose to do?" asked Leonard glumly.

"The *Nonchalante* should be at Caudebec. I'm going to rest there till early tomorrow morning. I must rest."

"And the treasure? It will need a gang to handle a stone of that size."

"Tonight I'll send word to the Corbus to meet me tomorrow at Jumièges. Then I'll see to Ralph—unless—But don't bother me anymore now. I'm done," she muttered.

"But what about Beaumagnan?" he persisted.

"We'll set him free when I have the treasure."

"Aren't you afraid that that girl will inform the police? It would be an easy job for them to surround this old lighthouse."

"Nonsense! Do you think she's going to put the police on the track of her father and Ralph?" said Josephine.

She sat up on one of the chairs and fell back again with a groan. Some minutes passed. At last with an effort which seemed to exhaust her she succeeded in standing upright, and resting on Dominique, went to Ralph.

"He's insensible," she murmured. "Guard him carefully, Leonard, and the other too. If one of them gets away, the game's up."

She went away slowly. Leonard accompanied her to the old barouche and in a little while came back, after padlocking the gate. He brought with him a parcel containing food. Then they heard the sound of hoofs on the stony road.

Ralph had already discovered that he was securely bound. He said to himself: "The chief is growing rather feeble. Firstly in talking about the steps she proposes to take before witnesses; secondly in entrusting stout fellows like Beaumagnan and me to the care of a single man. Those are mistakes which prove that she's in a bad state of health."

All the same it was true that Leonard's experience would render any attempt to escape uncommonly difficult.

"Leave those ropes alone," he said to Ralph as he entered. "If you don't I'll plug you on the jaw."

This formidable jailor took every precaution to make his task easy. After running them through the back of a chair he tied together the ends of the two ropes which bound the prisoners. Then he propped the chair on two legs so that it would fall over easily, and on it he set the dagger that Josephine had given him. If one of the prisoners stirred the chair would fall over.

"You're less stupid than you look," said Ralph.

"Shut your mouth or I'll plug you on the jaw," said Leonard.

He set about making a meal.

Ralph chanced saying: "I hope you're enjoying it. If there's any over, don't forget me."

Leonard rose with his fists clenched.

"All right: I'll shut up," said Ralph.

Leonard sat down again.

The hours passed. It grew dusk. Beaumagnan appeared to be asleep. Leonard smoked pipe after pipe, Ralph scolded himself for having been so careless as not to have kept an eye on Josephine.

"I ought to have been distrusting her all the time," he said to himself. "I've a long way to go yet to make her value me at my true worth. But what decision! What a clear view of the reality! And what a freedom from scruples! Just one single defect which prevents the monster from being perfect—her nervous system of a degenerate. And lucky for me it is today that she has that nervous system, since it will allow me to get to Mesnil-sous-Jumièges before her."

He had not the slightest doubt that it was possible to escape from Leonard. He had observed that the bonds which bound his ankles were loosened by certain movements, and feeling sure of getting his right leg free, he considered with satisfaction the effect of a kick on the point of Leonard's jaw. After that, hell for leather to the treasure!

The darkness thickened in the room. Leonard lit a candle, smoked a last pipe, and drank a last glass of wine. After that he became so sleepy that he nodded first to the right and then to the left with such vigor that he nearly fell off his chair. Then he tried holding the candle in his hand in order that the hot wax should fall on it and wake him up. He took a look at the two prisoners, another at the rope that ran through the back of the chair which was to act as an alarm, and went to sleep.

Ralph worked away slowly and gently at the task of freeing himself, not without success. It must be about nine o'clock.

"If I can get away at eleven o'clock," he said to himself, "I shall reach Lillebonne by midnight, get some supper there, and at three o'clock in the morning arrive at the sacred spot. With the first light of dawn I shall put the strongbox of the monks into my pocket—yes: into my pocket. I've no need of the Corbus, or anyone else."

But at half-past ten he was practically at the same point.

Loose though the ropes were, he could not free his foot from them, and he was beginning to give up hope when of a sudden he thought he heard a slight noise which differed from all the whisperings that break the deep silence of the night, leaves that rustle, birds that flutter among the branches, murmurs of the breeze.

The noise came again; and he was certain that it came from the window he had opened, which Leonard had carelessly pushed to.

Then one side of the window seemed to be moving slowly forward.

Ralph looked at Beaumagnan. He too had heard the noise and was looking at the window.

Then the hot wax of the candle fell on Leonard's hand; and he awoke. He looked at the bonds of the prisoners and the rope of the alarm and dropped off to sleep again. The noise, which had for the while ceased, came again—it was plain that the movements of their jailor were being carefully watched.

What was going on? It was evident that since the gate was locked someone must have climbed over the wall; and it must be someone familiar with the light house who knew where to find a spot from which the broken glass had been cleared. Who? A peasant? A poacher? Was it a rescuer—some friend of Beaumagnan's? Or was it just a prowler in the night?

A head appeared, indistinct in the darkness; and then the figure of a woman slipped easily over the sill which was at no great height from the ground.

Before he saw her face, Ralph knew that it was none other than Clarice!

With what pride and delight and thankfulness did he regard her! Josephine had been wrong, quite wrong in supposing her rival too feeble to act. In her anxiety, unable to tear herself away in her fear for his safety, mastering her exhaustion and her fear for herself, she must have lurked in the wood in which the lighthouse stood, and waited for the night.

And now she was attempting the impossible to save the man who had so cruelly betrayed her.

Once more Leonard awoke. But fortunately she was directly behind him. Once more he fell asleep and she moved noiselessly forward till she stood beside him, reached forward, and picked up Josephine's dagger which lay on the chair which was to act as alarm and add by its jingle to the noise of its fall. Was she going to strike?

Ralph was terrified. Now that the light of the candle clearly illuminated her face, it seemed to him to be set in a cold ferocity. But their eyes met, and she obeyed the unspoken bidding of his will. She did not strike. Ralph bent forward a little so that the rope which ran through the back of the chair hung slack. Beaumagnan, seeing what he would be at, bent forward too.

Then slowly, with a steady hand, she cut the rope.

As luck had it, their enemy did not wake. Had he done so, she would assuredly have killed him. Her eyes, still holding that threat of death, never left him. She bent down, her hand fumbled about for Ralph's bonds. She freed his wrists.

He whispered: "Give me the knife."

She handed it to him. But a hand was quicker than his. Beaumagnan who for hours had also been patiently at work, loosening his bonds, snatched the knife from her.

Furious, Ralph gripped his arm. If Beaumagnan loosed himself and got away before he did, farewell all hope of seizing the treasure. There was a desperate struggle, in which either of them put forth all his strength, telling himself that the least noise would wake Leonard.

Clarice, trembling with fear, sank to her knees, quite as much in order not to fall to the ground as to beseech them.

But Beaumagnan's wound, slight though it was, rendered him incapable of prolonged resistance. He let go the knife.

At that very moment Leonard moved his head, opened his eyes, and gazed at the picture before him, the two men half risen, clinging to one another in a fighting attitude, Clarice on her knees.

His gaze rested on it several seconds, several terrible seconds, for there was no doubt that, seeing what they were at, he would shoot them down, and rid himself of them. But his open eyes did not see them; they were blinded by the clouds of sleep. His eyelids closed down again over them before the consciousness of what they rested on came to him.

Thereupon Ralph cut through the rest of his bonds. He was free. As Clarice rose, trembling, to her feet, he whispered: "Be quick! Escape!"

She shook her head and pointed to Beaumagnan.

It was plain that she was not going to leave him behind her, a prisoner exposed to the vengeance of Leonard.

Ralph protested; but he could not move her.

Tiring of the conflict, he handed the knife to Beaumagnan.

"She's right," he said in a whisper. "One must play fair. Here you are. Free yourself. And afterwards let each look out for himself. What?"

He followed Clarice to the window. One after the other, they slipped over the sill. Once in the enclosure, she took his hand and led him to a gap in the wall.

He helped her through it.

But when he had climbed through it himself, he no longer saw anyone.

"Clarice!" he cried. "Where are you?"

The wood lay in the darkness of a starless night. He heard a rustling among the undergrowth on his right. He plunged into it in pursuit and ran into tree-trunks and brushes that barred his way. He was compelled to return to the path.

"She flies from me," he said to himself sadly. "When I was a prisoner, she risked everything to free me. Now that I am free, she does not want to set eyes on me again. My treachery, that monster Josephine, and the whole disgusting business have filled her with horror."

As he regained the path, someone came tumbling over the wall. It was Beaumagnan, escaping in his turn. Then of a sudden reports of a revolver banged out from some quarter. Leonard had rushed to the gap and was firing at random into the wood. Ralph made haste to get out of range.

So, at about eleven o'clock at night, the three adversaries started from the same point to get to the Queen's stone, more than thirty miles away. What were their different mean of getting there? Everything depended on that.

On the one side were Beaumagnan and Leonard, both of them well provided with confederates, and at the head of powerful organizations. Beaumagnan's friends must be waiting for him; Leonard had but to get to Josephine; the spoil belonged to whichever was quickest. But Ralph was the youngest and most active. If he had not made the mistake of leaving his bicycle at Lillebonne, every chance would have been in his favor.

It must be admitted that he instantly abandoned his search for Clarice and that the pursuit of the treasure became his only care. Walking and running he covered the seven miles to Lillebonne in less than an hour. It was a little before midnight that he awoke the porter of his hotel, made a hasty meal. Then, having wrapped up two small dynamite cartridges in brown paper and thrust them into his pocket, he mounted his machine. Neatly rolled up and fastened below the handlebar was a canvas bag in which to bring away the spoil.

He made the following calculations: "From Lillebonne to Mesnil-sous-Jumièges is about twenty-five miles. I ought to be there before daybreak. The moment it is light I shall find the block of granite and blow it up with the dynamite. It is possible that Josephine or Beaumagnan may surprise me in the middle of the operation. In that case I go halves. All the worse for the third party."

Having passed Caudebec-en-Caux, he followed along the rising ground the road which runs through the woods and meadows to the Seine. Just as on the day on which he had first made love to Josephine, the *Nonchalante* was there, looming large through the dim light. He saw that the window of the cabin which she occupied was lit up.

"She must be dressing," he said to himself. "Her carriage will be coming for her. Perhaps Leonard has got to her and made her start sooner than she intended. Too late, my lady!"

He drove on the machine as hard as he could. But half an hour later, as he was riding down a steep hill, he felt his wheel meet some obstacle; and he flew over the handles, over a heap of stones by the road side, and came to a stop scratched and bruised, but with no bones broken, in a thick and thorny bush twenty feet down the hill.

Two men—he saw them dimly—came out of the bushes and hurried to his bicycle.

"It was him! It must have been him! The rope got the machine! I told you it would," cried Oscar de Bennetot in a tone of great excitement.

"Yes. But where's he got to?" growled Godfrey d'Etigues.

Ralph made haste to scramble up through the bushes to the top of the high embankment.

They heard him; but they could not see him. They rushed after him, cursing furiously. But they had little chance of finding him in that darkness.

Then Beaumagnan's voice came faintly from below: "Don't bother about him! We've no time to waste! Smash his machine! That puts him out of action."

They made haste to obey. Ralph heard them go bustling down to the road. Then he heard them stamping on the wheels of his bicycle.

Then Beaumagnan said: "Come on! The horse has rested long enough. We've got to get there quickly. Confound this wound of mine. The bandage has shifted; I'm bleeding like a pig."

Apparently they did as he bade them, for half a minute later there came a crunching of wheels and a carriage started and went down the hill at a good pace. Indomitable, Ralph took the canvas bag from the wreck of his bicycle, and set off after it at a steady trot.

He was furious. Nothing in the world would have induced him to abandon the struggle. It was no longer merely a matter of millions and millions which would make the rest of his life magnificent, his vanity was up in arms. Having solved the insoluble enigma, he must be the first to arrive at the goal. Not to be there, not to seize the treasure, to let someone else take it, would have been an intolerable humiliation to the day of his death.

So, indefatigable, he toiled on behind the carriage, and not so far behind it either, buoyed up by the thought that the enigma was not yet solved in its entirety, that his adversaries, like himself, had yet to find the actual place in which the block of granite stood; and in that darkness it was going to take time. While they were doing it, he might once more get the better of them.

Then Fortune relented and helped him. As he entered Jumièges he saw in front of him the wavering light of a lantern, heard the tinkle of a bell, and, where as his adversaries had gone straight through the village, he dropped into a quiet walk.

Then he met the priest of Jumièges, who, accompanied by a small boy, was returning from administering extreme unction. Ralph dropped into step beside him, asked where he could find an inn, and in the course of their talk as they went in the direction of that inn, pretending that he was an archæologist, spoke of a curious stone which he had been told he would find in the neighborhood.

"The dolmen of the queen, or something of that kind, they told me it was called," said Ralph. "You ought to know that object of interest, Monsieur le curé?"

"Of course I do, monsieur," said the priest. "I'm pretty sure that it must be what we call Agnes Sorel's stone."

"It's at Mesnil-sous-Jumièges, isn't it?" asked Ralph.

"That's where it is, about two and a half miles away. But it's hardly an object of interest—just a group of small rocks emerging from a mound, the tallest of which is three or four feet above the Seine."

"It's on common land, isn't it?" said Ralph.

"It was a few years ago, but the Commune sold it to one of my parishioners, a M. Simon Thuilard who wished to extend his meadow-land."

Immensely pleased, Ralph took his leave of the priest, provided with minute directions for finding the stone. They enabled him to avoid the big village of Jumièges, plunge into the network of winding roads which lead to Mesnil-sous-Jumièges, with the result that he got ahead of his adversaries.

"If they haven't taken the precaution to provide themselves with a guide, they're certain to miss their way," he said to himself. "It is impossible to take a carriage straight, such a dark night as this. And then how are they to pick the right road? Where are they to look for the stone? Beaumagnan is exhausted and Godfrey d'Etigues is hardly intelligent enough to find it by himself. I fancy I win this hand."

THE STRONGBOX OF THE MONKS

At a few minutes to three, he crossed the fence which ran round the property of Simon Thuilard.

A couple of matches showed him the path across the meadow. At the end of it he came to an embankment, which seemed to him of recent construction, along the side of the river. He arrived at the right end of it and moved down it to the left. Then, not wishing to use up all his matches, he waited for the dawn.

Already there was a strip of gray sky along the edge of the Eastern horizon.

He waited, full of a pleasant emotion which wreathed his lips with a smile. The block of granite was near him, not many feet away. For centuries, at this very hour of the night perhaps, the monks had come furtively to this very spot on the broad earth to bury their treasure. One by one, priors and treasurers had come by the subterranean passage which led from the abbey to the Manor. Others doubtless had come in boats along the old river of Normandy which ran through Paris and ran through Rouen, the waves of which broke against the estates of three of the seven sacred abbeys.

And now he, Ralph d'Andresy, was a sharer of the great secret. He was the heir of the thousands and thousands of monks who had worked in those distant ages, sown throughout the length and breadth of France and gathered in their harvest without a pause. What a miracle! To have at his age such a dream come true! To be an equal of the most powerful and to rule among the lords of the world!

In the paling heaven the Great Bear was fading. You divined, rather than saw, the luminous point of Alcor, the cabalistic star which, in the vast expanse of the Heavens, corresponded to the little block of granite on which Ralph was about to lay the hand of the conqueror. The stream babbled against the bank in quiet little waves. The surface of the river rose out of the darkness in shining patches of light.

He walked along the embankment. He began to discern the contours and colors of things. A solemn instant! His heart was beating quickly. Then of a sudden thirty yards away he saw a mound of ground which scarcely rose above the level of the meadow, and in which, among the grass which covered it rose some points of gray rock.

"It's there!" he murmured, moved to the very depths of his being. "It's there! I have reached the goal!"

His hands were fumbling with the dynamite cartridges in his pocket and his eyes were seeking wildly the higher stone of which that priest of Jumièges had spoken. Was it this one, or that? A few seconds would be enough for him to introduce the cartridge into the cracks which earth and plants choked. Three minutes later he would be heaping the diamonds and rubies into the bag which he took from his knapsack. If there remained a few crumbs among the debris all the better for his enemies.

He walked forward and the nearer he came to it the more the mound took on an appearance which did not at all conform to what he expected. There was no higher stone... There was no block which, in days gone by, would have afforded to her whom they called the Lady of Beauty, a seat from which to look for the arrival of the royal barque round the corner of the reach of the river. Nothing rose above the mound—on the contrary its top was level. What had happened? Had some sudden rush of the river, or some storm lately changed a spot which the storms of ages had respected? or had—

In two bounds Ralph crossed the ten paces which separated him from the mound.

An oath burst from his lips. The horrible truth was clear to his eyes. The center of the mound had been disembowled. The block of granite, the legendary block was indeed there, but smashed asunder into fragments, its debris on every side of a gaping hole full of blackened pebbles and tufts of grass. Not a single jewel! Not a scrap of gold or silver! The enemy had passed that way.

Ralph did not stand before this paralyzing spectacle for more than a minute. Motionless, speechless, he studied it absentmindedly, and mechanically gathered in all the traces and evidence of the work that had been done some hours before; he marked the prints of a woman's heel; but he refused to draw from them the only logical conclusion. He walked away from it, lit a cigarette and sat down on the bank of the dyke on the edge of the river.

He did not wish to think. The defeat, and above all the fashion in which it had been inflicted on him, was too painful for him to suffer himself to study its causes and effects. At such moments one can only strive to retain one's coolness. But, in spite of everything, the events of the preceding afternoon and evening forced themselves on his attention. Whether he wished it, or not, the actions of Josephine Balsamo unfolded themselves before his mind. He saw her striving firmly against that nervous attack and recovering all the energy necessary at such a juncture. Rest when the hour of destiny had struck? Not she! Had he rested? And Beaumagnan, wounded as he was, had he allowed himself the slightest respite? No! And Josephine Balsamo would never make such a mistake. Before nightfall she had reached the meadow with her agents; and then in the daylight and later by the light of lanterns, she had directed their work. And when he, Ralph, had divined her presence behind the curtained window of her cabin, she was not making ready for the final expedition; she had returned from it, once more victorious because she never allowed mischances, futile hesitation, or superfluous scruples to prove an obstacle between her and the immediate execution of her designs.

For more than twenty minutes, letting himself relax from his fatigue in the warmth of the sun which rose above the hills on the opposite bank, Ralph considered the bitter reality into which had sunk his dreams of domination. He must indeed have been deeply absorbed in those bitter reflections not to hear the noise of a carriage which stopped in the road and see the three men who got out of it, climb over the fence and cross the meadow till the very moment at which one of them, on reaching the mound, uttered a cry of anguish.

It was Beaumagnan; his two friends were supporting him.

If the disappointment of Ralph was deep, what must have been the despair of a man who had staked all his life on the mysterious treasure! Livid, with starting eyes, the bandage which ran across his shoulder oozing blood, he gazed stupidly, as at the most horrible of spectacles, at the spot on which the miraculous stone had been violated. One would have said that the world was falling in ruins about his feet and that he was gazing into a gulf of terror and horror.

Ralph came forward and murmured: "Her work."

Beaumagnan did not answer him. There was no doubt whatever that it was her work. Must it not be that the image of that woman mingled with everything disastrous and overwhelming, with every cataclysm charged with infernal suffering?

Had he any need, like his companions, to leap into the hole and ransack its chaos for some forgotten scrap of the treasure? No! After the passage of the sorceress there was nothing but dust and ashes. She was the great scourge which devastates and slays. She was the very incarnation of the Principle of Evil. She was nothingness and death!

He drew himself to his full height, always theatrical and romantic in his most natural attitudes, gazed round him with dolorous eyes, then, of a sudden, crossed himself, and drove into his breast the blade of a dagger—of the dagger which belonged to Josephine Balsamo.

The action was so sudden and so unexpected that no one could have prevented it. Before his friends and Ralph had even grasped what he had done, Beaumagnan tumbled into the hole among the debris of what had been the strongbox of the monks.

His friends sprang to him.

He was still breathing and he muttered: "A priest—a priest."

De Bennetot hurried away. Some peasants passed. He questioned them and sprang into the carriage.

On his knees beside his chief, Godfrey d'Etigues was praying and striking his breast. Doubtless Beaumagnan had revealed to him that Josephine Balsamo was still alive and knew all his crimes. The suicide of his chief on the top of that revelation had shattered his mind. His face was convulsed with terror.

Ralph bent down over Beaumagnan and in slow and measured accents said: "I swear to you that I will find her. I swear to you that I will take the treasure from her."

Love and hate still persisted in the heart of the dying man. Such words alone could prolong his existence for a few fleeting minutes. At the hour of his agony, in the shattering of all his dreams, he clung desperately to every chance of reprisal and vengeance.

His eyes summoned Ralph, who bent down lower and heard him mutter: "Clarice—Clarice d'Etigues—you must marry her. Listen—Clarice is not the daughter of the Baron—he confessed it to me—she is the daughter of another woman he loved."

Ralph said solemnly: "I swear to you I will marry her—I swear it."

"Godfrey!" said Beaumagnan.

The Baron went on praying. Ralph laid a hand on his shoulder and made him bend down to catch Beaumagnan's faint utterance.

"Clarice is to marry d'Andresy. I wish it."

"Yes, yes," said the Baron, incapable of resistance.

"Swear it."

"I swear it."

"By your eternal salvation?"

"By my eternal salvation."

"You will give him your money that he may avenge us—all the wealth you have stolen. Swear it!" said Beaumagnan.

"By the eternal salvation," said the Baron.

"He knows all your crimes. He has proofs of them," Beaumagnan continued. "If you do not obey me, he will hand you over to the police."

"I will obey."

"May you be accursed, if you do not," said Beaumagnan.

His voice was growing fainter broken by harsh gasps between which the words came more and more indistinct. Bent down, with his ear a little above his mouth, Ralph just caught them.

"You'll pursue her, Ralph... You must tear the jewels from her... She's a devil... Listen... I have discovered... At Havre... She has a vessel... The *Glowworm*... Listen."

He was at the very end of his strength. Nevertheless Ralph yet heard:

"Go... At once... Hunt her down... This very day."

His eyes closed, the death rattle began.

Godfrey d'Etigues still went on beating his breast, on his knees at the bottom of the hole.

Ralph left them.

That evening one of the Paris papers published in its final issue the following paragraph:

'M. Beaumagnan, a barrister well known in militant royalist circles, whose death in Spain had already been reported by mistake, committed suicide this morning at a village in Normandy of the name of Mesnil-sous-Jumièges, on the banks of the Seine. The reasons for this suicide are absolutely mysterious. Two of his friends, Baron d'Etigues and M. Oscar de Bennetot, who were with him, declare that they were spending the night at the château de Tancarville, where they were staying for some days, when Monsieur Beaumagnan awoke them. He was wounded and in a state of great agitation. He insisted on their harnessing a horse to a dogcart and driving at once to Jumièges and from there to a meadow near Mesnil-sous-Jumièges. Why? Why this nocturnal expedition to a lonely meadow? Why this suicide? Questions to which they can give no answer.'

The next day the Havre papers published accounts of an incident which are summed up fairly well in the following article:

'Last night Prince Lavosneff, who had come to Havre to try a yacht which he had recently purchased, witnessed a terrible drama. He was returning to the French coast when he saw a column of flame about a mile and a half away and heard a loud explosion—an explosion, by the way, which was heard at several places along the coast. The Prince at once steered his yacht towards the spot at which this sinister incident had taken place, and there he found fragments of a wreck. On one of them was a sailor whom they succeeded in rescuing. But they had hardly the time to learn from him that the wrecked vessel was called the *Glowworm* and belonged to the Countess of Cagliostro, when all at once he sprang overboard again crying: "There she is! There she is!"

'By the light of the ship's lanterns they perceived another fragment of the wreck, to which a woman was clinging, with her head just above the water. The man succeeded in swimming to her and getting hold of her. But she clung to him so tightly that she prevented him using his arms, and the two of them sank. All efforts to find them were vain.

On his return to Havre Prince Lavosneff made a deposition to this effect, which was also signed by four of his crew.'

The paper added:

'Later information leads us to believe that the Countess of Cagliostro was an adventuress well known under the name of Pellegrini and sometimes also under the name of Balsamo.

Wanted by the police, who had two or three times just missed capturing her in localities in the Caux country, where she had recently been operating, she must have decided to go abroad, and in this way perished with her confederates in the wreck of her yacht, the *Glowworm*. We must also mention, with all proper reservations, that there is a rumor to the effect that there is a close connection between certain adventures of the Countess of Cagliostro and the mysterious drama at Mesnil-sous-Jumièges. There is a story going about of treasure unearthed and stolen, of plots and documents of great antiquity. But at this point we enter the domain of fable. We will stop therefore and leave it to justice to throw light on the affair.'

On the afternoon of the day on which this article appeared, that is to say exactly sixty hours after the drama at Mesnil-sous-Jumièges, Ralph entered the study of the Baron Godfrey at Haie d'Etigues, the study into which he had made his way one night four months before. How many roads had he traversed since that night and how many years older had he grown than the stripling he then was!

At a small table the two cousins were drinking, at a considerable pace, a bottle of brandy.

Without beating about the bush, Ralph said: "I have come to claim the hand of Mademoiselle d'Etigues."

He was hardly wearing the correct costume in which to ask a lady's hand in marriage. He was hatless and dressed in an old fisherman's jersey and trousers much too short for him which revealed his bare feet in grass shoes without any laces.

But Ralph's costume and his errand were of very little interest to Godfrey d'Etigues. Hollow-eyed, with the face of one of the damned, he held out towards Ralph a bundle of newspapers and groaned:

"Have you seen them? The Countess?"

"Yes, I know all that," said Ralph.

He detested the man; and he could not refrain from adding: "All the better for you. What? The definite death of Josephine Balsamo must have lifted a heavy burden from your mind."

"But the sequel—the consequences!" stammered the Baron.

"What consequences?" said Ralph.

"The law. It's sure to try to get at the bottom of this business. People are already saying that Josephine Balsamo was mixed up with the suicide of Beaumagnan. If the police get hold of all the threads of the affair they will go further—to the very end of it."

"Yes," said Ralph in a jeering tone, "to the Widow Rousselin and the murder of Jaubert. That's to say to you and cousin de Bennetot."

The two men shuddered. Ralph set their minds at rest.

"You can drink at your ease, both of you," he said. "Justice will not throw any light on this dark story, for the excellent reason that it will do its best on the contrary to bury it in oblivion. Beaumagnan was protected by powers who like neither scandal nor the light of day. The business will be hushed up. The thing that troubles me much more is not the action of the law—"

"What is it?" said the Baron.

"The vengeance of Josephine Balsamo," said Ralph somberly.

"But if she's dead—"

"Even dead, she is formidable," said Ralph gravely. "And that's why I am here. There is at the bottom of the park a small keeper's lodge. I'm going to install myself in it—till our marriage. Inform Clarice that I am here and tell her to allow no one to visit her—not even me. Perhaps however she will accept this present from me since we are engaged; and I beg you to give it to her from me."

And he handed to the astonished Baron a huge sapphire, of an incomparable fineness, and cut as they used to cut precious stones in an earlier age.

XIV

THE INFERNAL CREATURE

"Let go the anchor and lower a boat," said Josephine.

A thick mist rested on the sea, which, along with the darkness of the night, prevented them from seeing the lights of Etretat. Even the lamp of Cape Antifer lighthouse could not pierce the impenetrable fog through which the yacht of Prince Lavosneff was groping its way.

"Why are you sure that we are in sight of land?" Leonard asked.

"Because I desire it so keenly," said Josephine.

He lost his temper: "This expedition is foolishness — pure foolishness," he said. "What? It's a fortnight since we succeeded and that, thanks to you, we gained the most extraordinary victory. The whole mass of those precious stones is safe in the strongroom of a bank in London. All danger is over. The Countess of Cagliostro, Madam Pellegrini, Madam Balsamo, the Marquise de Belmonte, are all at the bottom of the sea, as a result of the shipwreck of the *Glowworm* which you had the admirable idea of organizing and which you directed with such vigor. Twenty witnesses heard the explosion from the coast. To all the world you are dead, a hundred times dead, and I as well, and all your confederates. If anyone succeeded in bringing to light the story of the treasure of the monks, they would come to the conclusion that it had been scattered about with the fragments of the *Glowworm* at a place impossible to fix exactly, and that the jewels are strewn about in the bottom of the sea. And we may well believe that Justice is delighted with this shipwreck and our deaths, and that it is not going to look too closely into the matter, such efforts have been made in high places to hush up the Beaumagnan-Cagliostro affair. Everything then is going well. You are the mistress of circumstances and victorious over all your enemies. And it is the moment at which the most elementary prudence bids us leave France and to get as far as possible away from Europe. And that's the very moment you choose to return to the very place in which you have suffered your worst defeats, and to confront the only enemy who remains. And what an enemy! A genius of a kind so exceptional, that, without him you would never have discovered the treasure. You must admit that it's madness."

She murmured: "Love is a madness."

"Then give it up."

"I can't give it up. I love him."

She rested her elbows on the bulwarks, her head between her hands, and murmured in despairing accents: "I love him. It's the first time I have ever loved. The other men—they don't count. But as for Ralph but I don't want to talk about him. Thanks to him I have known the only joy I ever had—but also the greatest suffering. Before I met him I did not know what happiness was; but I did not know sorrow either. And then—and then the happiness came to an end; and only the suffering is left. It's horrible, Leonard! The idea that he is going to marry—that another is going to share his life, is more than I can bear. Anything rather than that! I would rather risk anything—I would rather die!"

He said in a low voice: "My poor Josine."

They were silent for some time. She leaned on the rail huddled together and despairing. Then when the boat was lowered, she drew herself upright, imperious and implacable.

"But I risk nothing, Leonard—neither death nor failure," she said.

"What are you going to do?" he said in a tone of patient resignation.

"I'm going to carry him off."

"You hope to do that?"

"Yes. Everything is ready. The smallest details have been worked out."

"How?" he said in an incredulous tone.

"By the agency of Dominique."

"Ah! I was wondering what had become of Dominique," he said.

"Yes; directly after the coup, even before Ralph went to La Haie d'Etigues, Dominique got employed there as a groom."

"But Ralph knows him."

"Ralph has seen him once or twice at the most; and you know how clever Dominique is at disguising his face. It's impossible that he should recognize him among all the staff of the château and the stables. Dominique then, following my instructions, has kept me informed of what is going on day by day. I know the hours at which Ralph goes to bed and gets up, how he spends his time, and everything he does. I know that he has not yet seen Clarice again, but that he has sent for the papers necessary for the marriage."

"Does he suspect anything?"

"As far as I'm concerned, he does not. Dominique heard scraps of a conversation which he had with Godfrey d'Etigues the day he came to the château. Neither of them had the slightest doubt about my death. But nonetheless Ralph wished them to take all possible precautions against me, though I was dead. Therefore he is on guard over the château. He is keeping watch, continually on guard, and always questioning the peasants."

"And Dominique has let you come?"

"Yes; but only for an hour. One bold swift stroke, at night, and immediate flight."

"And it's tonight, is it?" he said anxiously.

"Yes, tonight between ten and eleven. Ralph is living at an isolated keeper's lodge, not far from the old tower to which Beaumagnan had me taken. That lodge is let into the big wall of the park. And on the other side of it, which looks on the country, there is only one window, on the ground floor, and no door. If the shutters are closed, to get into it you have to go round through the park gates and along the inside of the wall. The two keys will be under a stone close to the park gates tonight. When Ralph is asleep we shall roll him up in his mattress and blankets and bring him here. The moment we've got him, we set sail."

"Is that all?" said Leonard.

Josephine hesitated before she replied: "That's all."

"And what about Dominique?"

"He will go with us."

Leonard bent forward, tried to see her face clearly in the darkness, and said: "You haven't given him any special orders?"

"What about?"

"About Clarice. You hate that girl. Therefore I'm afraid that you may have entrusted Dominique with some job."

She hesitated again before replying: "That's no business of yours."

"Nevertheless—" he said doubtfully.

The ladder was let down for them to get into the boat. Josephine said in a mocking tone: "Listen, Leonard. Since I created you Prince Lavosneff and provided you with a yacht splendidly fitted out, you have become extraordinarily discreet. But we'll stick to our agreement, if you don't mind. I command:

you obey. You have the right to an explanation. I have given it to you. Act as if it was sufficient."

"It is sufficient," said Leonard glumly. "And I recognize that you have laid your plans admirably."

"All the better. Let's be starting."

She led the way down the ladder and settled herself in the stern of the boat.

Leonard and four of their confederates followed him. Two of them took the oars, another the rudder-strings, she directed their course in a low voice.

A quarter of an hour later, though her followers had the impression that they were moving forward blindly, she said: "We're passing Amont harbor."

From time to time she warned the steersman of rocks that rose above the surface of the sea and directed his course by landmarks invisible to the rest of them. The crunching of the keel upon the pebbles was the first thing to inform them that they had reached the beach. They carried her ashore, then beached the boat.

"You're quite certain that we shan't meet any coast guards?" whispered Leonard.

"Quite certain. Dominique's last telegram was quite definite."

"Isn't he coming to meet us?" asked Leonard.

"No. I wrote to him to remain at the château among the other servants. He will meet us at eleven."

"Where?"

"Near Ralph's lodge. Don't talk anymore."

All of them were lost to sight in the priest's staircase. Once in it, Josephine lit a bull's-eye lantern she had brought with her. They mounted the staircase, in silence.

On the top of the cliff the mist was much thinner. At intervals there were gaps in it through which they could see the stars. Therefore Josephine was at once able to point out to them La Haie d'Etigues, many of the front windows of which were lit up. The clock of Benouville church struck ten. Josephine shivered.

"Oh, the striking of that clock! How well I recognize it! Ten strokes like the last time I heard it—ten strokes—one after the other! I counted them as I was going to my death."

"Well, you avenged yourself all right," said Leonard.

"On Beaumagnan, yes. But the others—"

"On the others too. The two cousins are half mad."

"It's true," she said. "But I shall not feel myself fully avenged for an hour. Then I shall be able to rest."

They waited for the mist to drift over again in order that their figures might not stand out against the bare plain they had to traverse. Then Josephine led the way along the path, along which Godfrey and his friends had carried her to the priest's staircase. The others followed in single file without saying a word. The grass had been cut; here and there stood large haycocks.

As they drew near to La Haie d'Etigues the path ran between high banks covered with bushes between which they marched with growing carefulness.

The wall rose in front of them. A few more steps, and the lodge, in which Ralph had taken up his abode, came into view. Josephine halted them with a gesture.

"Wait for me," she said.

"Shall I come with you?" Leonard asked.

"No. I will come back for you and we will go into the park together through the gate which is on the other side of it, on our left."

She went forward alone, therefore, setting down her feet so carefully that no stone rolled under her sole and no leaf rustled at the contact of her skirt. She came to the window of the keeper's lodge.

She took hold of the shutters very gently. The fastenings, with which Dominique had tampered, did not hold them together.

She opened them till a little light came through the opening. Then she glued her eye to it and looked into a room, on the further side of which was a recess with a bed in it.

Ralph was in the bed. A lamp, with a crystal globe and a cardboard shade on the top of it, showed clearly in the circle of its light his face, his shoulders, the book he was reading, and his clothes heaped up on the chair beside the bed. He looked young indeed, with something of the air of a boy who is giving all his attention to a task, but at the same time struggling against sleep. Several times his head dropped forward. He awoke, forced himself to read, and again dozed off.

At length he shut his book and put out the lamp.

Having seen what she wanted to see, Josephine left her post and returned to her confederates. She had already given her instructions, but she took the precaution of repeating them.

"Above all, no unnecessary roughness," she insisted. "You understand, Leonard? Since he has no weapon within reach with which to defend himself, there will be no need for you to use your weapons. There are five of you; and that's enough."

"But suppose he does resist?" said Leonard.

"It's for you to act in such a manner that he can't resist," she said coldly with a touch of menace in her tone.

She had learned her way about so thoroughly, from the maps with which Dominique had supplied her, that she led them without hesitating a moment to the principal entry into the park. They found the keys, of the park gate and the door of Ralph's lodge, at the place agreed upon. They opened the park gate and took their way along the wall to the lodge.

The key turned in the well-oiled lock of its door without a sound; noiselessly the door opened on well-oiled hinges. Followed by her confederates, she entered. On the other side of the tiled hall was the door of the bedroom. She pushed it open with infinite slowness.

THE INFERNAL CREATURE

It was the decisive moment. If Ralph had not been awakened but was sleeping still, Josephine's plot would be successful. She listened. Nothing stirred. Then she stepped aside to make way for the five men and by letting the ray from the bull's-eye fall on the bed, gave the signal to her pack.

The assault was so swift that the sleeper could not have awakened before all resistance was useless. The gang had rolled him up in his blankets and pulled the mattress round him, and wound a rope round it in less than ten seconds. In less than twenty seconds the rope was securely tied. There had not been a cry; not a piece of furniture had been knocked out of its place.

Once more Josephine was victorious.

"Splendid!" she said in a tone of excitement which revealed the importance she attached to this victory. "Splendid! We've got him. And this time every precaution shall be taken to prevent him from getting away."

"What are we to do now?" Leonard asked.

"Carry him to the boat."

"Suppose he shouts for help?"

"Gag him. But he can't shout. Off you go!"

The four men stood up, bearing on their shoulders a burden which looked like a great bundle of linen. Leonard came to Josephine.

"Aren't you coming with us?" he asked.

"No."

"Why not?"

"I told you: I'm waiting for Dominique."

She lit the lamp and raised the shade of it.

"How pale you're looking," he said in a low voice.

"Perhaps I am," she said defiantly.

"I suppose it's about that girl."

"Yes."

"Dominique's at work, is he?"

She nodded.

"Who knows? There may still be time to stop him!"

"Even if there were, I should not change my mind. It's made up. What will be, will be. Besides, the thing is done. Off you go!"

"But why shouldn't we wait for you?"

"The only danger comes from Ralph. Once he's safe on the boat, we've nothing more to fear. Be off and leave me."

She opened the window. They passed through it with their burden and disappeared in the darkness.

She closed the shutters and shut the window.

A few minutes passed and the church clock struck. She counted the strokes—eleven. At the eleventh stroke she went to the door of the lodge, opened it, and listened. There came a low whistle. She answered it by stamping on the tiles of the hall.

Dominique came hurrying to her. They went into the bedroom.

On the instant, without waiting for her to ask the question, he said: "I've done it."

"Oh," she said in a shaky voice; and she was so upset that she tottered and sank into a chair.

They stared at one another in silence.

Then Dominique uttered: "She felt nothing."

"She felt nothing?" she repeated.

"No. She was asleep."

"Are you quite sure that—that—"

"That she's dead? You may take your oath to it I am! I drove the knife into her heart—three times. Besides I had the nerve to wait to make sure. There was no need. She had stopped breathing and her hands were cold."

"Suppose they were to discover it?"

"It's impossible. No one goes into her bedroom except in the morning. Till then—they won't see."

They did not dare to look one another in the face. Dominique held out his hand. She drew from her bosom ten thousand-franc notes and held them out to him.

He almost snatched them from her and said: "Thanks. If it were to be done again, I should refuse. What am I to do now?"

"Get away. If you run, you'll catch the others up before they get back to the boat."

"They've got Ralph d'Andresy?"

"Yes."

"That's a good thing. He's been giving me a lot of trouble during the last fortnight. He was very suspicious. By the way—those jewels of the monks."

"We have them," said Josephine.

"Are they safe?"

"In the strongroom of a bank in London."

"Are there many of them?" he said greedily.

"A trunk full."

"Good! More than a hundred thousand francs for me, what?"

"Much more. But hurry up—unless you prefer to wait for me," she said.

"No, no. I want to get away from here as soon as possible and as far as possible. But what about you?"

"I'm just going to make sure that there are no papers here which would be dangerous for us, and I'll catch up with you."

Dominique followed the others out through the window. At once Josephine ransacked all the drawers in the room, and finding nothing, hunted through the pockets of Ralph's clothes.

She emptied his pocketbook out on to the table. It contained banknotes, visiting cards and a photograph—the photograph of Clarice d'Etigues.

Josephine looked at it earnestly with an expression no longer of hate, but cold and unforgiving. Then she stood still wearing the air of one who gazed upon some painful spectacle, while her lips retained their sweet smile.

The mirror on the toilet table was in front of her and she caught sight of her image in it. She sat down with her head resting on her hands and gazed at herself. Her eyes grew brighter and her smile sweeter, as if she was enjoying to the full her consciousness of her beauty. She drew forward on to her forehead the thin veil which always covered her hair and arranged it to bring out her resemblance to the Virgin of Bernardino Luini.

She looked at herself for a minute or two, then seemed to relapse into her painful reverie. The village clock chimed the quarter past the hour; but still she did not stir. You would almost have said that she was asleep, asleep with her eyes open, unwinking. Presently, however, her eyes grew less vague, as they gazed fixedly at something in the mirror over her shoulder. Just as it sometimes happens in a dream that one's ideas, thronging and incoherent, crystallize into one idea more and more precise, into an image more and more clear, so it happened to her now. What was that disconcerting image that she seemed to perceive, to which she tried vainly to grow used? It was in the alcove in which the bed was set, the walls of which were hung all round with curtains. Between those curtains and the wall there must have been a space, for one would have said that a hand was moving them.

Then a hand actually appeared, then an arm, then, above the arm, a head.

Josephine, accustomed to spiritist séances in which phantoms were materialized, gave a name to this spirit which her terrified imagination had summoned from the shadows. It was clothed in white; she could not be sure whether its lips were wreathed with an affectionate smile, or drawn back in an angry snarl.

She stammered: "Ralph—Ralph—what do you want of me?"

The phantom parted the curtains and came round the bed. Josephine shut her eyes with a groan, then opened them again. The hallucination was still there; and the phantom drew nearer with movements which moved a chair and made a noise. She wished to fly, but could not. Then she felt on her shoulder the grip of a hand which was certainly not that of a spirit; and a cheerful voice said:

"My dear Josephine, I should really advise you to get Prince Lavosneff to take you for a short, restful cruise. You need one, my dear Josephine. What? You take me for a ghost, me, Ralph d'Andresy! I may be in pants and a nightshirt, nevertheless you ought to know me."

He began to put on his clothes quickly. She stared at him and muttered: "You? You?"

"Goodness, yes: me."

He laughed gently at her frowning face and went on in a jeering tone. "Now, don't go pitching into Prince Lavosneff under the impression that he has let me escape again. He has not. What he and his friends carried away was simply a dummy stuffed with bran, rolled up in my blankets and mattress. As for me, I did not stir from the shelter in which I took refuge as soon as you left your post on the other side of the shutters."

Josephine remained inert and as incapable of taking action as if she had been beaten to a jelly.

"Hang it! You don't seem to be quite yourself," he went on, in the same jeering tone. "Would you like a little glass of liquor to buck you up? I quite understand that you're very much upset and I admit that I should not like to be in your place—all your little play fellows gone—no help possible for quite a while— securely shut up in this room with a gentleman named Ralph. It certainly is not a time to see the world in rose-color. Unlucky Josephine. What a mess you have made of it!"

He stooped down and picked up the photograph of Clarice: "How pretty my fiancée is, isn't she? It gave me the greatest pleasure to see how you were admiring her just now. You know that we're going to get married in a few days?"

"She's dead," said Josephine.

"As a matter of fact, I heard about that," he said calmly. "Your little friend who was here just now stabbed her in her bed, didn't he?"

"Yes."

"With a dagger, wasn't it?"

"Three times—through the heart," she said.

"Once ought to have been enough, you know," he suggested.

She said slowly, as if striving to assure herself of the fact: "She's dead. She's dead."

He chuckled: "What can you expect? It happens everyday. But you can't expect me to change all my plans for a little thing like that. Dead or alive, I'm going to marry her. And we must manage as best we can. You managed splendidly."

"What do you mean?" said Josephine sharply, beginning to grow yet more uneasy at his careless bantering tone.

"What do I mean? Why look at you. First of all the Baron drowned you, next you were blown up and then drowned in the wreck of your vessel the *Glowworm*. But all that drowning doesn't prevent you from being here. Therefore the fact that Clarice has been stabbed through the heart three times is no reason for my not marrying her. Besides are you quite sure that your statement is accurate?"

"One of my own men stabbed her," she said.

"Or at any rate he told you that he'd stabbed her."

"Why should he have lied?"

"Why, to get hold of the ten banknotes you handed over to him."

"Dominique is incapable of betraying me! He would not betray me for a hundred thousand francs! Besides he knows quite well that I can lay hands on him. He's waiting for me with the others," she said fiercely.

"Are you quite sure that he's waiting for you, Josine?" said Ralph; and the jeering note in his voice was louder.

She shivered. She had a feeling that she was struggling in a narrowing circle.

He shook his head and said thoughtfully: "It's odd, the blunders we've made, you and I, with regard to one another. You must be uncommonly simple to think that the blowing up of the *Glowworm*, the Pellegrini-Cagliostro shipwreck, and the rubbish related by Prince Lavosneff took me in for an instant. How on earth did you fail to guess that a fellow who is not an imbecile to begin with, and has had the advantage of a course at your school—and what a school!—would read your game as easily as he would an open Bible? That shipwreck was really much too convenient. One is accused of dozens of crimes, one's hands are red with blood, the police are hunting one hard. Then one blows up an old vessel; and all the past, the crimes, the stolen treasure, the wealth of the monks, all sink in a lump along with it. One passes for dead. One grows a new skin. And then one begins again, a little further off, under another name, to murder, to torture, and to bathe one's hands in blood. That may take in other people, old girl, but not me. When I read about your shipwreck, I said 'It's time to keep one's eyes open wide,' and I came here."

He paused, smiling at her, a chilling smile; then went on: "But hang it all, Josephine, your visit was inevitable! And it was inevitable that you must clear the way for it by the help of some confederate. It was inevitable that the yacht of Prince Lavosneff should come cruising off this coast one night. It was inevitable that you must climb the staircase in the cliff which you had once descended on a stretcher. Well, I took my precautions; and my first care was to look about to see if there wasn't somebody I knew in the neighborhood. A confederate, it's the very first step in the art. And at once I recognized our young friend Dominique, since I had happened to see him, a detail of which you were ignorant, on the box of your carriage waiting at the door of Bridget Rousselin. Dominique is a faithful servant; but the fear of the police and a sound thrashing softened him to such a degree that he transferred all his faithfulness to me; and he gave proof of it by sending you false reports and by digging for your feet, in concert with me, the pitfall into which you have stumbled. As for his reward: why, there are the ten banknotes, out of your pocket, which you will never see again, for your faithful servant has gone back to the château and is under my protection. That's how we stand, my dear Josephine. I might indeed have spared you this little comedy and welcomed you here openly, for the mere pleasure of shaking you by the hand. But I wished to see how you would direct the operation, remaining myself in the background, and above all I wished to see how you would receive the news of the supposed murder of Clarice d'Etigues."

Josephine shrank away from him. He was no longer joking; bending over her he said quietly: "Just a trace of feeling—just a slightest trace—that was all you showed. You believed that the child was dead, dead by your order; and it did not move you at all. With you the death of others does not count. One is twenty, with all one's life before one... with charm and beauty... You crush all that, as if you were cracking a nut. Your conscience does not make one protest. It is true that you do not laugh; but none the more do you weep. In reality you do not give it a thought. I remember that Beaumagnan called you a daughter of Hell—a designation that revolted me. Now I see that he was right. Hell is in you. You are a kind of monster about whom I can never think again without horror. But what about you, Josephine? Aren't there times when you feel that horror yourself?"

Still sitting at the toilet table, her head resting on her hands, in the attitude of which she was so fond, she did not stir. Ralph's pitiless words did not provoke that access of indignation and fury for which he was looking. He felt that she was at one of those moments in life at which one sees into the deepest depths of one's soul and cannot turn one's eyes from the sight.

He was not greatly surprised. Without being frequent, such moments could not be very uncommon in the life of this unbalanced creature, whose nature, impassible on the surface, was now and again ravaged by nervous convulsions in its depths. Matters were turning out so different from what she had expected, and the apparition of Ralph was so disconcerting that she was unable to rise to struggle with the enemy who was so cruelly outraging her.

He took advantage of her weakness, and went on in a voice that demanded an answer: "Isn't it a fact, Josine, that at times you terrify yourself? Aren't there times when you are full of horror at yourself?"

The distress of Josephine was so profound that she murmured: "Yes—yes sometimes. But you're not to speak to me about it. I don't want to know. Be quiet—be quiet!"

"But on the contrary, it is necessary that you should know," said Ralph. "If such acts fill you with horror, why do you commit them?"

"I can't help it," she said faintly in an extreme lassitude.

"You do try then?"

"Yes. I try—I struggle—but it is never any use. I was taught evil. I do evil as other people do good. I do evil just as I breathe. That was what they willed."

"Who?"

"My mother," she muttered in a low voice.

"Your mother? The spy? The woman who made up all this Cagliostro story?"

"Yes. But you're not to blame her. She was very fond of me. Only she had not succeeded... She had become poor and wretched and she wished me to succeed... and grow rich."

"Yet you were beautiful. And for a woman beauty is riches. Beauty is enough."

"My mother was beautiful too; and yet her beauty was of no use to her," she retorted.

"You were like her?"

"You could not tell one from the other. And that was my ruin. She wished to carry out through me her great idea—Cagliostro's legacy."

"And had she documents?"

"A scrap of paper... the list of the four enigmas. One of her friends had found it in an old book; and it really seemed to be in Cagliostro's handwriting. She was intoxicated by it and by her success with the Empress Eugenie, from whom she got most of her information. So I had to carry on the work. She put that into my head when I was quite a child. My brain was trained to hold only that idea. That was to be my livelihood—my destiny. I was the daughter of Cagliostro. I was to take up the life she had led, the life he had led a life as brilliant as he leads in the romances in which he figures—the life of an adventuress, adored by everyone and dominating the world. No scruples—no conscience. I was to take vengeance for all that she had suffered. On her deathbed her last words to me were 'Avenge me.'"

Ralph reflected. Then he said: "But your crimes—this lust to kill?"

He could not catch her answer, and again he did not catch it when he said: "Your mother was not the only person to bring you up and equip you for evil. Who was your father?"

He fancied he caught the name of Leonard. But did she mean that Leonard was her father, the man who had been expelled from France in the days of the second empire—it was likely enough—or that Leonard had trained her in crime?

He learned no more. He had loved her; and he had not the heart to force his way into those obscure regions in which evil instincts come to birth and are fostered, in which ferments everything that unbalances, ruins, and disintegrates, all the vices, the vanities, and bloodthirsty appetites, all the cruel and inexorable passions which escape from our control. He asked no more.

Weeping silently, she caught his hands; and he was weak enough to abandon them to her. He felt her kisses and her tears rain on them. Insensibly pity filled his heart. The evil creature became a human being, a woman delivered over to a diseased instinct, the victim of the law of irresistible forces, one whom he ought perhaps to regard with at least a little indulgence.

"Do not drive me from you," she said. "You are the only being in the world who might have saved me from evil. I felt it at once. There is something so sane and healthy about you. Love is the only thing that has ever appeased me; and I have never loved anyone but you. So if you cast me off—"

Her lips filled Ralph with an infinite languor. Pleasure and desire embellished that dangerous compassion which weakens the wills of men. And perhaps if Josephine had contented herself with that humble caress, he might have succumbed of himself to the temptation to bend down and once again taste the savor of those lips which offered themselves to him. But she raised her head, slipped her arms round his neck, and gazed into his eyes. And that gaze sufficed to enable him to see in her no longer the woman who implored, but the woman who desired to seduce and was employing the tenderness of her eyes and the enchantment of her lips to that end.

Looks link lovers. But Ralph knew so well what lay behind that charming, ingenuous, and dolorous expression. The clearness of the mirror did not redeem all the ugliness and ignominy which he saw so plainly in it. Little by little he recovered. He withdrew from temptation and releasing himself from the siren who enlaced him he said:

"Do you remember, one day on the barge, that we feared one another, as if we were trying to strangle one another?

It is the same today. If I fall again into your arms, I am lost. Tomorrow—the day after, it would be death."

She drew herself up of a sudden hostile and dangerous. Once more pride took possession of her and the storm once more rose suddenly, causing them to pass without any transition from the kind of torpor in which the memory of their love lulled them, to a bitter constraint of enmity and hatred.

"Yes," Ralph went on. "At the bottom of our hearts, from the very first day, we have been ferocious enemies. Neither of us thought of anything but the defeat of the other. Especially you! I was the rival and intruder. In your brain my image was mixed with the idea of death. Voluntarily or not, you condemned me."

She shook her head and said in an aggressive tone: "Not till now."

"But now you have, haven't you? Only a new fact presents itself; and that is that now I can laugh at you, Josephine! The pupil has become the master; and that was what I wished to demonstrate to you by letting you come here and accepting the battle. I offered myself, alone, to your attack and to the attack of your gang. And now that we are face to face with one another, you can do nothing to me. Defeat all along the line. What? Clarice alive. Myself free. Come, my dear: clear out of my life. You are hopelessly beaten; and I have a contempt for you."

He flung these insults at her like the blows of a scourge which scarred her. She was deathly pale; her face was distorted; and for the first time her unchangeable beauty showed signs of withering and decay.

"I shall avenge myself," she said between her clenched teeth.

"Impossible!" said Ralph with a careless laugh. "I have cut your claws. You're afraid of me. That is the real miracle I have worked today: you are afraid of me."

"I'll devote my whole life to avenging myself," she muttered, scowling at him.

"Nothing doing," he said confidently. "I know all your tricks. You have failed. It's all over."

She shook her head and said fiercely: "I have other means."

"What are they?" he asked contemptuously.

"That incalculable fortune—those riches I have won."

"Thanks to whom?" he said lightly. "If ever there was a spark of real intelligence in that strange adventure, didn't I supply it?"

"Perhaps. But it was I who knew how to act and to take. And that's everything. As far as words went, you were never at a loss for them. But what was wanted was deeds; and those deeds I did. Because Clarice is alive and you are free, you shout: 'Victory!' But Clarice's life and your liberty are but little things beside the great thing which was the stake for which we fought. That is to say the thousands and thousands of precious stones. The real battle was there; and I won it, for the treasure is mine."

"Can one ever be quite sure?" said Ralph in a mocking tone.

"Yes: the treasure is mine. With my own hands I heaped the countless stones into a portmanteau, which was fastened and sealed before my eyes, which I carried to Havre, which I hid in the bottom of the hold of the *Glowworm*, and took away before I blew the vessel up. It is now in London in the strongroom of a bank, tied up and sealed as it was at the beginning."

"Yes, yes," agreed Ralph readily. "The rope is unbroken, still tight in its place. There are five seals, the sealing-wax is violet, with the initials J. B.—Josephine Balsamo—on them. As for the trunk it's of plaited wickerwork, with leather straps and handles—one of those simple things which attract no one's attention—"

Josephine stared at him with frightened eyes and said: "You know?... How do you know?"

"We spent a few hours together, I and that trunk," he said, laughing.

"Lies!" she cried. "You're talking at random. The portmanteau did not leave me for a second between the meadow of Mesnil-sous-Jumièges and the strongroom in London."

"Yes it did, since you let it down into the hold of the *Glowworm*."

"I sat on the iron hatch which closed the hold and one of my men kept watch over the port through which you might have entered it, all the time we were in the roadstead at Havre," she declared.

"I know that."

"How can you know it?"

"I was in the hold."

It was an alarming sentence! He repeated it and then, thoroughly enjoying his narrative he said to the stupefied Josephine: "In the face of the shattered block this was my reasoning: 'If I hunt for my good Josephine, I shall not find her. What I've got to do is to guess the place where she will be at the end of the day, to get there before her, to be there when she arrives, and to avail myself of the first opportunity of scooping up the precious stones. For, with the police on your trail, hunted by me, eager to get the treasure into a safe place, it was inevitable that you must take to flight, that is to say, get away abroad. How? Why, by means of your vessel, the *Glowworm*.'

"At noon I was at Havre; at one o'clock the three members of the crew who were on board went off, to drink their coffee at a bar. I slipped across the gang way into the hold and hid myself behind a heap of cases, barrels, and sacks of provisions. At six o'clock you arrived and let the portmanteau down by a rope, so putting it under my protection."

"You lie! You lie!" stuttered Josephine in a furious voice.

He went quietly on: "At ten o'clock Leonard joined you. He had read the evening papers and learned about Beaumagnan's suicide. At eleven o'clock you weighed anchor. At midnight, out at sea, a yacht met you. Leonard, who became Prince

Lavosneff, presided over the disembarkation. The crew and the packages containing everything of value were transferred from the deck of one vessel to the deck of the other, in especial the portmanteau which you hauled up from the bottom of the hold. And then to hell with the *Glowworm*!

"I must admit that I spent some devilishly unpleasant minutes. I was alone. There was no longer any crew or helmsmen. The *Glowworm* seemed to be steered by a drunken man, holding himself up by her wheel. One would have said that she was a child's toy which has been wound up and which goes round and round. And then I guessed your plan—the bomb in one of the cabins, the mechanism exploded it, the explosion.

"I was perspiring freely, I can tell you. Was I to throw myself into the sea? I had just made up my mind to do so, when, as I was untying my shoelaces, I nearly fainted with joy at the sight of a dinghy in the wake of the *Glowworm* fastened to her by a rope. It was my salvation. Ten minutes later sitting quietly in it, I saw a flame leap up in the darkness about three hundred yards away, and heard a roar roll across the sea like a peal of thunder. The *Glowworm* had blown up.

"The next night, after having been tossed about a bit, I came in sight of shore not far from Cape Antifer. I slipped into the water and swam to it, and that very day I came here—to get everything ready for your visit, my dear Josephine."

She had listened to him without interrupting with an air of serenity. She had the air of saying: "Words again—nothing but words." The essential thing was the portmanteau. Supposing that he had hidden himself on the vessel and afterwards escaped shipwreck. It was of no importance.

She hesitated however to ask a definite question. She knew very well that Ralph was not the kind of man to risk everything to obtain no other result than to save himself. She was very pale.

"Well, haven't you any questions to ask me?" he said.

"What questions? You said yourself that I had taken the portmanteau. And afterwards I put it in a safe place."

"And you didn't make sure that it was all right?"

"Gracious, no. What was the point in opening it? The ropes and seals were intact."

"You didn't notice the mark of a hole in the side—an opening made between the strands of wickerwork?"

"An opening?" she said faintly.

"Goodness, you don't suppose that I spent two hours with a portmanteau full of jewels without doing anything? Come: I'm not such a fool as that."

"Then—then—" she said in a yet fainter voice.

"Then, my poor friend, little by little, patiently, I extracted all the contents of the portmanteau with the result that—"

"With the result that?"

"—when you open it you will find nothing inside but a roughly equivalent weight of trifles of no great value—just what I had to hand, finding them in the sacks of provisions—a good many pounds of lentils and haricot beans—merchandise for which it is hardly worth your while perhaps, to pay the rent of a strongroom in a London bank."

She struggled not to believe him and protested: "It isn't true! You can't have been able—" Her voice died away before this paralyzing revelation.

He reached up to a shelf and took down a little wooden bowl, from which he poured into the palm of his hand two or three dozen diamonds and rubies and sapphires and carelessly made them dance and sparkle and clink.

"And there are others," he said with an air of satisfaction. "Undoubtedly the imminence of the explosion prevented me from bringing the lot of them away; and the bulk of the treasure of the monks is scattered about the bottom of the sea. But all the same there's something to amuse a young man and help him to bear up. What do you think, Josine? You don't answer...

But hang it all! What's the matter now, confound it? You're never going to faint! Oh, these infernal women! They can't even lose a thousand millions without going off. What milksops they are!"

Josephine did not "go off," as Ralph had phrased it. She drew herself up, livid with raised arms. She wished to insult him. She wished to strike him. But she was suffocating. Her hands beat the air like the hands of a drowning man waving above the surface of the sea; and she fell upon the bed, moaning hoarsely.

Unmoved, he waited for the end of the attack. But he had still something to say to her.

"Well, have I beaten you? Have madam's shoulders touched the mat? Are you knocked out? Defeat all along the line. What? That's what I wanted to bring home to you, Josephine. You will go away from here completely convinced that you can do nothing against me and that it is best to give up all idea of plotting against me. I shall be happy in spite of you, and so will Clarice, and we shall have lots and lots of children. So you will have to make up your mind to face these facts."

He began to walk up and down and went on in accents that grew more and more cheerful: "Moreover what would you? You struck a streak of bad luck when you went to war with a stout young fellow who is ten times as strong and smart as you, my poor girl. I'm often astonished myself at my strength and smartness. Heavens! What a marvel of cleverness, cunning, intuition, energy, and clearsightedness! A veritable genius! Nothing escapes me. I read the minds of my enemies like an open book. Their slightest thoughts are known to me. So, at this very moment you've got your back to me, haven't you? You're spread out on the bed and I cannot see your charming face. All the same I'm perfectly well aware that you're slipping your hand into your bodice and pulling out a revolver and that you're going—"

The sentence was not finished. Suddenly Josephine twisted round, revolver in hand.

The report rang out. But Ralph, who was ready had time to grasp her wrist and twist it back—towards herself. She fell back wounded in the bosom.

The scene had been so brutal and the dénouement so unexpected that he stood speechless before this suddenly inert form which lay before him, the face colorless.

However he felt no anxiety. He did not believe that she was dead; and as a matter of fact, when he bent down and looked into it, he found that her heart was beating steadily. He cut away the top of her bodice with his nail-scissors. The bullet, striking aslant, had glanced off after ploughing through the flesh, a little above the black mark on top of her breast.

"It isn't a serious wound," he said to himself, thinking that the death of such a creature would have been only right and desirable.

He stood over her, still holding the scissors in his hand, and asking himself if it was not his duty to destroy this too perfect beauty, to mangle that charming face and so to rob the siren of her power to injure. A scar in the shape of a deep cross across her face, which raised ridges of skin would render indelible, what a just punishment and what a valuable precaution! What evil deeds avoided and what crimes prevented!

He had not the courage to do so; he did not wish to arrogate to himself the right to do so. Besides he had loved her too well.

He stood for a long time motionless, gazing down at her with infinite sadness. The struggle had exhausted him. He found himself full of bitterness and disgust. She was his first love, his first real love, and that passion to which the innocent heart brings so much freshness and of which it retains so sweet a memory, had brought him in the end nothing but rancor and hate. All his life his lips would retain a slight curl of disenchantment and his soul the impression of a scar.

She breathed more easily and opened her eyes.

At once he felt an irresistible urge never to see her again, never even to think of her.

Opening the window, he listened. He fancied that he heard hurrying steps from the direction of the shore. Leonard must have discovered, on reaching the beach, that all the fruits of the expedition had been the capture of a dummy, and doubtless, anxious about Josephine, he was returning to help her.

"Let him find her here; let him carry her away!" he said to himself. "Let her die or let her live! Let her be happy or unhappy! I don't care a rap. I don't want to hear anything more about her. Enough of this hell!"

And without a word, without a glance at the woman who held out her hands and implored him not to leave her, he went away.

Next morning he paid a visit to Clarice. In order not to reopen wounds which he knew must be so very painful, he had not yet seen her again. But she had known that he was there; and at once he perceived that time had already done its work. A warmer color mantled her cheeks; her eyes were shining with hope.

"Clarice," he said to her, "from the very first day you promised to forgive me everything."

"I have nothing to forgive you, Ralph," she said, with the remembrance of her father's crimes in her mind.

"Yes you have, Clarice. I have hurt you cruelly," he protested. "I have hurt myself very little less; and it is not only your love that I ask but also your care and your protection. I need you to help me to forget horrible memories, to restore my confidence in life, and to combat many ugly qualities in me which urge me to a path I do not wish to tread. With your help I am sure I can be honest; I am certainly going to try hard. And I promise you that you shall be happy. Will you be my wife?"

She held out her hand.

EPILOGUE

As Ralph had supposed all the vast network of intrigue woven to acquire the legendary treasure was never brought to the light of day. The suicide of Beaumagnan; the crimes of Madam Pellegrini, the mysterious personality of the Countess of Cagliostro, her flight, the shipwreck of the *Glowworm*, all these divers facts, Justice could not, or would not, link together. The memorandum of the Cardinal Bishop was destroyed, or disappeared. The associates of Beaumagnan disbanded and did not speak. The world knew nothing.

Necessarily the part that Ralph had played in the affair could not even be suspected; and his marriage passed unnoticed. By what miracle did he succeed in marrying under the name of the Vicomte d'Andresy? Doubtless one must attribute this exploit to the formidable means of action afforded him by the two or three handfuls of precious stones saved from the treasure. With those means one can get many things winked at.

And it was by those means evidently that one day the name of Lupin was found to have vanished. On no register and on no documents was there any longer any trace of Arsène Lupin, or of his father, Theophrastus Lupin. Legally there was only the Vicomte Ralph d'Andresy; and that Vicomte went on his travels through Europe with the Vicomtesse, née Clarice d'Etigues.

In the course of their travels news came to them of the death of the Baron d'Etigues. He perished, along with his cousin Oscar de Bennetot, while they were out rowing. Was it an accident? Was it suicide? During the last days of their lives the two cousins had been reckoned mad; and it was generally agreed that they had committed suicide. But there was also another version which hinted at crime. There were people who declared that a yacht had run down the boat and disappeared. But of this there was no proof.

Whatever the facts might be, Clarice would not touch her father's fortune. She divided it among charitable institutions.

The years rolled on, delightful and careless years. Ralph kept one of the promises which he had made to Clarice: she was profoundly happy. The other promise he did not keep: he was not honest.

Honesty seemed to be beyond his power. He had in his blood the need to take, to scheme, to mystify, to dupe, to amuse himself at other people's expense. He was by instinct smuggler, filibuster, marauder, pirate, plotter, and above all chief of a gang. Besides, in the school of Josephine, he had discovered, not without pride, really exceptional qualities in himself which rendered him practically without peer. He believed in his genius. He conferred on himself the right to a fantastic destiny, and one contrary to the destiny of all the men who were his contemporaries. He would be above all of them. He would be the master.

Without the knowledge of Clarice then, without indeed the young woman's having the least suspicion of it, he carried on enterprises and brought to success affairs in which his authority grew stronger and stronger and his really superhuman gifts developed.[4]

But before everything he told himself, the repose and happiness of Clarice! He respected his wife. That she should be, and that she should know herself to be the wife of a thief, that he could not allow.

Their happiness lasted five years; at the beginning of the sixth year Clarice died in giving birth to a son called Jean.

The very day after her death that son disappeared, without the slightest clue which allowed Ralph to discover who had entered the little house at Auteuil in which he lived or how they had been able to enter it.

As for the matter of guessing whose hand had struck the blow, there was no need to hesitate about that. Ralph, who had never doubted that the drowning of the two cousins had been brought about by the Countess of Cagliostro, Ralph, who yet later had learned that Dominique had died of poison, Ralph regarded it as settled that the Countess of Cagliostro was the author of the abduction. His grief transformed him. Having no longer either wife or son to restrain him, he flung himself with all his heart into the course to which so many forces impelled him. From that day on he was Arsène Lupin. There was no longer any reservation, any compromise. On the contrary: scandals, challenges, arrogance, an unbridled display of vanity and mockery, his name written on the walls, his visiting card in strongrooms. Arsène Lupin, what!

But whether he was passing under this name or under any other of the different names it pleased him to assume, whether he called himself Count Bernard d'Andresy (he had stolen the papers of a cousin of his family, who had died abroad) or Horace Velmont, or Colonel Sparmiento, or the Duke of Charmerace, or Prince Sernine, or Don Luis Perenna, always and everywhere, in all his avatars and beneath all his masks, he hunted for the Countess of Cagliostro, he hunted for his son Jean. He did not find his son. He never saw Josephine again. Was she still alive? Did she dare to risk entering France? Did she continue to persecute and to kill? Could he admit, considering what she was, that the menace eternally held over him since the very moment of their rupture would not take effect in some vengeance yet more cruel than the abduction of his son?

All the life of Arsène Lupin, wild enterprises, superhuman trials, unheard of triumphs, unmeasured passions, extravagant ambitions, all these had to run their course before events permitted him to answer this formidable question.

And so it came about that his first adventure linked itself, more than a quarter of a century later, to the adventure which it pleases him to consider today his last.

ENDNOTES

1. The first enigma was solved by a young girl (see *The Secret Tomb*, by Maurice Leblanc). The two next were solved by Arsène Lupin (see *The Island of the Thirty Shrouds* and *The Hollow Needle*). The solving of the fourth is the theme of this book.
2. Hitherto none of the biographies of Josephine have given any explanation of the fact that she in a way fled from Fontainebleau. Only Monsieur Frederic Masson, scenting the truth, writes: "Perhaps one day some letter will be found which will demonstrate the physical necessity of this departure."
3. There is no doubt that the well-known legend of the Thousand Millions of the Congregations had its origin in this tithe.
4. The acquisition of the treasure of the Kings of France, the second enigma of Cagliostro, and the discovery of that impenetrable retreat from which, fifteen years later, he could only be dislodged by the help of a flotilla of torpedo-boats, dates from this epoch.

A fan of Sherlock Holmes?
Then meet Solar Pons

The original fan fiction from the great August Derleth—the Sherlock Holmes of Praed Street.

"the best substitutes for Sherlock Holmes known."
– Vincent Starrett

"an excellent series of adventures in detection in their own right." – *The Chicago Tribune*

For more details and a full list of titles:
visit https://www.hachetteindia.com/home/yellowbacks